HOPE IS
DAFFODIL BRIGHT

Zoë Jasko

Printed edition:
Also available in multiple e-book formats.

Published by:
The Endless Bookcase Ltd,
Suite 14 STANTA Business Centre, 3 Soothouse Spring,
St Albans, Hertfordshire, AL3 6PF, UK.

More information can be found at:
www.theendlessbookcase.com

ISBN: 978-1-914151-66-8

Cover design: Zoë Jasko and Morgana Evans

Front cover photos: Daffodils and coffee –Pixabay (Iona Motoc), soldiers at Grantchester – Zoë Jasko (top), W.V.S. volunteer - ©Imperial War Museum (FX 12216) (bottom)

Back cover photos: Little Nella – Zoë Jasko (top), Grantchester c.1943 – Zoë Jasko (middle), Lady Alice and Sir Lawrence Bragg – used with the kind permission of A.M. Glazer (bottom)

Author photo: Andrew Mason

This is a work of fiction. Certain characters in this work are historical figures, and the events in which they are portrayed are used imaginatively. All other characters are fictitious, and any resemblance to real persons, living or dead, is purely coincidental.

For my mother, Eleanor

I love you with all my heart.

AUTHOR'S NOTE

My grandmother was a member of the Women's Voluntary Service (W.V.S.) in the Second World War. She founded and ran the W.V.S. canteen for the Heavy Anti-Aircraft (HAA) soldiers based in Grantchester, a picturesque village 3 miles outside Cambridge. When she passed away, I inherited a box of letters on which she had written, *'Soldiers letters from the second world war – some historically interesting.'* I had recently graduated with a joint honours history degree and enthusiastically took possession of the box. Somehow, I never had the time to look in the box, as work and family life became all-encompassing. At the time of the 80th anniversary of the Battle of Britain, my mother, now an old lady herself, began to reminisce about her wartime childhood. Her stories of the canteen and the soldiers reminded me of the box, and I took it out from the back of the wardrobe where all miscellaneous items were stored and discovered a treasure trove of characters and events. What a wonderful starting point for an author!

As I learnt about the W.V.S. in Cambridge, I heard the voice of Lady Alice Bragg in a contemporary newsreel. She was the leader of the organisation in the city and later the city's third female Mayor. She was an exceptional woman. As too were the women who volunteered alongside her.

This novel is the dramatized biography of Alice Bragg. It is also a work of historical fiction inspired by the Grantchester canteen – a story set against the backdrop of the war on the Homefront and the post-war years. *In my book, the majority of characters in the Alice/Cambridge story lived, although in some instances I have had to give the characters authentic names as they have not been named in the records; the characters in the Jean/Grantchester story are entirely fictitious.*

To hear the voice of Lady Bragg, Mayor of Cambridge, listen

to this newsreel footage from 1945:

Britishpathe.com: Lady Alice Bragg bestows the Freedom of the Borough on the Cambridgeshire Regiment https://www.britishpathe.com/video/a-cambridge-freedom-to-county-regiment

Research for this book has been wide-ranging but could not have been written without the following sources:

Dobinson, C., *AA Command: Britain's Anti-Aircraft Defences of the Second World War*. London: Methuen Publishing Ltd., 2001.

Glazer, A.M, & Thomson, P., *Crystal Clear: The Autobiographies of Sir Lawrence and Lady Bragg*. Oxford: Oxford University Press, 2015.

Graves, C., *Women in Green*. Kingswood: Windmill Press, 1948.

Royal Voluntary Service WVS/WRVS Narrative Reports: Cambridge, 1940 to 1945.

Unpublished family letters, papers and photographs belonging to the author.

www.capturingcambridge.org
www.ww2civildefence.co.uk

The Women's Voluntarily Service has since become the Royal Voluntary Service: The UK National Volunteer Charity. For more information about their work see www.royalvoluntaryservice.org.uk

ABOUT THE AUTHOR

Hope is Daffodil Bright is Zoë's first novel and comes hot on the heels of her first book, an anthology with a twist, *What the Wind Saw: Short Stories from the Heart of Hertfordshire* (The Endless Bookcase, 2022).

A trained singer, she is co-founder and creative director of the Hertfordshire-based Felici Opera, and now, in addition to performing, enjoys turning her storytelling skills to writing.

Zoë has a BA in French and History (University of Exeter) and an MA in Victorian Studies – 19th Century art, history, and literature (Birkbeck College, University of London). She has been an active member of a marvellous book club since 2008.

She lives in Hertfordshire with her husband and four children.

www.zoejasko.com

ENDORSEMENTS AND REVIEWS

"... a cracking story ... Jean comes across as an engaging and fascinating person who led a life that pushed the boundaries of what was possible for someone of her background and sex at the time, [a character that] achieved so much and knew some fascinating people, not least Alice Bragg and Lady Reading. The story of her [Jean's] relationships with both Albert and her husband ring very true and captures well the tensions between her hopes, her frustrations and her sense of duty and loyalty. The book tells a good story too about the war, preparations for it, and how the WVS, despite many finding it inconceivable that women could do the arduous work that was demanded, stepped in and saved lives, offered comfort, and famously 'tea and sympathy.' Zoë has done a great deal of research, and it shows."

Professor Lynne Berry C.B.E.

"A heart-warming story about the WVS, the can-do women who did so much more than make endless cups of tea, but kept the country on its feet during the Second World War. As well as a fascinating insight into the history, this is a touching story of an ordinary woman's hopes and sorrows, and of the shadows cast by war."

Kate Miller, author

"Zoë Jasko's novel brings to life the essential, often uncelebrated, roles of women in wartime, and shows us how their contributions went beyond merely 'doing their bit.' It tells how their many kindnesses, selflessness and tireless efforts were vital in making life bearable for soldiers, evacuees and those who had lost their homes. The women's stories are packed with historical detail: from supporting firecrews and the injured during the Norwich Blitz, to helping internees contact their families, and the everyday privations endured on the Home Front. But Zoë Jasko applies her extensive research with a very light touch to evoke the period, in a way which never slows down the narrative. This is a rare

skill. A satisfying read, which also teaches us how these unsung, ordinary women served their country in remarkable ways."

Dr Elaine Saunders, social historian

'When World War II twisted the kaleidoscope, everyone's life was affected in unforeseeable ways. With incredible attention to historical detail, and using original source material, Zoe Jasko has written a book which captures both the essence of that time and shortly afterwards. Vignettes of interesting events and characters involving the village of Grantchester, the women of the Women's Voluntary Service, and the soldiers of the Heavy Artillery Battery who camped there are well described and cleverly blended together to create an engaging and most enjoyable read."

Charles Bunker – author, essayist and former-proprietor of the Orchard Tea Garden, Grantchester.

"An evocative blend of fact and fiction that shines a light on the often unsung role of the WVS during World War Two and takes us into the heart of one woman's life choices."

Louisa Treger, historical novelist.

1.

JEAN

TIME FOR CHANGE

Grantchester, December 1963

"Are you sure you can manage without me this afternoon, Mum?" Eleanor fussed anxiously as she buttoned up her camel coat by the front door.

"Yes, of course I can, darling. Don't you worry about me," Jean replied.

"Well, don't try and shift anything heavy. I'll do that when I'm back," Eleanor instructed, and glanced around the hallway for something for her mother to do which didn't require her help. Her eyes came to rest on the parish magazine lying on the walnut table next to the coat stand where Jean had left it absentmindedly when it had arrived a few weeks ago. Eleanor picked it up and smiled inwardly at the pen and ink design of the church, drawn by her mother a good twenty years ago – a black and white sketch that no one, not even her mother, had thought to update. She felt her stomach lurch in a strange resurgence of grief that grabbed her seemingly from nowhere. It wouldn't matter what happened in the village from now on because soon it would no longer be their home.

Forming a plan, she found, was always a useful antidote to sadness, and she would feel better about going out for the afternoon if she knew that her mother was busy. Busy-ness leaves no time for tears. In any case, there was so much to do to get everything packed up and ready for her mother's move. There was no question of allowing the afternoon to be lost to inertia.

"Maybe you could make a start on sorting out Daddy's

1

magazines in the study? And you've got lots of papers you need to go through too. There isn't room to take everything with you," she suggested.

Jean ignored her.

"Don't worry, Eleanor," she replied smiling. "You haven't seen Angela for months. Go and enjoy yourself. I'll be fine, and honestly, I have plenty to do that I can do sitting down."

"Well, if you're sure …"

Eleanor, grateful for a few hours off, picked up her umbrella and was gone, leaving Jean alone. Alone in her large house. So full of furniture and things but so empty. Jean sighed and went to the kitchen to make herself a cup of tea, waiting patiently for the whistle to blow as the water came to the boil on the gas hob. It was December, and it was cold. As she waited, she fiddled with her grey-blue cardigan, checking that all the buttons were done up, checking that her clean hankie was caught under the cuff of her blouse, ready to catch the tears that took her by surprise so often that they couldn't be counted as a surprise anymore.

So, no shifting furniture or anything heavy. She had strained her back during the week without one of the girls to help her. Not that Barbara, at eight months pregnant with her fourth baby, was any more able to lift boxes than she was herself – but Eleanor was here now. Objects were easy. They either would be kept because they were useful, claimed by one of the girls as an inheritance, or they would be consigned to the accumulating boxes destined for a jumble sale. Memories wrapped up in newspaper, obscuring their shape, so they were already as good as gone before they had even left the house. But the papers. So many papers – letters, receipts, documents. Where should she start? And what would she find amongst them when she did?

The water was taking its time to boil. Jean knew that

hidden inside the kettle small bubbles would be starting to form, the cold water from the tap straining and fighting against the heat from the gas until the gas won with a triumphant whistle. She moved over to the window as she waited and looked at the rain still falling on her already soggy garden. It was a good thing that Eleanor had taken the umbrella, it would be a wet walk to the bus stop, but at least the tea room in Cambridge where she was meeting Angela, her school friend, would be dry. Jean slowly traced a raindrop the length of the windowpane with her finger, avoiding the decision to start sorting out the papers.

As if mirroring the raindrop on the windowpane, two briny tears leaked from her eyes, and she felt them descend from wet eyelashes to her cheekbones, there to fall, as from a cliff, onto the kitchen floor. She reached for the hankie caught at her cuff and wiped the remaining wetness from her eyes.

How different last December had been. Looking forward to Christmas Day, anticipating a fun family day together with the twins, Barbara and Maeve, their husbands, Christopher and Bill, and all her precious grandchildren, wondering if maybe she ought to have invited Eleanor's new boyfriend, feeling guilty, knowing he was alone in London at Christmas, but relieved at not having to make the effort when Eleanor didn't raise the issue.

"You can't freeze him out, Jean," Alan had lectured her from the breakfast table this time last year, newspaper folded beside him.

"But I just don't feel comfortable," she had replied, spreading raspberry jam thickly on his hot buttered toast for him as she did every morning since he had retired.

"Time passes, Jean. We have to move on."

She remembered looking at him sharply at his comment, surprised at his softening. She had scrutinised his face as he continued to read his paper, as he bit into his toast and jam, still with his eyes glued on *The Cambridge Daily News*, unaware of how hard she was trying to read him. Was it really what he felt inside, or was it what he thought he should say? After several moments of silence, she gave up trying to understand and asked him what time he would be back for lunch. She was leaving her middle years behind her, but she knew him no better than she had as a girl before they were married.

She had dwelt on Alan's words all day, hearing them turn around her head, feeling them probe into a closed-off part of her psyche, a part of Jean Barnet that was locked away from the world. A secret place, hidden deep within.

"Time passes. We have to move on."

The words were a light that she had neither the desire nor the ability to switch on.

Yet her mind chewed the words, polished the words, gave the words so much meaning that by the time her daughter Maeve popped in with her boys in the late afternoon, Jean was troubled and anxious.

"It's the mood of the country, Mum," Maeve had laughed.

Maybe it was, Jean pondered as she sat listening to Maeve's complaints that the boys were growing so fast that she couldn't keep up with providing new shoes and clothes to fit.

There seemed to be so much change nowadays that it made Jean dizzy. There had been new houses built in the village. Parts of Cambridge were almost unrecognisable, with the dwellings, offices and college buildings that had sprung up in the last few years since the austerity of the 1950s faded from experience to memory. Her daughters were no longer little girls, living lives so dissimilar to anything that she could have imagined when she was their age. Eleanor had been to

Spain last year on holiday – for two weeks, by aeroplane! And the year before, Maeve had chosen to go back to work at the university labs in Cambridge as she said her little boys were 'old enough'.

"But wouldn't it be better for the boys if you were at home to look after them?" Jean had worried, hardly able to comprehend that her daughter could make the choice – that she had the opportunity to make the choice.

"It's interesting. I enjoy it. It makes me a better mother. We need the money – how else could we afford the car?" Maeve had responded, irritated at her mother's comments. "Anyway, it's not as if you didn't work," she sniped.

"I don't know what you mean by that, Maeve," Jean was quick to answer. "I've never worked other than to look after my family – and twins are hard work, believe me!"

"Of course, you worked. What else were you doing for the W.V.S. when we were children?"

"That's different. That's volunteering. It was for the Women's Voluntary Service. Volunteering isn't working. Anyway, it was the war, and we didn't have a choice. It was our duty."

"Well, I enjoy going to work, Mum, and I'm grateful for the opportunity. I don't need you telling me that I should live my life any other way."

Maeve had gathered her sons together then and hastened home; another pleasant afternoon clouded in a different outlook.

Jean sighed and raised the lid of the kettle before her on the hob. Inside, tiny bubble families were uniting with other bead-like families to form small crowds of heating water. Maeve choosing to work full-time at the labs was another way the country had changed. In her day, when a girl married, her husband provided her with everything she

5

needed or wanted, and what couldn't be provided was gone without. There were no thoughts of professional work if you were lucky enough to get a husband. Of course, a few of her cohort from her grammar school, the ones with fathers that were prepared to pay for their daughters' education and considered it money well spent, had gone to universities, mainly to the new colleges in London, but a couple had come here to Cambridge. Others had trained to become teachers. She had started a course at art school in a flimsy hope of becoming a textile designer, knowing that her parents would prefer her to become an art teacher if she had to work at all. To show willingness, she had given private tuition to the vicar's daughters in the evening while she spent her days covering sheets of paper in floral patterns for possible Liberty prints.

For most of her friends, these educational establishments were merely a way to meet suitable young men, but she hadn't met Alan at her college. A friend at the art school, Charlotte Dawlings, lived in a big house in Islington. North of the River, Islington could have been another country to Jean, who, apart from an annual holiday expedition to Brighton, knew no other part of the land than her south London suburb and a few streets around the art school at the city's heart.

"Mother and Father are throwing a party for Christopher's birthday, do come, won't you, Jean darling? It's going to be ever so much fun, dancing and such a gay time," she had gushed.

"I don't know," Jean had faltered, wondering how she would get from Catford to Islington and back again, wondering what to wear for a 'gay time', wondering if she dared.

Her parents had been more supportive of the invitation than she had supposed, her father ordering a taxi cab for both journeys at what she presumed must have been a
6

considerable expense. To her surprise, her mother returned from the draper's with a length of beautiful soft dark blue velvet, the colour of the sky at the moment when it is no longer day, but neither could it yet be called night. Eileen, her younger sister, insisted on presenting her with patterns from *Woman* magazine, but Eileen's ideas for a style were considerably more racy than Jean's. Jean only wanted to fit in. She didn't want to be noticed.

The party was for Charlotte's brother Christopher's twenty-first birthday, and the whole Dawlings clan was celebrating. Music and light poured from the first-floor windows onto the street below where Jean stood. She hesitated on the doorstep, midnight velvet swinging at her calves, and she pulled her borrowed black wrap tighter around her bodice, uncomfortably flat-chested in what Eileen had assured was fashionable underwear for the modern look. The undergarments had been an unnecessary expense in her opinion, but she had submitted to Eileen's direction when even her mother had insisted.

Her finger hovered lightly over the doorbell. She felt deep within herself that by pressing the button and sounding the bell, her life would change forever. She shivered, not sure that she wanted her life to change. She was enjoying the course it was flowing – days filled with glorious drawing, new friendships with fun and interesting girls, plus some welcome shillings in her pocket from the art lessons.

"It is so important that you make a good impression at this party," her mother had declared as she had laid the velvet out flat on their dining room table and started to cut the panels for the dress. She had raised her eyes at Jean's silence.

"You do know about the Dawlings family, don't you?"

Jean shook her head, wondering how her mother could know about a North London Islington family when she lived sheltered by middle-class South London Catford.

"Families like the Dawlings move in the best circles," her mother Anne continued. What is more, one of the Dawlings married a Rothschild, I understand."

How did she know this, Jean wondered?

"They are a good family, and there are bound to be some brothers or cousins to whom you could be introduced," Anne added thoughtfully, leaving unsaid what she and her daughters knew, that if Nicholas had returned, his very presence would have facilitated introductions. The never-ending, razor-sharp ache gripped Anne's heart, and for a second, her hands refused to work the scissors, leaving them stranded in mid-air.

"If it were me going to the party, I would wear red taffeta with silver beading," Eileen announced into the aching silence, "I would swing my necklaces and wear a white ostrich feather on a headband in my hair. I would make all the young men look at me. But I know what you'll do, Jean. You will hide in the corner and not even try to talk to anyone or even dance."

"That's not true!" Jean contradicted her younger sister. "I like to dance."

"You won't learn the steps for the new dances, so how can you dance at a party?" Eileen observed.

The sisters never argued. There never raised their voices at each other. Jean merely retreated to silent thought, leaving Eileen to continue unthwarted in her voiced desires or opinions.

"You'll never get a husband. Sometimes I wonder if you even want one," Eileen gave her last word and left the room as if exiting the stage.

But that wasn't true. Jean did want to be married. She wasn't fussed about the wedding; a simple affair would do with a pretty dress and a long net veil, with flowers – lily of the valley – and her family around her. And a husband. Someone to look after her. A home of her own, close to her parents, in Catford. And children, yes, she'd like children.

Now Jean stood on the Islington doorstep, finger lightly brushing against the doorbell.

"It's not going to ring itself," a man said stiffly behind her, and without turning to look at the speaker, Jean applied the pressure of change through her forefinger and heard the bell ringing behind the closed door.

The large first-floor living room was crowded and hot. Jean found herself parted from her wrap and with a glass of fizzing liquid thrust into her hand. She slipped unnoticed into the corner of the room where she stood next to a large bookcase and watched the golden bubbles in her glass rise to the surface and burst, rising and popping, rising and popping, before she lifted her eyes to look around the room. A small group of young men was gathered around the gramophone, taking sleek black disks from their paper sleeves, bantering enthusiastically about the merits of each, and debating without decision the order in which they should be played. Charlotte and some of her friends, whom Jean did not recognise, were dancing in the middle of the room whilst more middle-aged relatives were sitting on sofas and chairs pushed against the walls to make space for the dancing. A maid, dressed smartly in black with a pristine white apron, was offering more glasses of the fizzing liquid to the Dawlings' guests, and another was circulating with a tray of tiny morsels of food. Jean hoped she could escape the offer as she was unsure what the food was or whether she would like it. She bent her head and assiduously studied the bubbles in her glass so that the maid would pass her by.

"It's not going to get drunk by itself," the stiff voice remarked next to her elbow. Jean gave a momentary start. She had not noticed the man come alongside her.

"You are a funny one, aren't you, not ringing doorbells, not drinking champagne?" he observed flatly, in a tone that was neither critical nor teasing.

Jean looked at him shyly. He seemed quite a bit older than herself but surely not past thirty. He was smartly dressed in a dinner jacket and white tie, but he, like her, did not seem entirely comfortable in his party attire. She was struck by the stiffness that pervaded his whole body and, looking down, saw that he held his left leg taught and rigid as he leaned his weight against an ebony walking stick in his right hand. The stiff man had been injured. Her heart softened, and she raised her blue eyes to him and smiled. In reply, he offered her his hand.

"I'm Alan Barnet," he introduced himself, and in so doing, like her ringing of the bell, her life changed forever.

The whistle sounded from the triumphant kettle, calling Jean back to it. She angrily brushed aside the tears leaking from her watery eyes. She liked her kettle. Maybe it seemed strange to enjoy such an everyday object, but the kettle had always been there in her kitchen, providing routine, providing comfort. Maeve had given her an electric kettle for her birthday in November.

"You are always so difficult to buy for Mum, but you do like your tea, and I'm sure this will be useful," Maeve, who liked everything modern, had said as she watched her mother carefully take the wrapping paper off the box so that she could reuse it on another present.

"Mummy's not difficult to buy for," her twin sister Barbara had protested. Barbara had given her mother toiletries which Jean had put in the downstairs toilet for everyone other than herself to use.

The twins, although identical, somehow contrived to look utterly unalike. Maeve had short, dyed hair, whereas Barbara's was longer and natural. Barbara carried more weight than her sister even when she wasn't pregnant and clung to the pretty styles of the 1950s, whereas Maeve took a utilitarian approach to clothes, favouring trousers.

This new type of kettle could reach the boil, and it would turn itself off, Maeve had explained, which meant that you could continue doing what you were doing and not need to go back to the hob to turn it off. Jean didn't like the kettle. It meant you could do several things at once more effectively. It meant you could go to work and abandon your children. It meant you could get on with something else and forget you were on the point of making tea. No, Jean would keep her whistle kettle, and she would give the electric one, in its new box, to the next jumble sale, and if Maeve ever asked, she would say the box must have got put in the wrong pile when all the sorting out was taking place.

Jean poured some of the newly boiled water into her china teapot covered in purple and yellow pansies, quite the wrong flower for a dank December afternoon, but she loved it. It had been a wedding present all those years ago.

Theirs had been a short courtship. Everyone seemed to take it for granted that they would marry almost as soon as they had met at Christopher Dawlings' twenty-first birthday party. Alan wasn't a Dawlings, and he wasn't a Rothschild. He was a friend of Christopher's cousin, Hugh. They had served together at Ypres, where a piece of shrapnel had lodged itself into Alan's thigh, inflicting years of pain but letting him escape with his life. Jean's parents never said if they were pleased or disappointed that Alan was neither a Dawlings nor Rothschild. He had completed his degree after returning from the war, followed by his solicitor's articles. He was a member of the Church of England. He had his own small house in Cambridge, a legacy from his parents, now deceased, and he had an office to go to every day. What more was wanted?

Of course, there was no point in completing her art

11

studies now that she was going to be a solicitor's wife in Cambridge. Nothing was said. Jean just found that she was no longer going to classes and then no longer enrolled. The end had justified the means. A small wedding, a honeymoon on the south coast, and then she was in Cambridge, joined quickly by the babies. At least it was a version of her expectations. She was lucky. And she knew it.

She swirled the hot water around the teapot to warm it and then poured the cooling water down the drain, its task fulfilled. She put two teaspoons of black tea leaves from the caddy on the shelf into the teapot before pouring on the remaining not-so-boiling water from the kettle and stirring it with a teaspoon. Finally, she put on the white china lid with its ring of tiny pansies. The teapot was more sturdy than it looked, as it had survived what, twenty-seven years? Then she waited, counting to ten under her breath. Everyone needs a good cup of tea.

2.

EVERYONE NEEDS
A GOOD CUP OF TEA

"Everyone needs a good cup of tea," Mrs Fielding, the vicar's wife, had pronounced all those years ago as she poured the hot brown liquid into six teacups, sitting politely on their exquisite rose-bud saucers.

Jean was sitting in the large Victorian drawing room at the vicarage in Grantchester, where Mrs Fielding presided over her flock. Mrs Harding and Mrs Roberts sat together on the Victorian sofa, Mrs Weston and – how strange – Mrs Appleby, Mrs Fielding's daily help, the woman who did her cleaning and laundry, were sitting on velvet armchairs near the hearth. Mrs Appleby seemed uncomfortable, as if she wanted to jump up from her seat at any moment, whilst Mrs Weston surreptitiously edged her chair, little by little, towards the sofa to unite herself with the group to which she felt she belonged.

Why was Mrs Appleby included in a Grantchester ladies' tea party, Jean had wondered? But then, why was she there when she hardly knew these other older ladies? She had accepted Mrs Fielding's invitation to tea, not finding anything unusual. Mrs Fielding had been a great help to her since she had moved from her little terraced house in the centre of the city to the big house in the village of Grantchester, a move facilitated by Alan's promotion to partner in his solicitor's firm and by many years of careful saving. Overnight, she had found her status in the social pecking order to have been raised, but inside herself, she feared that she was an imposter. Mrs Fielding had surrounded her in Church of England warmth and had extended a hand of friendship to the young mother, saying,

"I come from Catford too," when she had found out where Jean had spent her childhood. The vicar's wife hadn't elaborated on this statement leaving Jean to wonder whether they were bound together in a secret club or whether admitting to coming from South London when living in a Cambridgeshire village was taboo.

Now she was drinking tea in the vicarage at what was clearly not a tea party. No daily help would ever be invited to afternoon tea. This was a meeting.

"Isobel, how was it last night?" Mrs Roberts asked as she accepted a homemade shortbread biscuit from the plate that Mrs Fielding was offering.

Isobel – Mrs Fielding – was delighted to be asked, for that, of course, was the reason for the tea party.

She sat down on the lone straight-backed wooden chair close to the coffee table where the teacups had been assembled only a few minutes earlier and took a bite into her shortbread before answering. She hesitated before speaking, enjoying not only the taste of her biscuit but also the fact that each one of her guests was waiting in expectation for her to finish it and learn the reason for their presence in the vicarage drawing room.

"You may know that I went to the meeting at the Guildhall yesterday evening," she began.

There were murmurs of affirmation and surprise from the ladies. Jean remained silent.

"Mrs Bragg was speaking. I don't know if you know her. She is the wife of Lawrence Bragg, the physicist who's at – well, I forget now which college."

"He's the head of the University Physics Department at the Cavendish Laboratories," Mrs Weston corrected.

"Thank you, Lavinia … The Cavendish Laboratories,

not particularly important as far as we are concerned."

"Isobel!" Mrs Weston interrupted again, eyebrows raised in shock. "He's a very important scientist, and Cambridge is lucky to have him. He's the youngest-ever winner of the Nobel Prize, and his research is nationally important – x-ray crystallography, you know," and so saying, she swept the gaze of the gathered ladies, conscious she was giving them essential information.

"You know I can't keep up with academics," Mrs Fielding laughed off the comment, embarrassed by her mistake and waving her mostly-eaten shortbread biscuit in the air. "Now, what was I saying? Ah yes, his wife, Mrs Bragg, has been selected to run the Cambridge branch of the Women's Voluntary Service. It seems she is a friend of Lady Reading, the founder. Have you heard of her ?"

Jean shook her head, as did Mrs Appleby, whilst Mrs Roberts' face looked entirely blank.

"She is Stella Isaacs, Dowager – Marchioness Reading. Her husband was Ambassador to the United States. Apparently, she's quite formidable. She was asked by Lord Hoare at the Home Office last year to found a women's service to assist with Air Raid Precautions if there is war," Mrs Weston informed the meeting tea party.

"Mother would have known that," Jean thought fleetingly before the unease of talk of war settled on her, as it seemed to have done upon the whole group, like snow falling quietly in winter, icy and cold. Mrs Appleby, Jean noticed, shivered visibly at the turn in the conversation.

"There won't be another war, Isobel. Chamberlain put all that business to rest last year," Mrs Roberts stated naively. Mrs Fielding turned a look of disbelief on her friend.

"My dear Elspeth, surely you don't think that Hitler will go along with all that 'peace in our time' for much longer?

No, ladies, war is inevitable, and like it or not, we will all have to be ready," Mrs Fielding pronounced dramatically. Her words stifling any response from the ladies present as snow muffles sound, each woman momentarily staring into the abyss of what another war could mean to herself and her family. For a while, there was silence except for the fast tick-tocking of the carriage clock on the mantlepiece and the sound of Mrs Fielding munching a second piece of shortbread.

"I was a bit suspicious before I attended the meeting, as friends aren't always the best choice to get a job done," Mrs Fielding continued at length.

Jean looked down at her feet and tightened her grip on her tea napkin.

"Mrs Bragg told us that Lady Reading is seeking to recruit half a million volunteers across the country, principally for A.R.P. – that stands for Air Raid Precaution."

"Half a million women? That won't be possible," Mrs Harding said, astonished.

"Well, if you had heard Mrs Bragg speak last night, you wouldn't think that. It seems the nation is beginning to galvanise. She said that although it felt like we could not do much to support our boys and the war effort, every little bit of help we could give would go a long way. Ladies, war will come to us whether we like it or not, and we must be ready to protect our homes and families and help each other. All it would take would be for Hitler to walk into France or Belgium, or the Netherlands even, and we would be a sitting target for invasion – most likely from the sky."

"I don't think I would be able to assist with anti-air raid precautions, whatever they are exactly, I'm far too old," Mrs Roberts asserted. "And I can't see how you will be able to either, Isobel. You are far too busy with the vicarage and parish work."

"I agree," Mrs Fielding said simply, realising that each lady present was probably thinking of any number of reasons why they would not be in a position to help.

"There are going to be many different roles for the Women's Voluntary Service," she continued, "which is how I come to cups of tea." She paused again for effect, and each lady, on cue, raised her cup to her lips for another sip.

"It seems that there is an urgent need for canteens for the soldiers, and this is something that can be organised and delivered by us older married ladies. After the meeting, Mrs Bragg approached me. She said that she knew my husband, the Reverend Fielding, and she asked me personally to set up a canteen here in Grantchester for the anti-aircraft gun battalion." Mrs Fielding drew herself up proudly as she spoke, as if to show that being asked by a friend of Lady Reading's to found an airman's canteen in a little Cambridge village was the highest of honours.

"Of course, without hesitation, I said that we would run a canteen in the village staffed by village women. I am sure that you will all want to be involved. Naturally, you will all need to join the W.V.S."

Jean shifted her weight uncomfortably on her chair, still looking firmly down at her shoes and holding tight to her napkin.

"I don't think that we are going to need a canteen," Mrs Roberts said, unconvinced by Mrs Fielding's reports. "The Prime Minister won't let us be drawn into another frightful war, and anyway, there aren't enough soldiers at the base to warrant a canteen."

"Not yet, I grant you," Mrs Fielding replied. "But when war comes, their numbers will be augmented. If this is going to be an air war, then Cambridge airport will be a prime target for the enemy."

"But we have three Public Houses in the village, Isobel," Mrs Roberts commented. "Surely that is sufficient?" She felt that if she involved herself in the planning, she was somehow signing up to the view that war was inevitable. Therefore, if she could resist any changes, then she could resist the possibility of the war arriving unwanted.

Isobel Fielding raised one eyebrow icily and imperceptibly. She knew that there would be war, and she was not one to be caught out by inactivity. She began to explain to Mrs Roberts, as if she were a small child,

"Elspeth, there could be hundreds of men here in a matter of months. Our three small village pubs will be overwhelmed. In any case, it would not be appropriate for the men to find comfort and sanctuary in such places whenever they are off-duty. There are too many temptations in public houses. We must provide an alternative. It is the Christian thing to do," she added, as if she had remembered at the end of her lecture that she occupied the social and moral position of Vicar's Wife.

"I would be happy to help, Mrs Fielding," Mrs Appleby volunteered. She had been silent throughout, until now.

"Thank you, Mrs Appleby," Mrs Fielding acknowledged, somewhat surprised. She had thought that Mrs Weston would be the first to agree to the proposal.

But Mrs Weston was not to be upstaged by a home help and immediately and enthusiastically gave her support. Mrs Harding nodded her agreement. Mrs Roberts, arguments defeated, and allies deserted, reluctantly assented.

"And you, Mrs Barnet? Would you be prepared to help?" Mrs Fielding asked Jean, leaning towards the younger woman, her voice coaxing, like a teacher encouraging a correct answer from a bashful pupil.

"I don't know," Jean replied truthfully, "the girls, you know, they need me."

"Of course, your children need you. No one is saying that they don't," Mrs Fielding countered, "but you do have your mother living with you now, don't you, to help you with the children, so you probably have more time than you think you have. Serving tea a few times a week to these poor boys far from home isn't too much to ask?"

"I don't know," Jean repeated, cross with herself that she didn't have the words to express why she didn't want to get involved.

"... Alan." She landed upon the idea of her husband. "He likes me at home," she added feebly.

"Don't they all, dear," Mrs Weston interrupted. She was itching to do something for the war effort, and here was an opportunity right on her doorstep.

Jean breathed deeply. There was no avoiding it. Mrs Fielding had decided that she should be part of the Grantchester canteen delivery party, and resistance was futile. So, in surrender, she said,

"Maybe I will be able to find a few hours each week. Where will the canteen be?"

There was only one reasonable place in the village to house a canteen: the village hall, next to the vicarage. The six women put their tea aside and left the vicarage to inspect it.

The village hall was hardly more than ten years old, and the villagers were very proud of it. It was a single-storey black and white building with a straw roof, hiding its newness so that it would fit in with an ancient village. Inside was a large room, known as 'the hall', a kitchenette, and the 'Reading Room,' a smaller room, open every morning for whoever wished to read the daily newspapers.

"Now," Mrs Fielding announced to her entourage, "as

19

we can't give the entirety of our hall over to the army, I suggest that we use the Reading Room for the soldiers. We could serve from the kitchenette and store provisions at the vicarage, as this kitchenette is rather small."

Mrs Appleby had moved away from the canteen committee and was looking at the furniture in the room, weighing up each piece's value to the project.

"Some of this furniture will need to go, Mrs Fielding," Mrs Appleby commented.

"Really? Do you think so?" Mrs Fielding replied, somewhat surprised as the room seemed adequately furnished to her.

"It's not particularly comfortable for men needing to relax," Jean chipped in. "There ought to be a few more armchairs with cushions."

"… and coffee tables," Mrs Appleby added.

Mrs Fielding smiled and squeezed Jean warmly on the arm. She had felt that Jean Barnet would drift in the right direction before not too long.

"Excellent suggestion, my dear. Perhaps you and Mrs Appleby could see to helping us sort out the room and the kitchenette."

Later, once the girls were all in bed and the evening meal had been cleared away, Jean sat with her husband and mother in their comfortable living room overlooking the garden. Although it was late, the early August light still lit the house, and there was no need for any lamps. Alan was re-reading that morning's edition of the *Cambridge Daily News,* and her mother was knitting for Eileen's new baby. Later they would listen to the nine o'clock news on the wireless before turning in for the night.

"Alan?" Jean asked softly.

"Yes, my dear," he looked up from his reading.

"Do you think there is going to be a war?"

It seemed strange to be asking such a question when there was so much peace in her house, no girls awake laughing and crying, no maid working clattering pans, and so much peace coming in from the open windows as the day was drawing to a close and birds too were bedding down for the night.

Alan put his book down, his face severe and clouded.

"Yes, I do," he said flatly.

"May God save us," Anne whispered into her knitting, bowing to the inevitable and to her source of sustenance.

"I've decided to join the Women's Voluntary Service," Jean announced suddenly.

Memories of her brother Nicholas had floated through her mind since Mrs Fielding had spoken of the 'poor boys'. He was a bright lad, the oldest, and the siblings' leader. He was quick to copy any accent and had his younger sisters and brother in stitches with his rendition of the Irish butcher or the cockney bus conductor. When they had been children, he and Jean had mounted puppet show plays for Eileen and Tom to watch. Their father had constructed a box tall enough for young Nicholas to stand in unseen and reach his hand up to bring the puppets to life accompanied by accents from around the country and around the world. Anne had sewn a red velvet curtain to cover the stage and had helped the children make the puppets; the old woman selling fish, the little boy with a kite, the businessman on his way to his office in the City with a bowler hat and briefcase. Jean had covered reams of paper in beautiful designs to pin at the back of the box as scenery, and she had spent a whole glorious weekend painting the box, decorating it with patterns and swirls so that it was as stunning as any provincial Theatre

21

Royal. During the performance, she would kneel beside Nicholas, hidden in the theatre box, passing him each puppet as he needed and sometimes assisting with the female voices. Unobserved, she smiled in delight that Eileen and little Tom were roaring with laughter or cowering behind sofa cushions in enjoyable fear at the twists and turns of Nicholas's puppet performance.

Years later, he had been posted to Passchendaele and had never returned.

At bedtime, Jean had bathed little Eleanor, only three years old, and read her favourite story, the one about Rufus the horse and Percy the hedgehog. She covered her with kisses before shutting the curtains firmly. It was hard to go to sleep when there was still daylight. Leaving the little girl chatting to her teddy bears, she crossed the corridor to check that the ten-year-old twins, Barbara and Maeve, were reading in their bedroom. She paused on the landing. Her beautiful daughters. Her beautiful house. What would happen to them if the bombs fell and fell and fell? Or worse still, if to fall was the fate of the country, and German soldiers invaded and occupied?

She knew she must do something.

"I've decided to join the Women's Voluntary Service," she repeated.

Her husband and mother both looked up at her blankly – maybe her mother didn't know about Lord Hoare and Lady Reading – although she doubted it.

"I mean," Jean faltered, "to help with the war effort – if there is a war."

Alan looked at his wife steadily, offering no words of encouragement or opposition.

"You do think I should, don't you, darling?" she asked meekly but not weakly.

She looked so young and girlish still, despite all her babies, with her blonde hair delicately framing her temples and her pretty, floral summer dress skimming her slender frame, that a lump came to Alan's throat along with an overwhelming desire to protect her.

He reached down unknowingly to his injured thigh and rubbed it silently as Jean and her mother waited for his response.

"I think that we will soon all be called upon to help in whatever ways we can, and in more ways than we can even begin to expect. And it won't be easy."

It wasn't.

"Everyone needs a good cup of tea," Jean remembered saying sympathetically, reaching her hand out to the old man during the Baedeker raids of 1942, when the mobile canteen had been called all the way to Bedford. By then, the war had sucked her into much more than rotas at the village canteen. She squeezed his trembling hand, shaking not from cold but from shock. There was dust and debris in his hair and beard. Somehow, he had managed to pull trousers over his pyjamas, but his feet were bare. He had not had time to find any slippers.

"Thank you so much," he whispered hoarsely. "Please, I need to ..." He fumbled through his trouser pockets, retrieving a shilling which he tried to press into Jean's hand.

"No, sir, we're W.V.S. We are here to help. You don't need to pay," she replied.

"Ah yes," he responded and took the tea, "but you need ... you need this," He tried to hand Jean the shilling for a second time.

"The poor love's confused," said Fiona Larkin, who was working the shift with Jean.

"Sir, let me help you find your way to the rest centre.

People will help you there. Come with me."

Then turning to Fiona, she said, "Fee, I'll only be a minute. Can you manage?"

Quite a queue had built up behind the elderly gentleman in his pyjamas. Firemen, dusty and strained, who had been working through the night trying to contain the fires that the Luftwaffe's fury had unleashed, wearily accepted much-needed refreshment from the mobile canteen, now that they had dampened down the flames.

"Don't be long," Fiona said before serving the next in the queue with a warming cup of hot tea from the urn.

Jean steered her old man through the debris on the streets, avoiding the shards of shattered glass and the puddles of water. Piles of rubble smoked where houses once stood. Hideous mangled shapes of furniture remnants and collapsed walls and floors punctured premises left strangely untouched by the night's outrage. Here and there, a lone fireman, in a dark uniform and tin hat, was still directing his heavy spurt of water on a smouldering section of somebody's home.

"It's all gone," the old man whispered. Jean leant in to catch his words.

"I know," was all she could reply.

At the end of the next street stood another W.V.S. volunteer in her recognisable grey-green flannel uniform dress, long-sleeved and buttoned to the waist, fastened with a belt, practical and economical. On her breast pocket, the distinct insignia W.V.S. CIVIL DEFENCE below the red embroidered crown of King George VI. Jean felt a surge of relief. Maybe that was what other people felt when they saw her. It was comforting to think so.

"Hello," she said, "I'm on the mobile canteen, but this gentleman needs urgent help."

The unknown colleague looked grimly at his bare feet, his shrunken, dazed body, his confusion, and said,

"Come on, love, let's get you warm. We'll see if we can get you sorted with some shoes, then we'll find somewhere for you to sleep, do you have any relatives?" she spoke gently, soothingly, authoritatively, and the old man relaxed into her care as he shuffled beside her.

Jean mouthed the word "thank you" as she turned away.

When Jean returned to the canteen, she found Fee dealing with a young mother wailing as loudly as her baby.

"How can I feed him? The pram's gone. His clothes are gone. Where's Phil? Oh, where's Phil?" The distraught woman cried as she clung to her tiny bundle. Jean felt sorry for her and yet slightly irritated. It was hard to lose all one's possessions, but her baby son was alive. No one knew yet how many had not survived the night, but she hid her tetchy thoughts under her well-used soft and caring smile.

"How old is your baby?" she asked, trying to distract the lady.

"He's not yet two months, and I can't feed him. I can't feed him. Oh, where's Phil?"

Suddenly, the Phil in question appeared at the front of the mobile canteen queue alongside Jean and the wailing woman. He was covered from head to toe in dust but bore a baby's bottle in triumph. The three women looked at him in astonishment.

"Oh Phil, you've got it!" the wife declared joyously.

"Sir, if you searched through the rubble for the bottle, then that was a very reckless and foolish thing to do," Jean scolded. But he wasn't listening. He had provided for his family, and his wife was content. Jean sighed and made them a cup of tea before directing them to the rest centre at the end of the following road, where her unknown colleague would help this newly homeless family.

It was a long night. Endless cups of tea were poured, and all the sandwiches ran out. There was a seemingly never-ending stream of poor, unhappy people and wet, tired firemen. Yet happily, as the thin early light became full day, it was reckoned that the actual number of casualties was low – although every loss was a tragedy, untold grief for the people that loved the person who was now a statistic.

"Nobody complained," Jean said to Fee after they had thanked an equally tired fireman for helping them to attach the canteen to the car, ready for the journey home to Cambridge, and climbed in, Fee to the driver's seat and Jean to the passenger side.

"I should hope bloody not!" was Fiona's opinion. "Best cup of tea outside of the Savoy is what we offer."

Jean found a scrap of energy to laugh at Fiona's description of W.V.S. tea. At the start of the war, she would have shrunk back from anyone who swore, and she certainly would never have been friends with a factory man's wife. How much had changed!

"No, I mean, no one complained about the raid or how we sort this mess out."

"What, not even the wailing mother?"

"She wasn't complaining. She was crying because she'd been so scared during the raid and because it's going to be such a job to replace all the things she's lost."

"Well, I don't know about you, Jean, but I need a hot bath and a good sleep. Come on, let's get this thing back to base," Fiona said as she started the dark blue Austin's engine. "At least we can't get lost in the daylight," she chuckled, and Jean smiled too at the thought of the number of times they had pitted their wits against streets and lanes bereft of lights.

The war of the mobile canteen versus the darkness.

She had rubbed the ridge on her forehead where her tin hat had bitten her skin throughout the shift, shut her eyes heavy with sleep, leaned her head against the car window to the sound of Fiona's chatter, and drifted off.

3.
A PLACE TO RELAX

The brewing tea in the pansy teapot was ready. Jean took a matching cup and saucer and a little milk jug down from the cupboard next to the hob. They were all three parts of a tea set given to her by her aunt and uncle for her wedding, but now only five cups and saucers of the original eight remained, along with the milk jug and the sugar bowl without its lid. Then she took the glass milk bottle from the fridge and poured some into the little pansy milk jug. She returned the milk to the fridge before pouring milk from the jug into her teacup. Silly really, she could have put the milk directly from the bottle into the teacup, but then that wouldn't be proper tea, would it? And anyway, she might want a second cup. She poured the brewed tea on top of the milk. To keep the pot warm for the possible second cup, she pulled the knitted sheep tea cosy over the spout and handle, smiling as she did so at the strangely shaped sheep knitted by Barbara when a little girl and still being used.

She took her cup of tea to the drawing room and put it on the small side table next to her favourite place on the sofa while she went over to the fireplace and picked up the fire iron and stirred the embers of the fire that Eleanor had made for her earlier in the afternoon, adding a few more pieces of coal from the copper scuttle. Then she returned to her sofa and sipped her tea slowly as she watched the golden flames rise in the fireplace, their reflection dancing and gleaming on the copper scuttle. She played with the patterns they made in her head. Memories of Mrs Appleby (dear Mrs Appleby), Mrs Fielding, Fiona Larkin, the soldiers in the canteen, the old man in his pyjamas after the air raid danced together in her mind with the pretty flames reflected in the scuttle. She wondered what had raised these shimmering ghosts to the forefront of her mind this afternoon. Had it been the remembrance of the conversation with Maeve about the W.V.S? Or was it that she felt particularly sad this afternoon, troubled that the moorings of her life were being cut piece by piece and that she was about to drift into the unknown? Was it this that was compelling her to find comfort in something so simple as making and drinking tea, and that, in turn, reminded her of how she had given comfort to those who most needed it during the war? She wasn't sure, and feeling it was too complicated, too dangerous, to examine more closely, she snipped her musings in the bud and let her eyes continue to delight in the copper flame patterns.

The village council approved the plan for the soldiers' canteen in the Reading Room at the village hall at speed after the tea party meeting, thanks to Mrs Harding, whose husband was chairman. Mrs Finlayson from the W.V.S. central office in Cambridge gave considerable advice on how to set up the canteen, explaining that the canteens were to be a place for refreshment and relaxation when the soldiers were off duty. Light suppers, afternoon tea, and the suchlike could and should be served at low prices for the soldiers to purchase. Additional costs incurred would need to be supported by fundraising.

August floated past the ladies in a holiday haze. There was no use in actioning any of their plans with so many away, the children at home from school, and extended family members staying with them on their holidays. But Alan had been correct – conflict was imminent. The holidays ended, September arrived, and with it, war. The expectation of German air attacks jolted the country into a shocked frenzy of preparation. Millions of gas masks for the whole population, including special ones for babies, issued the year before, now had to be treated seriously, taken out from the cupboards and down from the shelves where they had been stored when Chamberlain had assured the country of peace.

The light was to be imprisoned. Thick blackout curtains covering each window, incarcerated electric light, candle-light, torchlight. Light would not guide the path of the Luftwaffe's night bombs. Shelters needed to be found: secure cellars identified, sturdy furniture put in place, dug-outs excavated in gardens. Places of safety had to be made ready to welcome the frightened for hours on end, any time of the day or night – should the siren sound.

For the first weeks of the war, Jean was so tired from all she had to do that she fell asleep the instant her head hit her pillow, only to wake in the small hours, her pulse racing and her body shaking with fear; the fear of losing those she loved, as she had lost Nicholas and being powerless to prevent it. But nothing happened. Yesterday was just the same as the day before and the day before that, and the realisation came to her that tomorrow would surely be the same. There were no bombs. There was no invasion.

August laziness followed by the need to prepare their own homes for war, caused a slight delay in the preparations for the canteen. A delay which was understandable but not ideal, as troop reinforcements could be expected any day. So it was that on a bright morning towards the end of September, Jean waited for Mrs Appleby outside the village hall. It was the first day that September revealed it was prepared to consider that October might be around the corner. There was a hint of a chill in the air, and the sunshine was golden.

"Thank you for coming to help," Jean welcomed Mrs Appleby from where she was waiting outside the village hall door, but then wished she hadn't opened the conversation in such a way, as she couldn't be sure that she wasn't there to help Mrs Appleby. It was, after all, Mrs Appleby and not herself whom Mrs Fielding had entrusted with the key.

"That's quite fine, Mrs Barnet. I'm pleased we can get this up and running for the boys," Mrs Appleby responded simply and with practical goodwill.

Mrs Appleby's first point of call was the kitchenette. After putting on her apron and gloves, which she took from her bag, she asked Jean to take out all the cups, saucers, and plates from the cupboards and all the cutlery from the drawers and place everything on the large table in the Reading Room. Then Jean was to make a list of all the items while she cleaned the tiny kitchen from top to bottom.

"I've made the list," Jean said when it was complete and handed it to her new colleague, wondering if what she was doing was of any use or whether Mrs Appleby just wanted her out of the kitchenette while she worked.

Mrs Appleby frowned when she looked at the assortment of crockery and cutlery on the table and Jean's list.

"It's not going to be enough, and we have to allow for breakages," she commented, adding, "there aren't enough serving plates neither. You won't believe how much cake and sandwiches men can get through."

The two ladies replaced it all in the now clean cupboards. Mrs Appleby had worked fast, Jean thought, to have the whole kitchenette clean so quickly.

They then turned their attention to the Reading Room. It was probably larger than it seemed as a long wooden table occupied the centre, two huge bookcases lined the walls, and an old, rather enormous sideboard had been pushed up against the window.

"It's difficult to know what the men are going to want exactly," Jean commented as she surveyed the room, pondering how best to rearrange the furniture.

"I think most boys are the same," Mrs Appleby said wisely. "They're going to need a place to relax – feel like they're off-duty."

"So, it has to be comfortable," Jean continued, "with

31

more easy chairs, as I suggested to Mrs Fielding …"

"… and some writing tables so they can write letters home …" Mrs Appleby continued.

"… or eat a sandwich and have a cup of tea …"

"… but some might want to sit together and chat while they eat their supper …"

"… so, we will need to keep the long table."

Without realising, Mrs Appleby and Jean were beginning to start and finish each other's sentences as together they imagined the canteen and how cosy it could be. The first step was to find some of the larger pieces of furniture a new home.

"But we should keep one of the bookcases because the soldiers might want to borrow books to read in the evening," Jean proposed.

"Or play games."

"Board games?" Jean said, surprised, but then why not? It was their spare time when not on duty.

"Yes, we could put them on the lower shelves, and the boys can help themselves."

Jean thought about the evenings she spent at home in her comfortable drawing room. Something was missing. She knitted her eyebrows together and played at the sweet pea-patterned scarf tied around her neck, straining to think what else the boys could need.

It came to her. "A wireless!"

"Yes, and a gramophone and records," Mrs Appleby agreed.

"Really?" It wasn't an item on the top of Jean's list.

"Oh yes, Stanley would want a gramophone, Mrs Barnet,

most definitely, if it was him here."

It was quite a list: crockery, cutlery, easy chairs, coffee tables, board games, a wireless, a gramophone and records.

"We'll never get it all," Jean worried.

"Don't you worry, Mrs Barnet, I'm sure we will," Mrs Appleby announced confidently as she set to work cleaning the Reading Room – a task begun that day in September and completed every morning to come while the big guns were based in the heart of their picturesque village.

Mrs Fielding was energised by Jean's list and used her powers of vicarage persuasion to have the unnecessary furniture removed and second-hand armchairs and coffee-writing tables acquired. A notice given out by the vicar at the next Sunday service requesting board games led to a wonderful assortment of entertainments – ludo, chess, Monopoly, and the like – being donated from homes around the Parish. And, incredibly, a gramophone with a collection of records was also given. How lucky and how generous, the newly formed Grantchester branch of the W.V.S. agreed amongst themselves.

Mrs Finlayson at the Cambridge W.V.S. office recommended that all the crockery be the same type and colour so that any items straying inadvertently around the village could be recognised and repatriated. These would have to be purchased, as would a wireless.

"A jumble sale!" Mrs Roberts proposed at the next tea party committee meeting for the canteen.

"Excellent idea, Elspeth," Mrs Fielding agreed. "In the village hall. Mrs Barnet, you will make us some posters, won't you? I know you have quite a skill with a pencil and a paintbrush."

Jean felt her cheeks flush, and she fiddled nervously with her scarf.

"I'm not really … Not really sure what … what I'd draw," she stammered.

"Oh, that's quite all right for now. Mrs Appleby will no doubt give you some ideas," the older lady brushed off Jean's reticence.

Jean reluctantly agreed and then enthusiastically procrastinated.

A few days later, Jean found herself in another new experience with Mrs Appleby – sorting and pricing ornaments, books, clothing, utensils, a plethora of items cast off by one set of villagers to be sold to their neighbours.

"You've never been to a jumble sale, have you, Mrs Barnet?" Mrs Appleby couldn't hide her astonishment. "And what do you do with the things you no longer want?"

Jean felt irritated, slightly criticised. She prided herself on only buying what the family needed, so there was never excess to cast out. What was more, she made and mended the girls' clothes, keeping the twins' outgrown dresses and skirts for Eleanor. She preferred to borrow books from the city library rather than buy new copies in the numerous book shops, and she used utensils until they broke, at which point she fixed them or had them fixed. And if she did want to decorate her house with new ornaments, she would be horrified if what she had acquired had previously belonged to a neighbour.

"Well, of course, I've given to jumble sale collections," Jean answered apologetically, not telling the truth.

That evening Jean drew a poster picture of the village hall with a queue of villagers heading in to buy and others heading out with items in bags – she couldn't bring herself to draw the objects. Sometimes it is best to leave things hidden.

The sale was held in the main hall the following Saturday

morning. It was so much more fun than Jean could have ever expected. It seemed as if the whole village attended. Even old Mr Thomas, who could only shuffle around now with two walking sticks and smelt of stale urine, made his way slowly to the hall and was greeted warmly by Mrs Fielding, who cut him an extra thick slice of homemade cake for his tuppence.

The village children, under the supervision of Miss Edmunds, the teacher at the village school, had drawn a gallery of rather funny and quite attractive pictures of soldiers drinking tea in their new canteen, and these had been used to decorate the walls. Many of the village women had donated pots of their newly-made jam, and there was a buzz of buying and selling, gossip and chatter, as if this were a summer fête.

Jean served tea and cake for two hours that morning from the tiny kitchenette, the first shift of many, in a rota devised by Mrs Fielding. She would have liked to have worn her new W.V.S. uniform that she had bought and paid for herself, to show her little world in Grantchester that she was part of a bigger team, that in her own way, she too was volunteering for King and Country, but the thick overcoat was too heavy for early autumn and for being inside.

Mrs Appleby worked tirelessly alongside her. She must have been at least fifteen years older than Jean. Grey streaked her mousy hair, and she had deep lines around her eyes and mouth creeping down into her neck. Despite the inevitable middle-aged girth, her energy matched that of a much younger woman.

But the years caught up with Mrs Appleby.

Early in 1942 – how could Jean forget? – Mrs Appleby had arrived at her home to tidy the kitchen, help with the laundry, and make the beds. She had started to come and help Jean when Jean's maid had been called up, and Jean

35

found herself overwhelmed with her W.V.S. work as well as managing a home. Yet Mrs Appleby was busy herself, cleaning the W.V.S. canteen at first light before heading to the Barnet's and then to the vicarage. That morning the daily help's face was grey and filled with pain. She had aged twenty years overnight.

"Mrs Appleby, what's wrong?" Jean exclaimed, full of concern when she saw her.

Silent tears welled up in the older lady's steel-blue eyes, and the words stuck in her throat.

"Come in and sit down," Jean said kindly, leading Mrs Appleby to the chair at the kitchen table, "I'll make some tea," but before she could do so, the tears fell down Mrs Appleby's cheeks, and sobs took hold of her body.

"My dear, please tell me what's wrong. How can I help?" Jean soothed, while groping in mental darkness for what could have upset Mrs Appleby so much.

"Oh, Mrs Barnet – you haven't heard?" Mrs Appleby managed to utter.

"Heard what?"

"Singapore – the Japs have taken it."

The colour drained from Jean's face. Her hand flew to her mouth to suppress a violent urge to vomit.

Singapore, the gateway to the British Empire, un-assailable, unattackable – fallen! And – oh God no! The Cambridgeshire Regiment, local boys, only recently left from England to defend that country. Had they arrived? Were they safe? Her eyes became wide in frightened questioning.

Mrs Appleby seemed to crumple.

"The Regiment! They've been forced to surrender, Stanley!" And Mrs Appleby could speak no more as the sobs strangled her until she could scarcely breathe.

"Oh, my dear," Jean whispered softly, putting her arms around her domestic help, her colleague, and her friend.

What could be said? Nothing.

"You know I lost Bernard too?" Mrs Appleby added when again she could breathe.

"Bernard?"

"My husband. At the Somme. Stanley never knew him."

Jean's heart bled for this poor woman, the loss she had suffered was overwhelming.

"I'm sorry, I didn't know." But then, neither had she ever thought to ask.

"I'll make you a cup of tea, my dear. It will make you feel better. Everyone needs a good cup of tea."

Mrs Appleby managed a weak smile at Jean's words.

"We must hope, we must pray," Mrs Appleby dug deep inside herself to find resolution, "and we must do everything we can to look after the boys that are sent to us to care for, and trust God that someone will care for Stanley and all our Cambridge boys."

4.

THE MAYOR IN THE BOX

The Second World War had all happened a generation ago. Enough years had passed for it to seem like a different era, but in some ways, it was only yesterday. For the six years of conflict, Jean had been filled with a purpose that she had never experienced before and had never experienced since. She had worked hard, and she had made friends, special friends. She wished those times could have continued, and then, as always, she felt guilty. How could a decent person wish that a war could continue? As if to change her thoughts, she rose and, with great agitation, poked and stirred the burning coals in the fireplace, causing soot and ash to rise from the fire and fall onto the hearth. She would have more to clean up tomorrow, but she didn't care. She returned to her place on the sofa, feeling even more alone in the large drawing room than she had done before. In not too many weeks, she would be gone, and she would have exchanged this large drawing room for a smaller one. Eleanor was right, there was still so much to do, but the need for activity only provoked inertia in her. Mrs Fielding and Alice would have had everything organised for a move by now.

The grandfather clock tick-tocked in the corner of the room, a bass accompaniment to the flame dance. At first, its notes were background, but then the tick-tocking became insistent, imposing, until the clock said strictly and clearly, "You-must-sort-out-the-papers Jean!"

"Well, if you insist," she conceded to the clock. She knew now which box she would start with.

On the top of the wardrobe in her bedroom, pushed right to the back, up against the floral wallpaper, was a box. At first, Jean tried to reach up just by stretching, but it was no use, as she knew would be the case before she started. So now she found herself balancing precariously on her dressing-table stool, trying to reach it. In front was the hatbox, which still contained the hat she had bought for Barbara's wedding and had never worn again. Now that was a box which could be dispatched to a jumble sale.

The boxes and the top of the wardrobe were covered in a thick layer of dust. Jean sneezed but thought better of taking her hand off the wardrobe frame to reach for her hankie stuffed up her sleeve in case that action put her further off balance. Gosh, Eleanor would be cross with her if she could see her now! With a bit of wiggling and another couple of sneezes, Jean retrieved the cardboard box she wanted and took it downstairs. She paused, holding the box outside the study door. Alan's desk was still next to the large bay window with the beautiful view across the garden. Despite the grey rainy afternoon, it was light and airy in the room – a lovely place to work. Instinctively she turned away to the kitchen, placed the old box on the table, and poured herself the anticipated second cup of tea, now only vaguely warm despite the knitted sheep tea cosy's valiant efforts.

She felt strangely nervous – a little like how she had felt when she had attended her school reunion a couple of years ago. Meeting old friends and acquaintances again, girls whom she had known in her youth but with whom she had not kept up, had brought a quiet sadness at missing out in their lives, but also a feeling of relief of not having to complicate her own life by following theirs. Regret and relief coexisted.

Jean hadn't looked inside this box for nearly twenty years – it felt like a lifetime. For some, it was. Gently, she eased the lid from its base with a rocking motion. It was a sturdy box in heavy-duty cardboard with thin strips of metal reinforcing the edges – built to last. The emblem of a local paper manufacturer was emblazoned on the lid. Inside was a pile of papers: letters in small brown envelopes, postcards, Christmas cards, photographs, posters, sketches, newspaper clippings, documents, and notebooks, in no apparent order. She knew what kind of memories were in the box, even if some of the memories themselves were hazy. She did not touch the papers, only looked at the pile in front of her, sipping her tea and gently massaging her aching back.

Mayor gives Freedom of Borough to Cambridgeshire Regiment

The headline shouted from the newspaper clipping on the top of the pile. This was the last memory that she had included in the box nearly two decades ago. Below the headline was a grainy photograph of a thin lady standing on the Guildhall balcony in the centre of Cambridge, surrounded by male dignitaries. The lady seemed out of place alongside so much uniformed and official masculinity. To her left stood a Regiment General, to her right a robed office-bearer in dress-suit and top hat, carrying the silver mace of Cambridge over his shoulder. Further along the balcony, the University was represented by the Chancellor in his robe and mortar board. The lady, probably in her mid-forties, looked like a skinny black cockerel in her oversized Admiral bicorne hat, dark robe, and heavy Mayoral chain, which lay harshly on her flat chest. Yet she stood in front of the microphone to address the crowd absurdly elegant and charismatically self-assured.

It had been a warm autumn day, Jean remembered. No need for coats. Perhaps September? Yes, a glance at the newspaper date, 30th September 1946, so the ceremony must have been the day before, on Sunday 29th. She had been part of the vast Cambridge crowd that day, lining the streets, honouring the survivors of the Cambridgeshire Regiment, waving and cheering, feeling full of admiration for the town's boys, those of this war and two prior – and also for the new mayor, a woman and a friend!

The town was alive. The excitement of celebration ran like an electric current through the streets. Jean stood with her daughters in the crowd. Eleanor, only ten and finding it hard to see, clutched her Union flag and slipped between adults, weaving her way to a space at the front where other children had also found their way to an unobstructed view.

All around, a town was coming together in celebration and honour. A thousand people, maybe more, formed a neat crowd, packed tightly into the square, spilling out into the arteries beyond. There were men in suits, ladies wearing their Sunday best and hats, shabby from years of war but special, nonetheless. An island of councillors and community representatives sitting on chairs waited patiently for the parade to commence. Friends, families, neighbours, and well-wishers of the Regiment chatted excitedly. On the Guildhall balcony, behind the railings emblazoned with the coat of arms of the city, dignitaries in assorted uniforms were beginning to assemble. A technician was making the final checks on the microphone. His efforts caused a whine and a buzz to be emitted from the loudspeakers, which made the eyes of the assembling crowd turn to the balcony, where nothing of interest was happening. The eyes turned away, and the mouths continued their conversations.

Alan was not with them. He had joined his former regiment for the parade despite his stiff leg and the hours of standing around that the ceremony would demand. That morning, he had brought out the military ribbons from thirty years before, showing them the light of day that they had not seen in all that time. He pinned them to the pocket on the breast of his jacket, much to Eleanor's delight and astonishment.

"Daddy, they're beautiful. How did you ...?" she said, as she reached out to touch what to her were masculine trinkets. She had grown so much recently, and her crown nearly reached his throat.

"Not now, Eleanor," he responded abrasively. "We'll be late." He was too full of his own thoughts to answer any of hers and hurried his family out of the door to the bus stop.

This was the last weekend that all the girls would be at home. The university term would start the next week, and the twins would be off. Maeve was heading to Manchester for chemistry and Barbara to London for history. Jean was proud of them. She was grateful to Alan that he thought it important and was prepared to finance their continued education, but she was nevertheless anxious that Maeve was going so far away. She would have preferred her to be at one of the London Colleges, like Barbara, who would be at UCL. But Maeve had done so well to secure a place on such a well-thought-of course, especially now that so many young men were coming home demobbed and wanting to continue their lives. Like these Cambridgeshire lads marching in their parade of honour, which they so much deserved. So much was changing – again.

The sound of a drum beating the rhythm for hundreds of pairs of feet pulsed into the square. Waving and cheering, the crowd greeted the regiment, watching it process and form lines below the balcony. The soldiers of the wars before took their positions behind. Maeve thought she could see Alan, but Barbara wasn't sure.

An expectant hush fell across the square as the mayor, Councillor Lady Bragg, began to speak into her microphone. Her voice was light, soft, and warm, every syllable of every word clearly and slowly pronounced. She always spoke as if you were the only person listening to her and as if you were her closest friend, Jean remembered.

The speeches were given, and the soldiers processed again. With Mrs Appleby standing alongside her, Jean waved and cheered with the crowd, so grateful that the wars were over, that these men, and others, were safely home and thankful that this day marked the end and perhaps even a beginning.

Jean put the newspaper clipping back on top of the pile of papers in the box. The December day was short, and although still only late afternoon, it was dark outside now. She went over to the window and looked out into the black garden. It was still raining. Eleanor would be getting very wet, she thought, as she pulled the curtain tight across, keeping the light safe inside with her.

5.

ALICE

A CALL TO DUTY

London, June 1938

Supper had been served, little Patience was in bed, and Lawrence was reading *The Enchanted Castle* with eight-year-old Margaret, curled up together on the chaise-longue in his study. In perfect contentment, Alice Bragg sat at her gilt Georgian writing table, putting the finishing touches to an article she was writing for *The Yorkshire Post*. She was in what she called her 'boudoir' – the small, light, bright room leading from the grand drawing room in their private government apartment on the second floor of Bushy House. The scent of the ancient magnolia, which covered the mansion's south wall with its creamy blooms, wafted deliciously through the open window transforming Alice's boudoir into a bower. In Bushy Park beyond, across the ha-ha, deer grazed peacefully, as they had done for hundreds of years.

The newspaper article was a humorous account of a trip to Paris. Alice enjoyed writing her 'bits and pieces' for newspapers and magazines, although nowadays, she found that she was pressed for time since so much of her day and many of her evenings too were taken up with social engagements in support of Lawrence's position as the Director of the National Physics Laboratory at Teddington. As an eminent civil servant and the youngest-ever winner of the Nobel Prize, there were many functions for them both to attend, as well as formal dinners to host in the even grander dining room on the first floor.

As she was reading, correcting phrases here and there,

she heard a car's tyres crunching the gravel on the drive leading to the house. Strange. They weren't expecting any guests this evening, and the scientists who worked in the laboratories on the ground floor had all gone home for the night.

Clipped heels on the drive and doorstep, followed by the mellow call of the doorbell, drew Alice from her desk.

"Sylvia!" she exclaimed in surprise when their maid had shown in the new arrival – an attractive woman with nut-brown short wavy hair, dressed in a chambray blue suit, nipped in by a belt at the waist and wearing a discreet hat, fashionably perched on the side of her head, and white gloves.

"What a surprise! But how delightful, do come in!" Alice held out her arms to embrace her friend.

"Sorry for not telephoning in advance, Alice. I hope I'm not disturbing you. I wanted to see you just as soon as I could, so I took a chance that you would be free, and anyway, it's a glorious evening for a drive."

"Is everything all right?" Alice asked anxiously. Friends did not usually drop in as Bushy House was somewhat remote, although they were always made to feel most welcome when they did – Alice loved a busy, people-filled home.

"Yes, absolutely fine, my dear, but I have something extremely important I want to talk to you about." She took off her hat and gloves and handed them to the maid as she spoke.

Sylvia Moulton-Fletcher was not an impetuous woman. She was a hardworking Girton College law graduate now called to the Bar and practising in the Chancery Division at the High Court. But the news she had to impart could not wait. There was a breathless urgency in her voice married to

45

a tone of excitement.

"Have you been keeping track of all this business with that ghastly man Hitler, Alice?" Sylvia questioned when the two were alone in the boudoir bower, the slight remembrance of her Connecticut childhood years lingering on the word 'ghastly' making the word even more pronounced to Alice's ears than the meaning of the word itself.

Alice nodded and replied sadly, "Of course, it's a bad business."

"I presume Lawrence is involved with planning for war? No, you don't need to tell me about it. I'm sure it's all top secret." Alice did not respond.

"I met a rather outstanding lady today. In fact, I should say two outstanding ladies," Sylvia continued. "I received a telephone call from the Home Office yesterday. It appears my name is on a list drawn up by Mary Smieton – she's about our age and rather a highflyer at the Ministry of Labour but has now been seconded to the Home Office."

"You're on a list?" Alice queried in alarm.

"Yes, it's a list of what you might call 'can-do' women identified as particularly able to assist Lady Reading with setting up a new women's organisation for civil defence. I was intrigued and a little flattered, so I agreed to meet with Lady Reading today. To cut to the chase, Alice, this new women's organisation is important. The talk today is of civil defence but with men called up and probably single women too, if you believe the rumours circulating in the city, then it's going to be a great deal more than civil defence. It's going to be about keeping the country on its feet. I've agreed to join, and I want you to too."

Alice felt a little thrill of excitement travel along her spine. She and Lawrence had been having long talks recently, in the evenings, when the girls were safely asleep in their beds. They both viewed with concern the political developments on the continent, and in the circles they moved in, they were privy to information and opinions that were not necessarily mainstream.

If there were to be war, it would not be like the last – everybody in the know said the same. Whilst aircraft had been new inventions in the Great War, mainly used for reconnaissance, now they were instruments of death and destruction. The grim news from Spain, gripped in a tragic civil war, gave a terrible forecast for any future war elsewhere in Europe.

It was clear that Lawrence would have a role to play in the national effort. But what would hers be? The thought had been nagging at her daily. She had only been a young girl in the Great War, and there wasn't much she could do, although she and Enid, her sister, had regularly dressed up and entertained the wounded soldiers under their father's care at the hospital in Manchester. Enid would play the piano, and she would sing songs like Ivor Novello's *Keep the Home Fires Burning* or the American tune *There's a Long, Long Winding Road*. But her favourite was a hit from the Music Hall *Which Switch is the Switch for Miss Ipswich*, which she sang word-perfect in her strong, clear voice, never falling over the words of the tongue-twister and acting out the comedy. Her father had bought her the gramophone recording made by the vaudeville singer, Bill Murray, and even now, from time to time, she would dress up and sing along:

> Which switch, Miss, is the switch for Ipswich?
> It's the Ipswich switch which I require.

It was flippant, she knew, but it hid the pain. It hid the pain of a dead brother, of dead friends, and somehow it had allowed her to go on.

"If Lawrence thinks it's a good idea, then I will go and

47

see your Lady Reading," she said, eyes twinkling at the thrill of the unexpected prospect of a new adventure.

A few days later, a quiet secretary showed Alice and Sylvia into the single-room office at Horseferry House, Westminster. It was a small room, evidently intended for one person, but had been commandeered as office space for three women: one sitting at the desk reading through papers with intense concentration, another making notes in front, and a typist, clicking furiously, under evident pressure in the corner. The lady sitting behind the desk dominated the office. She looked Persian, Alice thought, with short black wavy hair, a long aquiline nose, and high cheekbones. She could have been Athene in goddess draperies. She could have crowned herself with a helmet and held a pointed spear aloft to command ancient armies. She could have been woven into tapestries or sculpted in marble.

"Lady Reading, Mrs Bragg, and Miss Moulton-Fletcher have arrived," the secretary announced from the doorway.

The Athenian goddess looked up from her lists and, with a gracious smile, beckoned Alice and Sylvia into the small office, brushing the paperwork aside to be gathered up by the woman who had been making notes.

"Miss Moulton-Fletcher, I'm delighted to meet you again, and Mrs Bragg, thank you for agreeing to come. Do sit down." Lady Reading effused in her heavy foreign accent as if a continental society hostess. But her domain was nothing more than a shoe box, and the fact that only four chairs were in the shoe box had become embarrassingly apparent to the new arrivals.

"We feel like we are squatting at the Home Office," the note-taker explained with warmth. "I'm Mary Smieton, formerly from the Ministry of Labour," and she leaned forward to shake Alice and Sylvia's hands. "Please sit down. I am quite happy to sit on the floor."

Alice kept her face deadpan as if it were perfectly normal for a senior civil servant to sit on the floor during a meeting but stored up all the details to recount to Lawrence later.

"My rank entitles me to a carpet," Lady Reading said ironically. "A carpet in a broom cupboard," she added without rancour. It was what it was.

"Tea?" she questioned and rang a bell on her desk for the quiet secretary outside to deliver.

Stella Isaacs, Dowager Lady Reading, was neither young nor old – probably in her middle forties, Alice presumed. Dressed impeccably in a well-designed light tweed suit and cream silk blouse, she held court from her Home Office desk and scrutinised Alice with her dark eagle eyes.

"Mrs Bragg," she commenced, "I am sure Miss Moulton-Fletcher has explained to you that at Sir Samuel Hoare's request, I am founding a national women's organisation to assist with Air Raid Precautions. The threat of war is real and imminent. We have no foresight as to when war will be upon us or what war will mean to the people of this country. Each region, each town, and each village even, will face its particular challenges and needs. The women of Great Britain will have a crucial role to play, and their part, no matter how great or small, will keep the country together in this trial, keep the machinery of day-to-day life in motion, and women will bring comfort to all those in need around them. This organisation must be run by women at a local level, with co-ordination only from the centre. It is on the ground – in the streets and in the homes of this country – that the war will be fought and won."

Lady Reading addressed Alice from behind the desk as if from a podium. The shoe box office was not a chamber for conversation but a stage for oratory. She held Alice's gaze and paused momentarily, seeking to read the effect of her words on Alice's expression and, pleased with what she

49

found, she continued.

"Miss Moulton-Fletcher believes, Mrs Bragg, that you are the type of woman who would embrace such a cause. She thinks you will be able to assist me in recruiting volunteers. These volunteers will be trained to know what to do when the air raid sirens sound and how to assist whoever, wherever and whenever the bombs fall – for fall they will."

Alice had sat quietly throughout Lady Reading's opening speech of explanation. She was not afraid of the impending war. Her sense of duty, of Christian service to others, was the skeleton of her personality, as hard bones were the skeleton beneath her flesh. But she wasn't sure why Sylvia and now Lady Reading thought that she was of the calibre to be in the advance guard of this new women's brigade. Not that she doubted her ability in any way, but she was the first to admit that she was not the same type of woman as Sylvia. Sylvia was a hard-working and clever barrister who was respected for her intellect and efficiency. Sylvia was the obvious choice to assist Lady Reading. Alice had partied and flirted her way through her degree course at Cambridge. Even now, at nearly 40 years old and a mother of four, she still relished parties, dinners, and theatrical performances. She liked to travel with her husband and work in her garden, read stories to her daughters, and enjoy the escapades of her sons. Not that she was lazy – not at all, she just enjoyed being with people and all the glorious social interaction people of all ages and classes had to offer.

But Lady Reading's intense, insistent message delivered through her heavily accented words was invigorating. It was as if her coal-black eyes and dark voice had cast a spell over Alice. It led her to the platform before the ancient army, equipping her with helmet and spear, then presenting her as the soldiers' new captain under the command of herself, Lady Reading, the Major-General.

"Lady Reading, please tell me what you would like me to

do."

The Dowager Duchess nodded in satisfaction at the addition of a worthy recruit to her ranks, and Miss Smieton smiled her agreement from the carpet.

"I want you to go to Manchester, Mrs Bragg." The Major General gave her orders. "I understand from Miss Moulton-Fletcher that you know a great many people in the city. I intend to travel there to recruit in July. I need you to prepare the way."

And indeed, Alice was the obvious choice for this task, as all the women present knew, perhaps even the typist in the corner whose fingers relentlessly tap-tapped the keys of her machine as if her life depended on it. Alice, who had lived most of her thirty-nine years in Manchester. Alice, the intelligent socialite who made and kept friends easily. Yes, Alice would know who to ask, invite, and persuade.

"You were a pupil at St Leonard's, were you not?" Stella Reading asked abruptly.

"Yes," Alice replied, unsure at the change of wind.

"I find that women from public schools such as St Leonards, Roedean or Cheltenham are good organisers – reliable and responsible too. Women such as you, Mrs Bragg, are a safe choice. For originality, I would probably look elsewhere."

At Bushy House later that evening, Lawrence was silent after Alice had described her visit to the Home Office in theatrical detail.

"I'm not sure I like the sound of your Lady Reading, darling," he finally offered. "But you are bound to succeed, my dear, as you have perfected the art of delegating, and there is nothing you can't persuade people to do. I have every confidence in you." And so saying, he bent a face full of adoring love to his wife's lively face and placed a kiss on her lips. A kiss which sealed his support for her endeavours, whatever they might be and for however long they might last.

6.
RECRUITMENT

Manchester, July 1938

Alice stood at the doors of the Baptist Church hall, neatly dressed in a navy summer suit and with a bright, welcoming smile exposing her slight buck teeth. A poster advertising the event she had organised was pinned to the street-facing noticeboard at her shoulder. 'WOMEN WANTED for A.R.P.' was the catchy title, in green capitals on a cream background, accompanied by the date, time, and place of the meeting. So far, only half a dozen middle-aged ladies had arrived and chosen their seats, avoiding the front row. A brighter, more noticeable, more enthusiastic poster would have been better, Alice thought regretfully, but there had been no time and no one available with design talents – yet.

The last six weeks had passed in a whirl of activity. Lady Reading had officially launched her Women's Voluntary Service at a Press Conference at the House of Commons on Saturday, 18th June, to coincide with the anniversary of the Battle of Waterloo. *We won that battle; we can win this*, was the clear rallying cry. And later, on the wireless at 9 o'clock, she had addressed the nation. Alice and Lawrence listened to the radio broadcast together in their drawing room, Lawrence trying to imagine the woman belonging to the deep Mediterranean tones and Alice imagining housewives of all classes listening to the broadcast in their homes and wondering what they would think. Would they be stirred to act, to join, to help? How aware was Britain that a terrible crisis was hovering like a great buzzard circling above a tiny field vole?

It was so good to return to Manchester. Alice had grown up here and, until recently, had spent all her married life in the city. It was a little holiday despite the circumstances – lunches, teas, and dinners with friends and family. Each engagement was an opportunity to spread the word of the W.V.S. and to encourage those she knew to play their part.

Today at the church hall was different. Today she was reaching out to unknown women with unknown reactions and opinions.

"Good afternoon, welcome," Alice greeted another two ladies arriving at the meeting – friends, one with a face of anticipation, the other with a face full of reticence, as if she had been cajoled into accompanying her friend. They were smartly dressed, but to an eye interested in fashion, it was easy to tell that their attire was not expensive. Shop managers' or office workers' wives, Alice concluded.

"Please do come in and join us for a cup of tea," she continued in the same tones to two total strangers as if she had been welcoming well-known guests to her own home.

"Thank you so much," the cheerful lady replied and, turning to her friend, said, "Come on, Betty, let's find out what's what," before linking her arm through Betty's to ensure that Betty made it through the entrance and into the hall.

"I don't know why I've come, Nora," Alice could hear Betty grumble as the two passed through the doors. "It just isn't going to be as bad as you think. No one wants a repeat of last time."

Last time! A trauma so awful, losses so terrible, no language for the pain that was still twenty years raw for them all. But Germany had re-occupied the Rhineland and now reunified with Austria. Hitler was rearming. The terms of the Peace Treaty were broken. At where would Germany stop?

"Good afternoon," a new voice addressed Alice. A plump middle-aged lady in a maroon silk print summer dress, immaculate white silk gloves, and elegant summer hat with a dark red Peter Pan feather sitting aslant on her short permanently waved hair. "Is this the women's meeting?"

"Yes, please do come in," Alice greeted.

"I'm a good organiser, you know," the lady informed Alice and entered the building.

A good organiser, a good delegator, a good team member, good at getting on with whatever needed to be done without making a fuss. Alice knew that all these qualities would be necessary.

"'Scuse me!"

Alice turned to a young, desperately thin woman of about twenty or so resting her bird weight on the frame of a large, battered pram. Inside, a baby girl lay on her back asleep, cheek turned to the left, arms to either side of her head – an infant weight-lifter, dreaming of raising an imaginary bar in her pram. A little lad, probably not much past two, peered around his mother's shabby skirts and looked at Alice suspiciously.

"Can I help?" Alice inquired, expecting to be asked the way to a shop or a park.

"Is this the meeting about the war help?"

"Yes, it is."

"I'm sorry I had to bring the babies," the young woman rushed. "Gladys, my sister couldn't mind them today, she got called in for an extra day's work, and I couldn't stop her. Lord knows how she needs the money, and Harry couldn't switch his shift. But I thought I'd come anyway, 'coz I want to help, and it's taken us over an hour on the bus." She looked nervously up to Alice, her tired eyes pleading not to be sent away.

"You don't think I can help?" the woman said, shoulders

55

drooping. "I do want to help, really, I do. You think just because I've got littl'uns I'd be no good at volunteering, but I can do lots. I can do first aid – I've learned it. And I can knit – see here I knitted Bobby's cardigan – I can knit socks for soldiers ..." her voice trailed off, and she bit her lip to prevent tears from welling in her tired eyes.

"My dear, you are most welcome at our meeting," Alice assured. "Let me help you with the pram up the steps, and you, young man, you must be Bobby? I expect you are hungry after your long ride on the bus. Mrs O'Connor is inside at the serving hatch. I'm sure she will find you an extra special biscuit."

With difficulty, the two women heaved the cumbersome pram up the steps without disturbing the sleeping child.

"What's her name?"

"Emily Ann," her mother answered proudly.

"She's lovely."

"Thank you."

"All women are welcome. All women are needed," Alice said. "Thank you for coming." Alice guided her to the refreshments.

Soon woman followed woman up the steps into the church hall. Singly, in friendship groups, with interest, with nerves. A few faces she recognised, but most she did not. With relief, Alice realised that the hall was filling up. Lady Reading would have a good-sized audience when she arrived in a few minutes. She was glad it was Lady Reading who would address the women present and not herself. For all her love of acting, giving speeches in public filled her with fear. Whereas Lady Reading was totally at home playing herself on stage.

The meeting went as well as could be expected. Many of the attendees enrolled. Some were motivated by the desire to protect their families and communities if the bombs did fall; others were excited by the opportunity to learn new skills – courses for driving in the dark, how to administer first aid, nursery-nursing qualifications to look after the young children of war workers. It was an adventure, a break from the norm, even if it was war. But other women remained tight-lipped, unconvinced. This wasn't for them. War wouldn't come. It wouldn't be that bad.

After the meeting, Lady Reading invited Alice to tea at the Midland Hotel, where she was staying. She would be leaving for Liverpool in the morning and to more recruitment rallies. The lounge was a picture of refinement. The plush velvet-covered chairs and artistically grouped ferns where the two ladies now sat were a far cry from the shabby church halls where they had been working together of late. Pristine waitresses served tea in dainty cups, delicate cucumber sandwiches, and slices of Victoria sponge cakes on finger plates. In the background, a young pianist with a mop of fantastically dark curly hair and a top lip pretending to hold a moustache played Debussy on an ebony black grand piano which reflected the light of the chandeliers.

"You have done an excellent job in Manchester, Mrs Bragg," Lady Reading said. "We have a good number of recruits, and where one woman starts, more will follow. That is the way of things."

"Thank you," Alice received the compliment with an elegant incline of her head.

The Dowager Marchioness surveyed the room; the table beside them was unoccupied. In the corner, an elderly couple were talking loudly – both deaf, no doubt. Close to the piano, a young woman was looking adoringly into the eyes of a young man who was engrossed in telling her a serious and complicated story. One of the waitresses had just picked up a tray of used crockery to take to the kitchen, and the other was heading towards the elderly couple with a notepad ready to take their order, which of course, would take some time and be a noisy affair.

Lady Reading leant forward towards Alice and said in a low voice.

"Evacuation, Mrs Bragg, that will be our first big challenge."

"Evacuation?" Alice whispered furtively in return.

Lady Reading nodded.

"We can't be sure that the children in the cities will be safe even with gasmasks and the shelters, and what will happen to them if they survive the bombings, but their homes are destroyed?"

Alice thought of the tired young mother at the meeting and her large pram with Emily Ann and Bobby.

"Is evacuation now part of our brief?"

"Not yet – officially. But, unofficially, Mrs Bragg, we can't wait to be directed by the government. We must have plans in place so that we are ready to jump when the government asks us to jump. As it stands, today we have access to thousands of volunteers, and we will be able to find homes to welcome the children in a way the Local Authorities couldn't possibly manage to arrange themselves if war were to be declared tomorrow."

"Let us hope not tomorrow," Alice replied optimistically.

"Indeed, for today we are not ready – isn't this delicious sponge, Mrs Bragg?" Lady Reading continued abruptly and loudly as the waitress approached their table.

"I do agree, a quite outstanding sponge," Alice added on cue.

"May I offer you more tea, ladies?" the waitress enquired.

"Yes, please," Lady Reading answered for them both.

They ate some more of the quite outstanding sponge in silence as the waitress removed the teapot to take it away to refill it with fresh leaves and hot water.

Alice had been pleased with what she had achieved in Manchester. Many women had joined the W.V.S. thanks to the talks that she had arranged and conversations that she had had. Seeds for the future had been sewn. Women who weren't ready to join now might volunteer in the future, now that the idea had been planted in their minds. She knew that Lady Reading was pleased with her efforts too. As Stella Reading had been telling Alice about the plans for the evacuation, Alice had the uncomfortable feeling that she was being primed for a new role. She thought it best to be upfront with Lady Reading before the suggestion was articulated.

"Lady Reading, I must tell you, Lawrence has received a promotion to the head of the Cavendish Laboratories. We will be moving to Cambridge in September," Alice explained.

For an instant, Lady Reading seemed disappointed. Alice's supposition must have been correct.

"It's an immense honour," Alice continued. "It's probably the one position he has wanted more than any other, and he will be able to continue his research alongside the world's best physicists."

"Congratulations to you both," the Marchioness said wholeheartedly. "It's a shame. I was counting on you coming to Head Office with the evacuation planning."

Alice tried to arrange her features in an expression that would convey the appropriate level of disappointment at missing out on this opportunity.

"But no matter, we need a strong Borough office in

Cambridge. You are just the person to get it off the ground and manage it." She took a sip of tea from her cup and added, "I think you will have an interesting war in Cambridge."

For a second, Alice felt a wave of apprehension. She could say, "no, thank you." After all, relocating a family and helping her husband settle into another important role would be quite an undertaking. She could say, "I'd like, please, to do a little nursing," or, "Lady Reading, my experience in Manchester has shown me that I only can spare a few hours a week – I'd be happy to assist in a canteen."

But she couldn't make any of these replies. It quite simply wasn't in her. Service to others, taught to her by her parents from infancy, combined with her love of adventure and drama and the thrill of meeting new people, made "no" impossible.

"I look forward to the challenge," she replied instead with a smile and quietly took a sip of tea from her cup.

Alice could not – and would never – say no.

7.
JEAN
SALVAGE

"Hello Mum, I'm back," Eleanor called as she opened the front door.

Jean opened her eyes with a start. She could hear Eleanor moving in the hallway, taking off her coat and putting her wet umbrella in the rack so the drips of rainwater would collect in the tray at its base and not form a wet puddle on the floor.

"I'm in the kitchen, darling," Jean called back. Almost without thinking, she reached into the bottom of the pile of papers in the box on the table in front of her, the box she had been looking through before she must have fallen asleep. Her fingers found a fat brown dogeared envelope. She pulled it out hurriedly and hid it in her skirt pocket before Eleanor entered the room.

"Oh, it was so wet," the voice from the hall continued, "but so much fun."

"How's Angela?"

"She's well. I'll tell you in a moment. Just changing my shoes."

Jean pressed her hand against the envelope in her pocket and waited.

"There!" Eleanor announced as she entered the kitchen. "Have you had a good afternoon?" She bent down to kiss the top of her mother's silvery head.

"What have you been up to?" she asked, noticing the box.

"You told me that I should go through papers and for once I have done as I was told."

"That's great," Eleanor replied enthusiastically, sitting down in the chair next to her mother. "Have you found anything interesting, and have you thrown anything away?"

"It's a box of papers left over from the war," Jean explained. "I've just started to go through it," she lied.

Eleanor picked up the *Mayor Gives Freedom of Borough to Cambridgeshire Regiment* with the photo of the cockerel lady.

"I remember that day!" she said excitedly, "There were hundreds of people in Cambridge, and we waved our flags at the soldiers. We went with Mrs Appleby, didn't we? Dear Mrs Appleby. I do miss her. I wonder if I remember anything else?" And without asking permission, she reached for the pile in the box and started to flick her way through.

"I wouldn't expect you to remember very much," Jean commented, hand flat against her pocket. "You were very little, only three when the war started and nine at the end."

Eleanor stopped her paper rummaging and said thoughtfully,

"I do remember being scared. Scared of the bombs. The sirens would go off, and then we would hear the booming of the anti-air raid guns and shrapnel falling. And I remember Granny looking after us as you were so busy."

"No, I wasn't!" Jean protested, "I always had time to look after you."

Eleanor could see her mother bristling. "Well, maybe it's just I remember having such fun times with Granny then," she said in a conciliatory voice. "And your war work was so useful and needed." She returned to the pile. "Are these things in any order?"

"I don't expect so," her mother replied. "I think I just

added what I thought I might like to keep, and I seem to remember having a pile of papers in my writing bureau, and I think another under my bed, then I guess at some point I must have amalgamated it all into this box."

"Well, you should talk to Barbara about how to organise it better and what things you should keep. This list of telephone numbers and addresses must be out of date," she said, waving a browning sheet of lined paper, "but these newspaper clippings and maybe the letters could be interesting to future historians or even to your grandchildren or great-grandchildren."

"Maybe," Jean concurred unenthusiastically. It was clear why Eleanor was quite the office manager in London that she was.

"My goodness me!" Eleanor exclaimed suddenly. "Is this a picture of you, Mum? With a piglet?" and she handed an extract of newspaper to Jean.

"Gosh, yes, don't I look young!" Jean took the clipping, jolted by a younger version of herself in her W.V.S. uniform standing next to a stall at the market in Cambridge and holding, as Eleanor had correctly said, a piglet.

"What a day that was! It was at one of the early salvage drives," she said, the memories flooding back across her face, but her lips remained closed as if nothing further needed to be said.

"Go on, tell me about it," Eleanor urged bright-eyed, almost like a little girl again waiting for her mother to tell her a story. "I'd love to know why on earth you are holding a piglet, Mum!"

Jean took her time to ready herself for the story. She was not one of those people who were forever talking about what they had done or someone who would recount stories of other people's escapades. She only volunteered information

– even about her daughters, who she was so proud of, and her precious grandchildren – if specifically questioned.

"Well, do you remember that during the war, we all had to be so careful not to throw anything away that could be used again or turned into something else – metals, rubber, rags, paper, kitchen waste ..."

Eleanor nodded her head and started to sing:

"Because of the pail, the scraps were saved,
Because of the scraps, the pigs were saved.
Because of the pigs, the rations were saved.
Because of the rations, the ships were saved,
Because of the ships, the island was saved
Because of the island, the Empire was saved,
And all because of the housewife's pail."

"Oh my!" Jean laughed at the end of Eleanor's recitation of the playground ditty. "I haven't heard that in ever such a long time."

"But what has that got to do with you and the piglet?"

"Salvage – the collection of all these things was one of our main areas of W.V.S. work. I met Mrs Finlayson from the Cambridge office when we started the village canteen in '39. She had seen my posters for the jumble sale we held to raise funds for it, and she asked if I would help her with some posters that she needed for other campaigns in Cambridge. Look, here's one I drew."

Jean reached further into the pile and picked out a poster with the words 'Games for the Minesweepers.' It had a picture of a minesweeper ship, with four large portholes, from which a cartoon crew shouted their requests for games – ludo, chess, monopoly – each word in a bubble with the captain adding 'thank you!' at the end.

"There are more here," she said, sifting further into the box, pulling out a second poster, a picture of a housewife in a pretty print dress, her hair tied up with a scarf, placing food scraps into a pail with the words 'Waste is taste for pigs.'

"These are very good, Mum," Eleanor said admiringly.

"Do you think so?"

"Yes, I do."

Jean looked closely at her old posters. She could only see their faults, lines she should have created differently, angles that now seemed wrong.

"Well, they did their job," she continued, "and it went from there. Once I started helping at the Cambridge office with the posters, I seemed to get more involved in other ways. There was always so much to do.

"Salvage was a real problem. As we are an island, we were used to importing so many products from overseas. Paper, for example. Most of our paper used to come from Scandinavia or Canada. But the Nazis were in Norway, and whatever shipping could make its way from Canada and the USA across the Atlantic needed to be safeguarded for food and other supplies."

"Yes, I remember how thin the paper used to be," Eleanor reminisced, "drawing or writing always showed through from the other side."

"And that's despite the book drives."

"Book drives?"

"The quality of the paper was decreasing as the paper was being repulped again and again. The Ministry of Supply realised that the best quality paper was in the books in libraries – householders' own and also institutions – so we held collections called book drives. I remember in '42 we ran a 'Mile of Books' around Great St Mary's."

"A mile in length?"

"Yes, we aimed to collect enough books that if we laid

65

them down end to end, they would stretch for a mile around the outside of the church."

"That's an awful lot of books. But what about valuable books? They weren't destroyed, were they?" Eleanor asked anxiously.

"No, of course not. There were some people in the town, especially at the colleges, who were very upset about the book drives at first because they thought old or important books would be torn up for paper, but we had all the books checked by experts before they were sent off for pulping.

"We decorated a lorry and sent it with the A.R.P. Messengers' band and a number of the younger W.V.S. volunteers to the outlying districts so that everyone in Cambridge and villages like ours could add their books. In the evening, the lorry came back loaded with books, as well as all kinds of other salvage – pots and pans, rags. And not just salvage but other items that we were collecting – gramophone records, blankets, prams. Everyone took advantage of the lorry, probably as it was getting so difficult to get petrol.

"Because we were only expecting books, we had nowhere to store all the additional items, so we had to unload everything and take it to the central office. It was the most astonishing collection of junk. Honestly, Eleanor, you could hardly imagine it – jam-jars, toys, and bicycle wheels. We were so glad Alice was on holiday that week as she did find it so hard to live with mess, even though she was so committed to salvage."

"Who was Alice?" Eleanor asked.

"Alice Bragg," Jean replied. "Don't you remember her?"

Eleanor shook her head, "I was only little, as you said yourself."

"Alice Bragg was in charge of the W.V.S. in Cambridge.

Her husband was knighted during the war for his services to physics, and she became Lady Bragg. But she always was a Lady. She didn't need the title. Alice was an incredible woman. She became the Mayor after the war," Jean said.

"So that's her in the newspaper giving the regiment the Freedom of Cambridge," Eleanor deduced. "You must have known her quite well, then?"

"Yes, we were good friends for a while."

"But you're not in touch anymore?"

Jean shook her head and sighed,

"No. That happens, Eleanor."

Eleanor nodded her head in agreement.

"Tell me about the piglet, Mum."

"We realised that people living in Cambridge didn't understand just what could be reused and were throwing things out unnecessarily. They were good about donating used clothes, but rags were going into the dustbin, and there was so much we could do with rags – knitted rags could be unpicked and turned into clothes and blankets, and even the worst, most disintegrated rags could be used in roofing. Do you know I heard that stiff white shirts were turned into five-pound notes? But I admit I found that hard to believe. It's like the iron railings."

"Iron railings?" Eleanor asked, puzzled. She was still waiting to hear about the piglet.

"The Ministry of Supply needed more iron for manufacture. There were an awful lot of railings in Cambridge at the start of the war. Volunteers from the W.V.S. visited all the landlords who owned the railings and pointed out to them how much the metal was needed as it could be melted down and reused for manufacture. But most were quite reluctant to give them up. Our own office had railings around the front, and we realised we could set an example. So Mrs Finlayson arranged a ceremony, and Lady Bragg invited the Mayor, who gave a speech in front of the railings to a little crowd that clustered about how important it was for us all to do our bit for the country. Then the Surveyor's men took the railings down and carted them off. Our ceremony caused quite a stir – many people offered their railings after that. We must have got several hundred promises, and most of them turned out well. But do you know, Eleanor, I heard after the war that the iron from the railings couldn't be used, and most of it was dumped in the Thames Estuary. But I'm not sure. It could just be a rumour."

"What a waste!" Eleanor exclaimed, "Surely they could have put the railings back."

"That would have been nice," agreed her mother, "but there was so much that needed to be rebuilt after the war. I suppose they didn't have time."

"You still haven't told me about the piglet, Mum."

"So," Jean picked up her story. She was finding her stride. "We knew that we needed to educate the townsfolk about salvage, so Lady Bragg secured us a stall in the market – we used my posters to decorate it and some from the Ministry of Supply and others from the W.V.S. headquarters and old bunting too. On the stall, we had samples of all the different kinds of things that could be salvaged – cloth, food scraps, you know, things like that. Lots of people stopped to look, and W.V.S. ladies explained what could be saved, how to store it, and how it could be collected or taken to a dump. It was a great success. But the biggest draw to the stall was the piglet. Alice borrowed it from a friend. It was about eight weeks old, and they put it in a crate next to the stall. It was so sweet. All the children wanted to stroke it. One young lad, probably about twelve years old, asked if he could pick it up, and without waiting for a reply, he picked the creature up and held it like a baby in his arms. But he wasn't used to how firmly one needs to hold piglets, and babies for that matter, and the creature squirmed and wriggled until the lad dropped it. The piglet bolted under the stall and across the square. We all tried to run after it. Some of the boy's friends dived under the stall, nearly upsetting the table and everything on it. Some of us tried to head the piglet off as it came out from under the table, but to no avail, because it was getting frightened by all the noise and dashed under a hardware stall, knocking over a pile of brooms and brushes. In all the confusion, ladies were dropping their shopping, and children were laughing. A policeman joined the chase but wasn't so spritely and quickly became out of breath. Eventually, the piglet, squealing horribly by now – panicked, I suppose, by all the fuss – reached a vegetable stall where the stallholder hastily dropped some cabbage leaves and the like, which waylaid the little piglet. It was me who finally picked the poor little thing up."

"You!" Eleanor exclaimed with astonishment. "You've never had anything to do with farmyard animals. At least that's what I thought."

"You're quite right," Jean laughed, "but I'd had a lot to do with babies, and I, for one, knew how to hold this little one – very firmly and very tightly. We took him back to his crate, where he remained safely for the rest of the day. But when the reporter came to take a photograph, Alice decided that I should hold the piglet up for all to see. So that's how I came to be in the newspaper." She gathered up the paper memories, shutting the lid tightly on her Pandora's box. "Now, tell me about Angela."

Eleanor had a great deal to tell her about Angela and the plans for her wedding in the Spring. She was going to be one of her bridesmaids, with dress fittings planned for after Christmas. For the rest of the evening, Jean listened to her daughter's excited chatter, pleased that it was distracting her daughter from the box, but wondering, guiltily, if Eleanor might be jealous, might herself be wanting to get married but not trying too hard to hear evidence of such in her child's tone of voice.

Jean took her box back to her bedroom for the night. She undressed slowly, folding each garment neatly and placing it on her chair. She would wear them again tomorrow as they were still clean – perhaps with a different, brighter scarf as it would be Sunday, and Barbara would be coming with her family for lunch, as they did most weekends.

In her long white flannel nightdress, with its raspberry embroidered cuffs and sleeves buttoned high to the neck to keep her warm from the night chills, Jean finished brushing her hair before getting into bed. The box was on her dressing table, and the brown envelope was in the pocket of her skirt. She sat on the edge of her bed, wondering what she would do. After several moments, which could have been minutes for all she knew, she went over to her skirt, removed the envelope, and put it under her pillow before turning off the light, leaving the envelope untouched, unread. She lay for a while on her side, eyes wide, staring into the darkness, listening to rain skitting on the window.

8.

ALICE

"NO, I CAN'T SEND THEM AWAY."

August 1939

This afternoon Alice was determined to write a long letter to Sylvia. It was quite disgraceful that she had let so many months pass without even scribbling a few lines. Her excuse felt lame – she had been busy. Sylvia, promoted by Lady Reading to lead the Birmingham and Coventry branch, was surely just as busy, yet she had managed to write twice since Whitsun. Although Sylvia didn't also have a husband and family to occupy her, Alice thought as she looked up, catching sight of Lawrence and the boys through the long French windows, setting up cricket stumps on the lawn to practise bowling and batting together. She would use this moment of peace and quiet on her holiday to write to her good friend.

Dearest Sylvia, she wrote,

It is so perfect here, so fresh, that we are all beginning to feel that we can forget our current anxieties,

She paused and turned her fountain pen in her fingers. Anxieties, she could write a great long list of those if she should choose – the impending war, her younger son David's delicate health – but why share them with Sylvia, who, without a doubt, had her own? Then, of course, not everything about this last year had caused anxiety. Returning to Cambridge had been a delight. It was perfectly wonderful to live close by to her parents, who had moved to the city when her father had taken up a post at the University, his last before retirement. It meant that she and her children could see them so much more regularly now.

71

And what a beautiful city to live in with the colleges and history! The Braggs had rented a large old house from Gonville and Caius College not far from the stretch of the River Cam, affectionately known as the Backs. Lawrence had acquired a college punt by the time the boys had come home for their long summer holidays. Within a couple of days, Stephen and David had both mastered the art of manoeuvring their punt as if they were Venetian gondoliers disguised as public school boys, transporting their sisters and their mother in a most gentlemanly fashion along the river; Margaret trailing her fingers in the cool water and Patience cuddling her doll Ingrid, while Alice told the family stories of the people who lived and worked in the beautiful old buildings which they passed and of her fun-filled life in the city as an undergraduate.

Christmas, too, had been perfectly charming. The girls had helped Alice decorate the house with armfuls of garden greenery: ivy, mistletoe, red-berried holly. She and Lawrence had made garlands from all the beautiful Christmas cards they had received from friends all over the world. Lawrence insisted on climbing the ladder to attach the garlands to nails which he discreetly banged into the lofty cornices of the drawing room and the dining room so that the nails could remain hidden there year after year for that purpose without the knowledge of the landlord.

Stephen and David helped their father bring in an enormous Christmas tree, which they manoeuvred with difficulty through the house to the large drawing room, dropping many needles on the way. Kitty, their maid, hastily swept up the offending articles trying to be stern with the family for making more mess for her to clear up, but wanting to join in.

Once in situ, the tree reached the ceiling and spread its arms out wide, demanding to be adorned. The family duly honoured it with garlands of tinsel, large red and gold glass baubles, and dripping silver strands, all put away carefully last Epiphany to come out again this Christmas Eve. It was a family affair, decorating the tree. Even little Patience was allowed to help, nestling chocolates in bright wrappers among the lower branches; chocolates sent from friends in Germany.

Friends and colleagues were included in the Braggs' Christmas celebrations. After Christmas and before New Year, Lawrence and Alice had held a party for all the Cavendish Laboratory scientists and their wives. There were more than eighty guests. Alice had had to engage additional help, as it would have been far too much for Kitty and Nellie, their cook, to manage. Oh, it was such fun! The house was full of merriment. Not least because Lawrence had invented a complicated intellectual paper game for his scientists to play rather than dance, as in his opinion, scientists were notoriously bad dancers. His scientists passed the evening in happy intellectual isolation, absent-mindedly taking their refreshment, perched on the stairs or sofas. One professor sat upright on a dining chair in the middle of the room, quite oblivious, in his concentration, to the party around him.

That particular professor had left the labs during the year. Like so many others, silently departing in a steady drain of scientific talent sucked into secret government war strategy. The Prime Minister, Neville Chamberlain, may have assured the country of peace when he returned from Munich last summer, but this was only a pause, a chance to take a breath, to take stock, to act under the surface, to prepare. War was creeping up determinedly and almost unobserved.

Alice placed the nib back on her pale blue writing paper and continued:

Hugh Lyons, our friend and Stephen's headmaster at Rugby, has lent us his beautiful house overlooking the Barmouth estuary for the month, on the condition that should war break, we will leave immediately and return to Cambridge so that the Lyons family themselves can evacuate to Wales. I cannot tell you how I am keeping everything crossed that this won't be the case. We have worked hard these past months at the W.V.S. Borough office to put as many plans as possible for evacuating the children of Cambridge and receiving evacuees.

She paused again, a flutter of fear in her stomach like a trapped butterfly. She didn't want to write any more on that subject. Turning her fountain pen round and round in her fingers, she studied her family beyond the window in the garden. Lawrence had just bowled David out on the lawn, and on the terrace, Margaret was reading to Patience, who was playing with Ingrid. Like all mothers, she wanted to keep her children safe, keep them close.

The antidote to fear, she realised, was to work. And how she had worked! She pressed the nib of her pen to the paper, and with a spurt of ink, she continued her letter:

You would laugh at me if you saw me nowadays, Sylvia, since, for the first time in my life, I have what you could call a proper job. Yes, really, I do! I can see you laughing already. Every weekday morning, I ride my bicycle to the shabbiest little office that the Borough Council could possibly have found for us, and there I spend my days compiling lists, contacting possible volunteers and matching skills to jobs. I have even managed to quell my fear of public speaking, and it is I who is frequently the principal speaker at our recruitment meetings. You should see how I exhort, encourage and persuade. I ride high when I can see that what I say has been taken seriously and good women join us, but I confess I am irritated by the apathy that still exists. I don't suppose that many people will prepare for this war until it is upon them.

That was enough of war. She finished the letter with a description of the house, the beautiful coast, and a long and pleasant walk the family had enjoyed the day before.

But the great demon of war was waking up and stretching its muscles, and there was no longer anything anyone could do to stop it.

Four days later, the Bragg family packed up their luggage and boarded the train back to Paddington, from where they would make their way to King's Cross and return home to Cambridge. It was going to be a very long day of travelling, so they had left early. The family had a carriage compartment to themselves, and Alice had made sure that there was a hamper full of sandwiches, fruit, and cake with bottles of ginger beer as a treat. Thankfully, there would be a trolley service for hot tea on the train.

Nothing seemed untoward when they left Wales. But it wasn't long before Alice noticed that the West Country stations seemed busier than they ought to have been and that the trains which passed on the opposite track, bound away from Paddington and on their way to Wales, were increasingly crowded – crowded with small people's pale faces. Children's faces. Alice looked intently at each train that passed them, at each station where their train paused. Had they missed a radio announcement? Had the war been declared, and evacuation started without them knowing? Lawrence had noticed too, and was thinking the same. They looked at each other in solemn silence, each knowing the other's thoughts, as their children waded their way through their train picnic and talked about cricket, Wales, dolls, and books – oblivious to the trains heading west.

At Paddington, the platforms thronged with groups of children in uniforms, herded by their teachers, each holding a small suitcase and boxed gas mask. Many children were laughing and playing. Some stood sadly – worried, alone. Despite trying to hurry her family through the station, theirs was a slow course. They wheeled their holiday luggage on trolleys, avoiding the varied groups waiting on the platform and the station atrium. The Bragg children looked around and took it all in.

"Mummy, why are there so many school children here when it's still the school holidays?" Margaret asked.

"I don't know, poppet. Perhaps they are going on trips to the seaside?" There was no need to worry her children when nothing was certain.

"The evacuation must have begun, Mother," Stephen concluded. Alice braced herself. This was not a helpful supposition on her son's part.

"Mummy, what's evacuation?" Patience reached for her mother's hand fearfully. It was too confusing, all these children, some happy and some crying.

"I'm sure the evacuation has started," Alice's young man added. "Look, I can see some of your W.V.S. over there. They wouldn't be here to help on holiday trips to the beach. It must be war."

"Stephen, we don't know that," Lawrence interposed sternly. "I'll buy a paper, and the situation might become clearer, and then we must press on to King's Cross. I would prefer to sleep in my own bed tonight and not be forced to stay in London."

The paper was bought. It was not war – yet. But how long now? Weeks? Days? Hours? The first children were being sent away from the East End in readiness for German attack. Better to be safe than sorry.

The holiday atmosphere had evaporated. The peace and sunshine of Wales were further away than a distant land. They were all tired now. Lawrence was concentrating unsuccessfully on a crossword. Now and again, his eyes flicked up to meet Alice's as they sought silently to reassure each other. The boys quietly and unenthusiastically played a game of cards, attempting to kill time rather than benefit from it. Margaret read, caught up in the adventure of her story. Patience had fallen asleep, nestled against her mother, and lulled by the rocking of the train on its homeward-bound tracks, gradually losing her grip on her beloved Ingrid until she let go and Ingrid tumbled to the carriage floor.

"I simply can't send my children away," Alice declared vehemently behind the closed doors of their bedroom late that night when all the children were in bed, and they could finally talk openly.

"But my darling, they won't be safe here."

"I can't. I just won't." Alice's voice was calm but strained.

"Alice, we must," he exploded in a whisper which threatened to become a full voice. He had kept the horror of it in all day so as not to scare the children, and now it burst forth.

"The Germans have taken back the Rhineland, united with Austria, marched in Czechoslovakia, and now they are perched on Poland. Sweetheart, it's highly possible that they will make their way to Britain and invade."

"They never will," she replied determinedly. "They will never be able to cross the channel."

"They have aeroplanes, darling. They can bomb us. They can land their troops. It is entirely possible that Germans could be here in East Anglia – within weeks."

"Now you are being dramatic," she answered wryly.

"What about if you went abroad with the children? You could go with them to America, Canada. There's still time."

"No!" she almost shouted. She took a deep breath; it would be no good for the children to hear their parents arguing. "No, I can't send them away – I can't. And I won't leave you."

She felt hot tears sting her eyes and Lawrence's strong and comforting arms around her. He pulled her close and held her, kissing her soft hair. No more was said. Much more was thought.

Alice rose late for breakfast the following day. It was

Friday and still officially her holiday. She had slept fitfully, the worries of the day filling her night-time world. The breakfast room was empty. Only her place remained laid. Lawrence had left the newspaper on the table for her to read, and she glanced at the headlines – no declaration, no war. She poured herself a glass of orange juice.

Kitty entered with a tray of freshly made toast in a silver toast rack, Seville marmalade in a glass bowl, rolls of butter in a square dish, and a pot of freshly made tea.

"Good morning, Mrs Bragg."

"Good morning, Kitty."

"Excuse me, Mrs Bragg, but this came for you just as Cook was preparing your toast. I thought I'd bring the two together," and, putting the tray down on the table in front of Alice, she pointed to a telegram.

"Thank you, Kitty."

"Will there be anything else, Mrs Bragg?"

"No, thank you, Kitty, not for the moment. Come back shortly, and I will have made my list for the day."

Kitty left to continue her daily chores, and Alice opened the telegram. It was from Chicago.

Dearest Friends, let us help. We will look after your children for the duration. They will be safe with us. P. Shaffner.

Peggy Shaffner and her son Paul. What wonderful friends to offer such help. But she couldn't send her family away – could she? Was it really necessary? What if it was? These friends in Chicago were certainly alarmed enough by Europe's distress to cable the offer. Not the boys. She couldn't send the boys away, well, definitely not Stephen. He was so near to finishing school and had his sights set on an engineering degree at Cambridge. Maybe the girls, then? Perhaps Nanny Hilda could be prevailed upon to accompany the girls to Chicago. No, that was too much to ask. No one knew how long this war might be. If she sent her girls away, they could be abroad for years – the family would be broken up. It was not to be considered.

Alice turned the problem over in her mind, forcing herself to look at the dilemma from all angles and disentangle herself from the fear of what the decision meant one way or the other. She spread her butter and marmalade to the four corners of her toast and tried her hardest to take her feelings out of the equation.

The doorbell rang, and Kitty entered with a second cable, this time from Lawrence's friend George Milroy Carrie in Ottawa.

Bragg – send us Alice with the children – they will be safe in Canada with us. Do not delay. Carrie. PS, if she won't leave you, send the children with their nanny.

She read it silently as Kitty waited near the table.

"Kitty, did Mr Bragg say he would be returning for lunch today when he left for the lab?"

"He's expecting to be back for lunch at 12.30, Ma'am," the maid replied.

"Thank you. I will be in the study if you need me."

"Yes, Mrs Bragg, was there anything else you wanted me to do, Ma'am?"

"Oh no," Alice said vaguely. She could hardly think her head was so troubled with the immediate, urgent decision of her children's future. It seemed incredible that she had been so involved with planning the evacuation of Londoners' children to Cambridge that she hadn't thought for one moment that the situation could be so dire that she would need to consider evacuating her own.

Lawrence returned for lunch, his usually cheerful face

79

lined with worry. He sought Alice in the study immediately.

"My love, I don't suppose you have been listening to the wireless this morning?" he asked.

"No, I've had other things to do." She was alarmed. Neither she nor Lawrence would normally listen to radio broadcasts other than in the evening.

"Germany has declared war on Poland – early this morning."

The words wrenched Alice's breath from her body

"Oh my goodness," she whispered. Great Britain was allied with Poland.

"Has Chamberlain declared war?" she asked huskily.

"Not yet."

Alice handed her husband the two telegrams that had come that morning. Saying, when he had read them,

"And I've had at least half a dozen telephone calls from the wives of other professors asking us what we are going to do about the children. I said we hadn't decided. What should we do, Lawrence? What should we do?" she looked up at him pleading to help her make this enormous, consequential decision.

"Frankly, darling, I think we need to take advice."

"From whom?"

"Sir William Spens," he replied grimly.

Later that afternoon, Alice and Lawrence mounted the narrow stone staircase leading up to a first-floor corner suite of rooms overlooking the central courtyard of Corpus Christi College. Lawrence knocked smartly on the heavy old wooden door.

"Enter!" a muffled voice called from within.

The Braggs entered as ordered. Alice knew Sir William but had never visited him at the University. He was the Master of Corpus Christi College and the Regional Commissioner for the Eastern Region. Should the land be invaded, should East Anglia be cut off from London, cut off from government, Sir William Spens would lead the eastern counties, doing whatever they could to repulse the enemy.

The room the Braggs entered was a den of papers – papers stacked high on a large desk, papers in piles on the floor, and papers on chairs around the room's edges. Only two simple straight-backed chairs with red upholstered seats were empty of papers. These had been placed opposite the desk's occupant, no doubt for students, college fellows, or university colleagues like themselves. Despite the window, the room was dark – the light eaten by the rows of double-stacked books on the bookcases climbing the walls.

Spens was sitting at his desk, pipe in hand.

"Ah Bragg, Mrs Bragg, what can I do for you?" he asked pleasantly, placing his pipe carefully on a maple leaf-shaped pipe dish, ready to be picked up and completed when the Braggs departed. He motioned towards the empty chairs for the Braggs to take a seat. Alice and Lawrence sat down.

"Sir William," Lawrence began, "we have come to ask for your advice."

Spens inclined his head in a nod of approval and encouragement.

"We have received telegrams from friends abroad urging us to send our children to them. But we are not sure if this is the right thing to do," Alice explained.

Spens looked at the Braggs with a steely firmness in his dark eyes.

"Absolutely not, Mrs Bragg! On no account should you send your children abroad!"

Lawrence and Alice exchanged a look of surprise.

"Sir William, are you quite sure?" Lawrence probed. "Will the children be safe if we are invaded?"

Spens maintained his steely firmness from behind the desk.

"It is not quite a question of safety. More a question of morale. Many Cambridge citizens think that we have inside knowledge at the University, that we know of Hitler's exact battle plans. Of course, we don't! We can suppose, we can guess, and we have to plan. Think what the message to the townsfolk would be if you, Lawrence Bragg, the head of the Cavendish Laboratories, a man respected by all for his work with the Admiralty on using crystals as piezoelectric devices to spot enemy submarines in the last war, sent his children abroad. Your action would spread fear and despondency. And you, Mrs Bragg, head of the Women's Voluntary Service here in this city, how could you credibly draw on the support of Cambridge women if you are seen to send your children abroad? If you are seen to draw on advantages that you have which they do not?"

He paused, noting their anxious, pinched faces.

"Have you friends or family in the West Country?"

Alice nodded. She could see it all and was strangely relieved.

"I would send your children west for a few weeks then, Mrs Bragg. That will comfort you and allow us all to see what will happen next."

9.

JEAN

DAUGHTERS

The next morning the sun had returned to the December sky, replacing the dankness of the previous day. Here and there, handfuls of sodden, beige leaves clung determinedly to the trees at the end of Jean's lawn. A lone, shrivelled red rosebud in the large southwest border was the only reminder of summer past. Yet, even though the year had three weeks more before it turned, tiny daffodil heads were already poking up beneath the trees and in clumps along the wooden fence where the bulbs had been planted so many seasons ago.

Barbara and Christopher arrived at 11 o'clock, Barbara's belly swollen with the baby expected in the new year. Sally, their eldest, had just started at the Perse Girls' School and had brought some classwork to show her Granny. Jean wondered what it would be today. A couple of weekends ago, when the family had visited, Sally had brought her algebra workbook, and Jean had concentrated heroically, listening to her granddaughter's excited chatter and trying to understand the mathematical language before her on the page. But it made so little sense. She had never been taught. She hoped today's offering would be a safe subject, art or perhaps English literature. She liked reading stories. Eight-year-old Graham and six-year-old Trevor tumbled into the house, wellingtons ready in a canvas tote bag. Jean welcomed her family with a kiss and a special biscuit for the boys to take to the swing at the end of the garden, both of which would keep them going until lunchtime.

"Now, what have you got to show me, Sally darling?" she asked, putting her arm around her tall granddaughter's shoulders and leading her to the drawing room.

Sally proudly produced a blue exercise book with the words *Le Français* carefully stencilled on the cover.

"French – excellent!" Jean enthused and thought silently, "Oh rats, I never was any good at French."

Meanwhile, Barbara waddled in search of Eleanor, who was preparing the lunch in the kitchen. She kissed her sister on the cheek and sunk heavily into the kitchen chair.

"Not much of a weekend off for you."

"Not really," Eleanor replied, "but it was fun to see Angela yesterday."

"Oh good, I'm glad you managed that. How is she?"

"She's fine. The wedding plans are going well."

Barbara looked up sharply at her sister, waiting to see if she would mention her boyfriend, Kurt, but Eleanor moved on to dress styles, and Barbara wasn't one to push a door that wasn't ready to open.

"Pass me those carrots, Eleanor. At least I can peel them sitting down."

Eleanor gave her sister a colander full of rinsed carrots and turned to put the kettle on, as it wouldn't be long before their mother would appear in the kitchen in search of a cup of tea.

"How do you think Mum is?" Barbara asked in a low voice, inviting the confidence of her younger sister.

"Well, her back seems to be getting better. I haven't let her lift anything, and yesterday morning before I went to meet Angela, we went through all the china in the sideboard. I'm hoping to get her to take a look at the books in the study this afternoon after you've all gone."

"That's great," Barbara replied, leaving aside the carrots

to ease her hands across the aching, stretching, itchy skin of her abdomen, letting her palms rest where she could feel baby hardness, arm, leg, or spine she couldn't tell.

"But what about in herself? How do you think she is in herself?"

"She hasn't said what she thinks about the move, if that's what you're asking," Eleanor replied.

"No, she never says what she feels. We have to look for clues with her, don't we? Sally's like that too," Barbara observed. "I know she's happy to come here today because she's brought her notebook to show Granny – it's a kind of semaphore."

"Mum did look at one of her boxes by herself yesterday – one from the war."

"Really?" Barbara was surprised. "What was in it?"

"All sorts of newspaper clippings, some of her posters, letters too, I think."

"Well, I never. Was it W.V.S?"

"Yes, and she even talked about the clippings and told me stories. Honestly, Barbara, you wouldn't believe it. She talked more about the war yesterday afternoon than I ever remember. More than she's talked in a long time about anything."

"That's great," Barbara said, shifting her bulk, searching for a position on the chair, which was bound to be just as uncomfortable as the first. "Maybe it means she'll talk about Daddy a bit now, or even start thinking about what kind of life she could have living in Cambridge."

"Don't hold your breath," Eleanor grimaced. "It's been hard enough just persuading her to give up this big house and move into the city. But maybe you could talk to her about how to arrange what she has in the box properly – you know, as a historian might like to find it in the future."

"Some hope!" Barbara snorted. "She won't listen to me any more than she'll listen to you. But I'd like to hear about what she did in the war."

"Don't you know?" Eleanor asked, surprised.

"Not really. I know Maeve, and I are older than you, and looking back on it now, I ought to have been more aware of what she did."

"Why weren't you?" Eleanor asked, finding it hard to believe her older sister, with a longer memory, wouldn't know.

"Well, I suppose I didn't see her do it."

Barbara remembered her mother putting on her uniform and then not being at home, or not being home, and then arriving home in her uniform, but she could not have described what her mother had done in the intervening hours. She knew about the canteen, it was part of the village's life. She'd been allowed to help out there, even as a little girl, washing up, and, on occasion, she had made cakes for the soldiers. But she couldn't remember what her mother did there. Make the tea – perhaps. She heard her mother talk about the mobile canteen. She had seen the Queen's Messengers for herself as she cycled past the field where the convoy was parked, but she had never seen it in action. She knew the outside of the office in the centre of Cambridge, where her mother volunteered two or three times a week, but she had never been inside.

It seemed so much more obvious to her now she was older and a mother herself.

"I think it takes quite a long time before a child fully realises that their parent has interests or concerns other than them," she continued. She thought of her own little boys who were so deeply involved in the ups and downs of their daily lives that they had faces full of sad astonishment when told, "Mummy is tired with the new baby coming, she needs to rest," or, "Daddy can't play now, the tap's leaking and he's got to fix it." Whereas Sally, on the other hand, was older and was beginning to notice these little things herself and alter her actions accordingly.

"And you know, Eleanor," Barbara continued, "we were caught up in what we were doing ourselves. Maeve and I had our school exams to take."

"And boyfriends!" Eleanor teased.

"Yes, those too," Barbara laughed in response, thinking of a certain young man on whom she had had what the family termed a 'crush' at the end of the war.

"Maeve and I both did our bits of war work too."

"Did you? I don't remember?"

"Well, you were very young."

"What did you do?"

"I used to help Granny with the knitting – it was called 'comforts for soldiers' – socks, gloves, hats and then later, during the Liberation, we knitted for the refugees in Europe. Granny taught me how to knit vests – vests for children. We must have knitted hundreds. I remember taking our vests into Cambridge once with Mummy and Granny, to be loaded up onto a van, ready to be sent to Belgium and Holland. Maeve worked on the camouflage nets – I guess that's a craft of sorts."

Eleanor had been working swiftly as they had been speaking, peeling, and chopping the apples for the sauce and the crumble. Now she cut the final green ball in half, then into quarters, sliced out the core, and stripped off the peel while Barbara scraped the remaining carrots. They worked well alongside each other and enjoyed each other's company.

"What about Dad? What did he do?"

"You know, I can't remember that very clearly either – gosh, I am rubbish." Barbara put her last carrot back in the colander, ready for chopping, and furrowed her brow, trying to remember a time that seemed so much longer ago than it was.

"He couldn't do much war work because of his leg, but he always seemed very busy with his clients – probably because so many men were called up, but people's legal matters still needed resolving."

"I miss Dad," Eleanor said, barely audible.

"I know. I do, too," Barbara reached over and took her younger sister's hand.

"I'm going to miss this place," Eleanor continued, her voice strained, as she flicked her eyes around the familiar room.

All the girls would. It was their family home, a place full of memories.

"But it's for the best that Mummy moves."

"Yes, it's for the best."

After all, the 1960s weren't staying still for any of them.

10.
THE QUEEN'S MESSENGERS

Sally had grown up since starting at the Perse School, Jean thought somewhat regretfully, as she led her granddaughter to the sofa positioned next to the crackling fire in the drawing room hearth. The child was a good couple of inches taller than she had been in the summer holidays, and she seemed to have left behind her little girl preoccupations at primary school. Children don't stay little for long, and Sally would soon become a little mother herself with the arrival of a much younger baby brother or sister in only a matter of weeks.

"Now let me see your book, darling and tell me all about your French classes," Jean urged, enjoying the warm presence of her granddaughter beside her on the sofa.

Sally beamed as she practised the sentences that she knew and explained how *Mademoiselle* came from the South of France and found England far too wet and cold.

"Can you speak French, Granny?" Sally asked.

"Only very bad school-girl French learnt a very long time ago," Jean laughed.

"Have you ever been to France?" Sally probed further.

"No, darling, I haven't travelled very much."

"Mummy and Daddy haven't been either. Do you know anyone who's been to France?"

Jean thought about the brown envelope under her pillow. To lie to a child or to tell the truth?

"Yes," she answered vaguely. "I knew someone who was there at the end of the war," and leaving no space for her granddaughter to ask any more questions, she added, "A

French soldier stayed with us quite near the beginning of the war, and I had to speak French to him. We had a lot of foreign soldiers visit Cambridge back then. They were stationed in various places over the country, and when they had leave, they had no homes to go back to, so the W.V.S. arranged for them to visit places of interest and have a little holiday, so to speak. There were quite a few Free French soldiers in England, and I volunteered to host one for a weekend here. Grandpa wasn't happy about it, but we had a spare bedroom and had to offer it up."

In truth, Alan hadn't been happy about it at all.

They were both standing in the scullery where she had found him sleeves rolled up, apron on, carefully spreading a minute layer of polish across his ageing leather shoes.

"Why are you always volunteering to do these things without consulting me?" he had said peevishly.

"I'm sorry," she replied, anxious to avoid a brewing argument, "I thought you'd be pleased. It will be fun."

"No, it will not," he snarled, rubbing the polish into the shoe. "You will want me to show this French Captain around the colleges, and I've got far better things to do with my weekend."

"I'm sorry," she repeated, "I know you're busy, I'll see if Fee can show him around, and then we'll just have him for board and lodging."

Had she given in enough? Had she held her ground? Alan picked up the brush and, with vigorous rhythmic sweeps, shined his shoe. She waited.

"All right," he had agreed finally. He probably knew that their spare room couldn't be spare for much longer.

"He was a very nice man, Sally. He spoke English marginally better than I spoke French. You should have seen his face when I told him at breakfast that he could have *confiture de souris.*"

"Why is that funny, Granny?" Sally asked.

"Because I should have said *cerise* – *cerise* means cherry and *souris* means mouse."

"Mouse jam!" Sally exclaimed, and both Jean and she giggled at that curious wartime food.

It wasn't long before the roast was ready, the savoury aroma of the joint reaching them before the meal had left the kitchen. Christopher stood opposite Jean at the head of the large dining table in Alan's place, her son-in-law, not her husband, now brandishing the carving utensils. In front of him on a cranberry-coloured dish was a large joint of pork. Apple sauce and gravy, in cranberry and gold-painted jugs, joined three large serving dishes of boiled potatoes, carrots and brussels sprouts, and together they spanned the length of the table. Her oldest son-in-law was a handsome man with chestnut hair now beginning to go ever so slightly grey around the temples. He used to sit on her left at family gatherings, but now, as the most senior male member of the family, he took Alan's place. But he was not as good at carving, Jean thought sadly.

"For what we are about to receive, may the Lord make us truly grateful," Alan had prayed before starting to carve the chicken. Jean had long since given up prayers of any description. It was no good requesting anything of a God who may or may not hear, not when He couldn't or wouldn't bring Nicholas back from the trenches in the last war and not when He allowed bombs to fall all over the country, bringing wretchedness and misery in this war.

"Amen," Anne concluded.

"Amen," Jean added, as no one else need know her private thoughts on the matter.

Alan manfully attempted to dissect the small chicken into enough pieces to feed the family around the table; his wife, his mother-in-law, his daughters Maeve, Barbara, and little Eleanor, and not forgetting himself. Jean hovered anxiously at his shoulder, ready to distribute the meagre amount of meat on the plate along with the potatoes, cabbage, and carrots which, thankfully, were plentiful since Alan had started to grow them in the garden.

"It was very clever of you to get a chicken this week, my dear," he commented once the task of carving was complete, "I am sure it will be delicious."

Jean smiled weakly in response. She was so tired. Their maid had been called up to compulsory war work months ago and had a job in a munitions factory near Peterborough. It was such a relief that Mrs Appleby could spare a few hours a week to help her, but it still meant the burden of cleaning, cooking, washing, and mending for six people fell to her – and she spent many hours each week volunteering.

Alan didn't seem to notice how tired she was nowadays. But then maybe he was tired himself. He was too old to join up or be conscripted, and his injured leg prevented him from heavy physical war work, he nevertheless accompanied the girls to school in Cambridge on their bicycles and home again each day, and he was growing quantities of vegetables in the garden and had taken on additional *pro bono* work at the practice.

"We had a demonstration of macaroni and noodles this week at the W.V.S. office," Jean mentioned as the family ate their Sunday lunch in silence.

"I beg your pardon?" Alan couldn't imagine what Jean was talking about.

"Macaroni and noodles – it's food that can be made from Italian paste – flour and water and egg powder. We think it's going to be very useful for the feeding centres and the canteens. Mrs Finlayson organised the demonstration, and we must have had, oh, at least 60 people in – cooks and canteen staff from our catering units, as well as from the schools and colleges."

"Great," mumbled Maeve, "so we've got that to look forward to at school now."

"I only thought you might be interested," Jean said, but she had seen that they weren't really. They were probably too hungry themselves.

"Mum, are you all right?" Eleanor asked. "You were miles away. Christopher's served your meat."

She hadn't been miles away – she had been in the dining room all along. But she had been years away.

"I'm fine. I was thinking about the war."

Barbara opened her mouth, about to say something, but Jean cut her short.

"You like eggs, don't you boys?" she asked, looking at Graham and Trevor both tucking into their roast meat, skirting around the vegetables – there would be a battle royal about that soon enough.

"I like eggs and soldiers," Trevor stated simply.

"Scrambled's best with oodles of butter," Graham grinned.

"Did you know, boys, it was very difficult to get eggs during the war? So the government decided it would be a good thing if we all used powdered eggs rather than fresh eggs because then at least people all over the country and especially in the cities could eat eggs in their cooking. A Professor at the Department of Zoology – I think it was a Professor Gray, but maybe it was Brown – anyway, a Professor, let's call him Professor Gray, came to our office one day and asked if we would help out with an experiment."

93

"What sort of experiment," Graham asked wide-eyed, imagining yolk-coloured liquid dripping into test tubes and explosions letting off eggy smells.

"A cooking experiment. The scientists had produced several different kinds of eggs, and Professor Gray and his colleagues wanted to know which kind ordinary housewives preferred. So, Mrs Richards and Mrs Thomas spent an entire afternoon in our office preparing and cooking scrambled eggs on toast. They invited six women from each of the wards in Cambridge to come at quarter-of-an-hour intervals and, when they arrived, gave each woman three kinds of scrambled eggs on toast to taste, and asked their opinion. The whole office smelt of eggs. There was so much coming and going that none of the rest of us could get on with our work, so we joined in with the tasting."

"Did it taste nice?" Trevor asked, munching a particularly delicious crispy roast potato.

"One of the varieties was pretty awful, darling, it made the egg look grey and lumpy, like glue paste for paper-mâché, and it didn't taste much better. Another was such bright yellow that it didn't look at all natural, but it tasted like eggs at least."

"And what was the outcome, Jean?" Christopher asked.

"The outcome was that all the women had a fun afternoon with a free meal and a full portion of powder to take home and cook with for their families with the obligation to report back a fortnight later. Professor Gray was very pleased and sent the office a lovely thank you letter. The government might have adopted one of the types of eggs. I'm not sure."

"But we didn't have to use powdered eggs because Mrs Harding used to let us have eggs from her chickens," Barbara added for her sons' benefit. "But we did have to eat our vegetables, boys," she noted, nodding at two plates bereft of meat and potatoes, where carrots and brussels sprouts were cooling in a puddle of gravy.

Then, turning to her sister, she asked, "Do you remember when we had oranges from America?"

"Alice Bragg gave us those," Jean added, remembering the juicy treats that Alice had gifted to her from American friends who regularly sent food packages from Chicago. "The Americans were very generous. They sent all kinds of food – we had an enormous delivery of tinned food arrive at the office once from the American Red Cross. It was very kind of them, and I'm sure they intended it to be useful, but we didn't know what all the food was or how to cook it."

"I seem to remember the Americans helped to fund the Queen's Messengers, didn't they?" Christopher asked.

"What were the Queen's Messengers, Granny?" the little girl still in Sally asked, imagining pretty winged fairies flying with golden envelopes sent by the beautiful young Queen.

"Let's hear about that over pudding – now boys, vegetables!" Barbara suggested. They took no notice.

"Boys! I said eat your vegetables up," she commanded.

The convoy had arrived in summer '41, Jean remembered – July, maybe August – paid for by the United States War Relief Fund and a donation from Her Majesty, Queen Elizabeth, Lady Elizabeth Bowes-Lyon as was, and now the Queen Mother. The day the East Anglian convoy had arrived, one of eighteen across the land, she had walked through the lanes from Grantchester to Trumpington to where the lorries had been parked in a field. It wasn't far, it only took a few minutes, and she was pleased she was wearing her W.V.S. summer uniform, a grey-green flannel dress, as it was hot.

Jean could hear the buzz of excited chatter before she arrived at Maris Lane and entered the field. There must have been at least forty W.V.S. ladies all in their uniforms and assembled not so patiently for the grand inspection of the formidable convoy on the cut dry grass.

"Hello Jean," Fee called out and waved. "Can you believe it?"

Her friend's face was full of excitement. Her W.V.S. hat bobbed jauntily on the black curls that naturally covered her head, not like Jean's hair that needed uncomfortable night-time curlers to produce any kind of wave or a perm at the hairdressers, an expense she found hard to justify when she didn't like the effect any more than her natural straight locks.

Fee was standing next to one of the blue and silver lorries with the words QUEEN'S MESSENGERS emblazoned above the windscreen and FOOD FLYING SQUAD GIFT of H.M the QUEEN below the hatch on the left side of the vehicle.

"This one's a canteen – look, there are four of them – guess that's where you and I will be, and over there are the kitchens," Jean looked to where Fee pointed in the direction of two lorries parked further along the line. "And the next two along are food lorries, and then two water wagons."

"It's amazing!" Jean said on her breath. And it was! Like Fee, she could scarcely believe her eyes. The lorries and the women who volunteered to work in them would now be able to feed hundreds, even thousands, of people following an air raid.

Fee was looking longingly up at the cabin. She was just itching to climb up and drive the lorry.

"Aren't you afraid, Fee?" Jean asked.

"Of what?"

"Of driving something so big, driving in the dark, driving to an air raid. The damage could be huge."

"Not a bit," her friend grinned, "I can't wait."

"I volunteered for the Queen's Messengers rota because the convoy was so close to home," Jean explained mid-way through her apple and pear crumble. "I know my way blindfolded along the Grantchester Road from here to Trumpington, even now, so of course, I could find my way there in the dark with no lights in the villages, I'd be one of the first to arrive, so it made sense. Grandpa was cross because I'd joined yet another rota, but as it turned out, the convoy wasn't used very much."

"Really, why was that?" Christopher asked. He was a north London boy and had remained with his parents in Edgeware throughout the war.

"Because after '41, we didn't see many bombings in East Anglia. Hitler had turned his attention to Russia, although we weren't to know that at the time," Jean explained. "But we did have one large Blitz – Norwich in April '42."

Jean had woken suddenly to the sound of the telephone in the study crying into the dark night. She hastily switched on her bedside lamp and groped sleepily for her alarm clock. The clear, round face told her it was only 4.15 a.m. Alan stirred in the bed alongside her and rolled over. The telephone was still ringing. Jean forced herself out of bed and hurried in slipper-less feet to the study, hoping the ringing hadn't woken the girls.

"Hello – Jean Barnet speaking," Jean said into the black receiver.

"Mrs Barnet," came an unrecognised female voice, "Queen's Messengers are called – Blitz in Norwich. Please go immediately to the convoy."

"Yes, of course," Jean replied, wide awake now and already going through her mental checklist of what she needed to do to be ready.

"And good luck," wished the voice.

"Thank you," she replied.

Jean hastily pulled on her W.V.S. winter uniform, stockings, and thick W.V.S. coat, knowing it would be cold on an April morning and wrote a note leaving it on the kitchen table.

Messengers called. Blitz in Norwich. Love you!

Then she ran the short way along the dark road to Trumpington and waited at the convoy for crews to arrive – by foot, by bicycle, a very few by car – as the night sky slowly turned from black to navy to grey.

The convoy progressed the seventy miles slowly to Norwich from Cambridge through Newmarket and Thetford and a countryside that was beginning to wake for the day. They could see the smoke on the skyline ahead many miles before arriving. As they approached, Jean sat in silence, looking at the pillars of smoke growing in size. Even jovial Fee, who was usually never short for comment, was hushed by the prospect of what they would find.

Fee, her face set in grim determination, drove her heavy lorry into the bombed city. She kept her eyes on the provision lorry in front of her, knowing that it was leading the way for her kitchen lorry and the water lorry following behind, each vehicle driven by a W.V.S. volunteer – A Queen's Messenger. A fireman's escort met them on the outskirts of Norwich, completing the relief convoy. Little by little, they made their way towards the city's centre. First, through roads that still looked like roads and then onto tracks that looked like no city centre at all – buildings crumbling, twisted piles of mortar and metal wreckage all around them, firemen pouring gallons upon gallons of water onto smouldering ruins of lives and livelihoods.

Jean and Fiona climbed down from their lorry. An eery

silence surrounded them – dazed bewilderment blanketed the city.

"It was bad," called a passing warden. "We've lost thousands."

"Lives or homes?" Jean asked.

"Too early to tell," he replied, running off in a hurry to help elsewhere.

"Bloody hell!" Fee said quietly.

She had a knack for finding the right words.

"I don't think I've ever worked so hard in my life as I worked that day and the next," Jean said, looking around the table at her family and their emptying bowls of crumble. "The Messengers acted as one big field kitchen to supply the rest centres for all the poor people caught in the bombing because so many of the Norwich centres themselves were affected. There was a team from Bury St Edmunds which was meant to relieve us, but they never came because they were having such a bad time themselves, as Bury was bombed too."

"The Germans bombed a lot of our cathedral cities in '42, didn't they," Chris observed. "What were they called? They had a nickname, didn't they?"

"We called them the 'Baedeker bombings'," Jean replied.

"That's a German word, isn't it, Mum? Why did they give those bombings a German name?"

"Because Hitler wanted to reduce our morale by bombing our beautiful historic cities, people said that Göring, the chief of the Luftwaffe, must have used the Baedeker travel guides to plan the raids. Who knows? But certainly, many lovely places suffered that spring along with Norwich and Bury – Bath, Exeter, York."

"Were you safe, Granny?" Sally asked. All this talk of war

and bombings alarmed her.

"Yes, I was darling," Jean answered. The only thing I had to face then was hard work. Since no other volunteers knew how to use the lorry kitchens, we had to plough on ourselves. We drove to Horning for the night to be safely out of the way in case there were more air raids. Thankfully there weren't. We returned to Norwich in the morning to continue helping. I hadn't been expecting to stay overnight. I had nothing with me but the clothes I was in, and I was so tired. We didn't arrive back in Cambridge until late that night. We'd been working for forty hours at least. And you wouldn't believe how much we had served. I still remember – nearly four thousand cups of tea and sandwiches and about six thousand portions of soup! I was bowled over when I heard the final count."

It was nearly midnight on the day after she had set out that she had returned home, taking the route in reverse through the night-time lanes to her lightless house. The sky was clear, and she could see the bright belt of Orion. No planes, no bombs, no heavy guns, no sirens tonight. She was exhausted and filthy. The house was utterly still, and her husband, daughters, and mother slept peacefully and safe within. Thank God – the God she silently raged against. On tiptoe, she crept along the landing and took a blanket from the airing cupboard to prepare herself a makeshift bed on the sofa. She was too tired to wash and too tired to create more laundry by slipping into the sheets beside Alan.

"You did a lot of war work then, Jean?" Christopher asked his mother-in-law, scraping the last remnants of custard from his bowl so that the bowl was as spotless at the end as it had been at the beginning. "You must have got lots of stories. You should share them. It's good for the children to hear what you did."

Barbara secretly applauded her husband for saying so naturally what she would have liked to be able to say herself.

"We were just children during the war," he continued. "You'll have different memories from us – it would be good for them." His bowl was now spotless, and he began to eye up the last tablespoon of crumble remaining in the serving dish. "There was a camp here in the village, wasn't there?" he asked.

"Yes," Jean answered simply. "Behind the Rose and Crown Pub."

"I don't suppose there's anything left of it?" he asked.

"No. It's all gone."

"That's not true, Mummy," Barbara interjected. "Don't you remember, the Officers' Mess was turned into the cricket pavilion when the war was over?"

"Interesting," Christopher commented.

Jean didn't think it was interesting. It was for the best that there was no trace of the men who had been there and the things that had happened.

"I think you must have done a wonderful job, Granny. I'd like you to tell me more about it," Sally said, in such an adult tone, that the adults around the table were surprised by the almost-not-a-child among them. She left her place, put her arm around her grandmother, and kissed her on the cheek.

"Honestly, darling, I didn't do very much." Jean laughed, caught out slightly by the unexpected loving gesture that her granddaughter had made. "Not more than anyone else did. Everyone who lived through the war has their own story, and everyone suffered and made sacrifices. And you know, I'm not one for telling stories. I prefer to listen to other people's stories – that's far more interesting."

But she knew that was not all of it. To tell stories of what had happened is to create memories, and to create memories

101

is to make history. Some things are better left unsaid and so forgotten.

11.

ALICE

FLEAS AND JAM JARS

Cambridge, October 1939

Hester Adrian was a woman of boundless energy and limitless enthusiasm. She possessed a delicate bone structure, the sort that would have made a young man beautiful but made a woman regal. She was quick to smile, and when she did, her face lit up with an ethereal warmth, but even then, her grey eyes, magnified behind her spectacle lenses, never lost for an instant their incisiveness and ability to read and understand the currents moving beneath conversations and situations.

Hester and Alice had struck up an immediate and life-long friendship when Alice arrived in Cambridge to begin the autumn term of 1938. They were of the same mould, and, to their amusement, they had led parallel lives. They had been born in the same year, had children of similar ages, and both, before the war, enjoyed travelling and entertaining. That could be said for many women and would be the foundation of true friendship, but their sisterhood went deeper. Hester's husband, Edgar, like Lawrence, had received a Nobel Prize, and held an important position in the life of the University, being Professor of Physiology and Master of Trinity. Both Alice and Hester were Oxbridge women with degrees in Modern History – Alice, a daughter of Newnham and Hester of Sommerville. It went deeper still. When they had been on the cusp of womanhood, they had stared death and paralysing grief in the face, their brothers ripped from them, slaughtered on Flanders' Fields, a sacrifice to the might and right of King and Country.

Lady Reading's rallying cry in the summer of 1938 had been answered by Hester, as it had by Alice, and Hester had become the first member of the Cambridge W.V.S. She might have been jealous when Alice arrived, appointed by Lady Reading, to lead the Cambridge branch, but she never said. If she had been, that jealousy had soon evaporated, like the mist warmed by the sun on an autumn day, under the sunshine of Alice's warm nature. In any case, Hester was more than happy to take on responsibility for one area of work rather than oversee a whole operation. Her duties were so complicated, so fraught with difficulty, that they absorbed her completely all day at the office and penetrated her dreams at night. The influx of evacuees from London, an incredible gigantic tangle of billeting needs, the unknotting of which she was in charge. It pushed the sadness of her absent children away from the forefront of her mind.

Like Alice and Lawrence, Hester and Edgar had faced a choice: to keep their children with them in England or send them to safety in America. Pennsylvania won the argument. All three children were dispatched on a ship from Liverpool to the sanctuary of the USA at the end of September 1939, under the guardianship of a first cousin. Hester regretted her decision when she kissed them goodbye and waved them off with a cheery smile, exhorting them to be good, pay attention, and write as much as they could. They would grow up without her.

And so, Hester and Alice, who had had so much in common, suddenly didn't.

Hester approached the office, first slowing down her bicycle by desisting to pedal and then applying the brakes. She had not reached a stop before a large woman, cross-armed and with a mutinous face, accosted her from the pavement.

"Mrs Adrian, I am not at all happy," the woman launched.

"Mrs Wiggins, whatever is the problem?" Hester responded, alarmed.

"I know it's not your fault, Mrs Adrian, but I won't put up with it. I just won't."

Hester parked her bicycle.

"Why don't you come into the office, Mrs Wiggins, and I'll see what I can do to help."

"The mood I'm in, Mrs Adrian, I'm just not minded to. I want you to get rid of them, find them somewhere else to go."

"Do come in, Mrs Wiggins. I'm going to make myself a cup of tea, perhaps you'll have one too, and you can tell me all about it."

Mrs Wiggins followed Hester reluctantly into the office. Alice had arrived already and was reading a report in preparation for a meeting she was to have in the middle of the morning with the head of refuse at the Borough about their joint salvage campaign. She raised her eyes and smiled as her friend entered, accompanied by Mrs Wiggins, who was exuding antagonism and a desire not to be placated.

At the desk by the door to the back office, Mrs Ghent was on the telephone, taking notes on a request for transport,

"... hospital, half past ten this morning, yes I've got that, we'll get a driver and car, no, I won't call you back, only if there's a problem ..."

Hester glanced at Mrs Ghent's paperwork as she passed her desk on her way to the office kitchenette to make the tea. There were already several names and times together with telephone numbers, and the list was growing. She made a pot for them all, wondering what could have riled Mrs Wiggins.

"... yes, how many children? Three. How old? Golly,

that's very young, and there's no adult? Yes, we'll get a driver who's used to small children – just try not to let them eat anything. There's nothing that upsets our women more than children being sick in their car."

Mrs Wiggins, meanwhile, was sitting like an immovable mountain at Hester's desk. Hester smiled confidingly but with the serious intensity of a GP.

"Now, Mrs Wiggins, how can I help?"

"You know, Mrs Adrian, I'm always one to do my bit."

"Of course you are, I know."

"And I willingly let them into my house."

"Yes, you did, and we are most grateful."

"But they have fleas. Those bloomin' kids have brought fleas with them."

"Oh dear, I'm so sorry."

"And these frightful boys wet their beds every night."

"Oh dear," Hester repeated. "Poor little boys, though, they are away from their parents. They must be most distressed. Bedwetting is natural and only to be expected in the circumstance."

She wasn't prepared for the tirade her comments launched. The children were lazy. They weren't bothered about correct toileting even when awake. They never washed their hands. They helped themselves to food from the kitchen cupboards without asking permission, and they deliberately provoked and fought with Mrs Wiggins' seven and eight-year-old sons – the older of whom was now badly bruised.

"I'm just not having those children in my house a day longer."

"… two prams! Thank you so much. Yes, of course, you

can't bring them both on the bus. We'll find a driver to collect them. It may be tomorrow now ..." Mrs Ghent punctuated Hester's billeting problem.

"I'm so sorry that the arrangement with the boys isn't working out, Mrs Wiggins. If you could please continue to look after them for a couple more days, I will find somewhere more appropriate for them. Now, how many are there and how old are they?"

"Four"

"Four boys or age four?"

"Four boys altogether."

"Goodness me, six boys in the house, no wonder you've had a challenging time! And how old are they?"

"Well, I wouldn't know for sure, and they don't seem to know either, but I think they must all be between five and ten."

"Oh dear," Hester sighed. "Let me see what I can do." She took out a thick file and started to read through the lists of names. It wasn't going to be easy to find a billet with a foster mother able to take four small boys so that the brothers needn't be separated from each other. Several telephone calls later, she had found a solution, not ideal, but a solution, nevertheless. Two families who lived a few doors apart from each other had space to take the children. The boys could not be billeted together, but at least they would be close enough to see each other every day, and who knew what the families would work out between them.

In less than half an hour, Mrs Wiggins left, assured that the four East End boys would be moving on and that her house would be fumigated to remove the unwelcome insects. Her temper had so much improved that she said,

"Thank you, Mrs Adrian. You know I'm always prepared

to do my bit."

"I wonder then, Mrs Wiggins, if, when you feel ready, might you be prepared to lodge one or two of the new hospital staff? We are expecting more to arrive, and there is no longer any hospital accommodation available?"

Mrs Wiggins departed – a round bundle of smiles. She would still be able to do her bit with a much more palatable set of lodgers.

"Well done, Hester," Alice praised her friend when Mrs Wiggins had left.

"She's not the only one to be upset, though," Hester replied.

"No, but I believe many billets are working out."

Hester screwed up her face in a sign to show she did not agree.

"Come on, Hester," Alice cajoled. "Only last week, you told me about a family of twins and their dog that you'd managed to house with the vicar at Trumpington and how happy he and his wife were since they missed their grandchildren so much since they moved to Scotland.

Hester sighed, then smiled. "Yes, Alice, you're right. It's so often only the problems we hear about in the office. It can be hard to remember all the success stories, where the children and families have settled in well, and Cambridge host families are content."

A knock sounded at the door, and both women looked up to see a lad struggling under the burden of a large cardboard box.

"Excuse me," he said. "This is the W.V.S., isn't it?"

"Yes, it is. How can we help?" Alice asked, walking over to him, her interest piqued both by the appearance of the youth and his box.

"My mother said you'd like these jam jars."

"Jam jars?" Alice queried.

"Yes. She doesn't want them, and she said you would. So here they are."

He placed the box on the floor, and Alice saw that inside were at least three dozen clean, empty jam jars.

"Thank you," Alice said, and the youth swiftly departed, not wanting to be caught in conversation with women the age of his mother, or older.

The jam jars caught the light streaming in through the office window, becoming diamonds in a cardboard case.

"Alice, what on earth do we want jam jars for?" Mrs Ghent asked, cradling the telephone beneath her neck, as she paused before dialling a volunteer to see if she were free to collect the 10.30 patient from the hospital.

"I don't know – yet," Alice replied. But knowing they would probably be useful in the future, she stowed the box neatly in the back room before leaving for her meeting on the question of salvage.

12.
GOD'S GLASS
WILL KEEP US SAFE

When Alice returned from her salvage meeting, a small woman, scarcely five feet tall with the straightest light blonde hair that Alice had seen for many a long year, was standing hesitantly at the doorway to the office, unsure whether she should enter. Her shoulders were slightly rounded, a little bit drooped, and she carried herself with her head forward, her head checking that the landscape was safe so that her body could follow. From her manner, she could have been one of the London evacuees except that her skirt and coat were cut from good quality cloth and the garments were well made, her shoes were newly polished and stylish, and she carried a leather portfolio.

The woman waited. She was not going to enter until invited. This, too, was strange, Alice thought momentarily, as most visitors to the office entered without appointment or announcement and launched straight into their list of problems and concerns, regardless of what the staff might have been doing before their arrival.

"Can I help?" Alice asked the stranger, knowingly adding warmth to her voice to put the newcomer at ease.

"Thank you," the lady replied. "I'm looking for Mrs Finlayson. I'm from the Grantchester branch. She asked me to come."

Mrs Finlayson was absorbed in cross-checking billeting lists at her desk hemmed in with filing cabinets. She looked up when she heard her name.

"Mrs Barnet, how nice to see you. Alice, this is Mrs Barnet."

"My name's Jean. I'd be happy if you called me Jean," Jean said nervously.

"Of course, Jean, I'm Alice, Alice Bragg," and the two shook hands.

"I asked Jean to come by the office last week when I visited the canteen they have set up for the artillery soldiers," Mrs Finlayson explained. "She's an artist and made the most beautiful posters for their jumble sale. I thought maybe she could draw some for us. Did you bring your posters with you to show Alice?"

"Yes," Jean replied, and with her hands shaking slightly, she placed the portfolio on Mrs Finlayson's desk and took out three posters, handing one to Alice, the other to Mrs Finlayson, and putting the third on the desk to be viewed by them all.

The poster Alice held was reminiscent of an illustration from a favourite storybook. It depicted a stream of happy customers leaving a jumble sale, their cloth bags bulging with purchases. The poster on the table was more avant-garde; a layered cake and cup of tea, both angular, like an art-deco sculpture. In the third, which Mrs Finlayson held, a soldier relaxed, reading in an armchair. His body and the chair extended to the borders of the design, making it a strikingly modern image.

"These are good," Alice said admiringly.

"Would you have time to help us, Jean?" Mrs Finlayson asked. "We're organising a jumble sale in two weeks to raise funds for the station canteen. There's such a need for better refreshment at the station with so many people coming and going."

"And we need to get social clubs off the ground for the evacuee mothers. And toys, we need lots of donations of toys for the babies and toddlers," Alice added.

"And prams – don't forget those. We're in desperate need of prams."

Jean's mind was racing as Alice spoke. Ideas for posters were forming in her mind's eye like genii escaping from their lamps.

"I'd love to," she replied, taking back her posters to put them away. Now that she had passed her perceived test and both she and her artwork had been welcomed, a smile of relief lit up her face, and her shoulders ceased to droop.

"She's very talented," Alice said to Mrs Finlayson when Jean had left.

"Isn't she!"

"She has the appearance of being a conscientious person, even though she's clearly shy. Did you say she already volunteered at the Grantchester canteen?"

"Yes, she does, but not every day, I think," Mrs Finlayson replied.

"I wonder if she could find time to help us in the office. There is so much that needs to be done," and with that, the centre manager and her deputy continued their tasks for at least five minutes before a sweating middle-aged lady walked in.

"I've come to see me gran'son, Charlie – check 'e's all right. 'e left wiv out enuff socks, so I brought 'im some more. 'e's stayin' in Cambridge somewhere. The man at the station sed you'd know."

"Do you have an address?" Mrs Finlayson queried.

"Lor' no, 'e's eight and can't write none too good."

Alice took a deep breath. It was going to be a long afternoon.

It was late when Alice returned home on her bicycle, her

head aching and looking forward to a reviving cup of tea. As she approached her house, she saw a large grey van parked outside her entrance with its doors flung wide. Two delivery men in overalls were unpacking something large and flat and obviously delicate.

"Easy does it, Mick," a very large man with protruding belly said to his partner, a tiny stick man with balding hair.

"I'm being easy, Len. Couldn't be anything else!" Mick replied.

"Afternoon, Ma'am," the large man called Len greeted Alice with a broad smile revealing a missing front tooth.

"Good afternoon," she replied and entered her front garden taking her bicycle to the porch at the side.

The front door was flung wide open, and loud voices were coming from inside.

"Watch your weight, Mal."

"I'm a watchin' it, but I can't see much down here."

"Can't nobody make sure we have more light, please!"

Alice was perplexed. What was happening inside her house?

She entered hurriedly and found Maggie, hugely pregnant sitting on the stairs and eating warm toast with honey, scattering crumbs over her and around her as she ate. Maggie was a bus-conductress, evacuated from London with nowhere else to go and a baby due in no time at all if she'd got her dates right, but then she wasn't quite sure of, you know, when she and Alf had done 'you-know-what', and her family went in for big babies. Alice sighed at the crumbs. She didn't like mess.

"Maggie, what is happening? Where is Mr Bragg?" Alice asked as she took off her coat and hung it on the hall coat stand.

"Mr Bragg's in the cellar."

"The cellar? Are you sure? What on earth is he doing down there?"

"'aven't a clue, Mrs Bragg. But I can tell you what, this is the best fun I've 'ad in days. You shoulda seen the first lotta fellas tryin' to take all of it down the cellar."

"Take what, Maggie?"

"Glass."

"Glass what?"

"Glass, like windows I expect 'coz of the size. Would you like some toast? I'm gonna go an' make meself some more," and she heaved herself up from the stairs and waddled off to Alice's kitchen.

Alice followed the voices down to the cellar. A lightbulb attached to a small thread of wire swung like a bell from the ceiling, throwing great shadows on the walls. The temperature dropped step by step until she felt quite chilled without her coat on. At least it was not damp.

The cellar was large. It was almost the entire size of their ground floor and was divided into several sections, which could almost be called rooms. As they did not need to use the cellar as storage space, the rooms were mostly empty, except for the one closest to the stairs, which Alice had designated as the family air-raid shelter. This was kitted out with small cot beds and blankets, a writing table, a couple of chairs, and other comforts and entertainments which might be useful. Nobody knew how long they would have to shelter underground.

Alice could hear Lawrence's voice in the room ahead.

"This will be quite fine, I think, for that pane. Do we

need more blankets to wrap it in? You have crates as well, don't you? Do be careful, gentlemen, as you step back."

She entered the room to find four more delivery men in their brown overalls and her husband in his everyday lounge suit standing around a very large length of something patently fragile on her cellar floor. Life in Cambridge was becoming increasingly extraordinary.

"Ah darling, I'm so glad you're here," Lawrence greeted. "We're going to need another pair of hands, and Maggie isn't quite up for the job."

"Of course," Alice smiled. "But Lawrence, my dear, perhaps you would like to tell me what we are all doing in the cellar? I love parties, but I do like some warning."

"Oh drat, didn't I tell you?"

"Tell me what?"

"I agreed with the Provost of King's that we would store the chapel glass in our cellar while the war goes on – in case there are bombs, you know."

Alice felt a little dizzy.

"King's College glass, in our cellar?" she clarified.

"Yes, darling, I hope you don't mind. We've got one pane in, and I believe another is making its way down the stairs now.

"What did I say about being easy, Mick?" Alice heard Len call on the stairs behind.

"I'm being as easy as I can," Mick answered, his voice straining, revealing the effort of carrying a priceless pane of antique stained glass down cellar stairs.

Two of the men already in the cellar went forward to assist Len and Mick so that they could safely store the two large panes in their new home. Wrapped in layers of cloth,

Alice couldn't tell what stories in what colours the panes depicted.

"How much are we expecting?" Alice asked.

Len scratched his head as he tallied up,

"Well, we got three of them panes down 'ere now and four more up in the van, Mrs Bragg, and there was another van being loaded with more in crates as we left. Should arrive any minute now, I expect."

"And are we expecting anyone else?"

"Only the driver, Mrs Bragg, 'coz we're all 'ere already."

"As I said – a party," Alice commented cheekily. "We should crack open a bottle of champagne to celebrate the successful removal and relocation of the King's College Chapel glass to the home of the Bragg family. But I think a cup of tea will be safer," and she left the men to it. Lawrence followed her up the stairs behind.

"You don't mind, do you, Alice darling?" he asked sheepishly, "I'm so sorry I forgot to tell you."

"Not at all," she replied, her eyes twinkling. "I think in the scheme of things that it is most amusing. And I don't think anything bad will happen to us here as long as we are the caretakers of God's glass."

13.

JEAN

ALBERT'S BOOK

George Woodbridge had whistled loudly as he had entered the village canteen for the first time.

"Oh my, lads, what a vision," he turned over his shoulder to the gunners following on behind.

Albert Dollis, at George's shoulder, spied Mrs Harding and Jean standing by the kitchenette hatch waiting to serve the troops.

"Take your hat off," he hissed into George's ear and scrambled to remove his own. "There are ladies here."

Young Bob Hastings, scarcely eighteen, followed suit, and all three entered, looking more like three little boys than three soldier men.

The 387 Battery D troop of the 121 Regiment of the Royal Artillery had arrived in the earliest days of Spring 1940 under the command of Captain Maltby. With a remit to protect the RAF trainee pilots and aircraft at the Marshall's aerodrome, the gunners took over the temporary base structure that had been erected six months earlier for troops from a sister regiment now departing, moved on to defend the South Coast.

The gunners came from all walks of life and from all over the country. A few were temporary reservists – part-time soldiers for many years, who knew the drill, knew the weapons, men who had volunteered. Most had been conscripted. The younger ones had hardly had time to fly on their own from their mothers' nests. The older ones had nests with babies of their own. Tents for sleeping, tents for offices, tents for army mealtimes, and tents for military stores created an alternative canvas village on the fields behind the Rose and Crown pub in the heart of picturesque Grantchester. Few complained. Certainly not the villagers, for these lads with their huge guns would protect the village and her ancient neighbour city from the hellfire that would come, surely soon, from the sky, and certainly not the gunners, who found themselves unbelievingly, as Alice entered Wonderland, stationed in a delightful country idyll.

For idyll, it was. Grantchester was beautiful. The peaceful Granta meandered past the village and through green meadows to the city of colleges and learning, hardly daring to leave, on its way to the sea. Willows bent over to waterfall their fronds into the calm water. Even in winter, it was beautiful, ice covering the water, hard frosts bedecking the willows so that they cried silvery tinsel. In the village, thatched white-painted cottages sleepily decorated the few village streets and the ancient Early English Parish church of St. Andrew and St. Mary called Christians to worship by its mere presence, now that its bells were silenced.

A handful of fellow newly-arrived gunners had already found their way to the Reading Room canteen. One was writing a letter between sips of his tea at a small table by the window, two more were engrossed in a game of chess, and a fourth was chatting to the women at the serving hatch. Someone had placed a vase of early daffodils in the middle of the long table in the centre of the room, and bright cushions called from the armchairs for gunners to sit down and relax.

"Welcome! Come in," Mrs Harding cheerily greeted the three soldiers at the door. "And do shut the door. You're letting in all the cold air."

Bob reached round immediately and, muttering an apology to the ladies at the hatch, closed the door to save the warmth.

"And you're not going to get any of this delicious cake standing on the doorstep, lads," the gunner at the hatch added, his mouth half full of sponge.

"Should've known you'da found the cake, Alf!" George retorted. "Always the first to find the grub ain't yer?" he teased. "But my, it's like the Crown and Anchor on a weekday afternoon," he said admiringly, looking around at the wooden furniture, the books on the shelves, the day's newspapers laid out ready to read.

"I'm not sure that's a compliment, young man," Mrs Harding laughed. She could have been his mother.

"It's more like the common room at school," Albert said with a fondness in his voice, appreciating the hall that was so welcome, so homely, and so not a military hut. For more than six months now, his home had been a metal cot under canvas shared with eleven other men, a separate tent for ablutions with, frankly, primitive washing facilities, and another larger tent for meals. And it was so cold in camp, so bitterly, bitterly cold.

"Well, I wouldn't know anythink about no common room seein' as I'm not a toff like you!" George replied quickly with a teasing twinkle in his eye.

Jean stirred the pot of tea she had just made before the newcomers had entered and surreptitiously took them in, memorising what they looked like so that she could learn their names. Mrs Fielding had said to the volunteers – and they knew that she was correct in this – that all the women must learn the full names and ranks of the troops from the first meeting; that each must be addressed as Gunner so-and-so or Mr such-and-such or even just by their Christian name, or surname alone, if that's what they preferred; each must be addressed in the way that they felt most comfortable, because whilst these boys (and in truth, most were fully grown men and had been for many a long year) were posted in Grantchester, the Reading Room canteen in the village hall was the closest place to a real home that they would have.

The joker was a squat broad-chested man probably in his mid-twenties with merry green eyes, freckles, and dark brown hair. He fidgeted with his cap and twisted and turned in repartee between his fellow troopers who viewed him with warmth, not irritation. For all his teasing, this man must be a good friend, Jean thought. The grown-up schoolboy was older, thirty perhaps. He had a wistful stillness about him. His blonde hair and pale skin looked out of place in his brown uniform, as white cherry blossom looks when fallen on the muddy earth. The last newcomer was the youngest – a child with a chubby round face and dimple in his left cheek when he smiled, a quiff of black curls that crowned his forehead like a Michelangelo cherub.

"I'm Mrs Barnet, and this is Mrs Harding. Would you like some tea?" she asked softly. "It's fresh."

"George Woodbridge at your service," the joker introduced, "and yes, please, Ma'am, I'd love a cuppa."

"Albert Dollis," the schoolman nodded.

"Bob Hastings," the soldier-child mumbled.

"There's coffee too if you'd prefer. We managed to get some this week," Jean offered.

"What do yer think we are, lady, yanks?" Gunner Woodbridge jibed. "Can't speak for the others, but give me a good, strong cuppa any day and a slice of sponge, and I'll be yer man forever."

Jean felt her cheeks flush, and unsure how to respond, silently began to pour three cups of tea for the soldiers.

"We can certainly provide you with the tea and cake,"

120

Mrs Harding responded good-humouredly, "but we are both married ladies and have our own men to keep us busy. That will be thruppence, young man."

"A good deal, if ever I 'eard one," Woodbridge grinned and winked at Jean.

The tea or their married status? Jean wondered silently, and her cheeks burnt bright as she cut three slices of cake.

When she looked up nervously at the soldiers, George had taken his cup and cake and was making his way to the chess players to disturb their game with his mischief. Albert Dollis had taken his place at the hatch and was counting his pennies out for Mrs Harding.

"Don't mind George," he said to Jean as he picked up his cup of tea and slice of cake. "Mostly, he says the first thing that comes into his head. Please don't let him offend you," he added, noticing that Jean hadn't replied immediately with 'of course' or 'chaps will be chaps'; noticing that her cheeks were red, that the face that had been so friendly at their entrance, had, for the last few minutes, been turned studiously on the cake; noticing that George's brashness had made her feel uncomfortable.

Mrs Harding was busy taking Bob's money and mothering the youth, who anyone could tell, just by looking at him, was more of a boy than a man. Jean looked up at Albert and tried to say with a smile, "I'm all right … thank you for noticing." He nodded and turned, taking his tea and cake in the direction of George, where the chess players now needed rescue from the joker of the pack.

"Woodbridge, how's your whist?" Albert asked, reaching for a pack of cards lying ready on the long table a little up from the chess, as a blast of icy air from the door announced the arrival of another half dozen or so men, themselves now off-duty and seeking comfort.

A full week passed before Jean's turn on the canteen rota coincided with when George, Albert, and Bob were off-duty. She had worked for three afternoons at the Cambridge office, copying out volunteers' information onto index cards so that the files could be cross-referenced. On one day, before returning home, she had bought eight yards of forget-me-not blue flannel from a fabric stall on the market, enough to make a dress for each of the girls with plenty of room to grow if she made each dress large by taking up the hems and putting tucks in the bodices. As she entered the village on her bicycle, fabric parcelled up in the basket attached to her handlebars, she thought she saw George and Albert on the road ahead, making their way to the encampment between Broadway and Grantchester Meadows. She was on the point of calling a friendly "hello" only to find that they were two uniformed strangers.

It was early evening when Albert arrived at the Reading Room, tired and cold from a long day at the gun emplacement. The skies had been silent all day, as they were most days, but the feeling of what could happen at any moment always hung tangibly in the air like an unspoken question, a gnawing fear. Sometimes he felt sick of waiting. He wished the Germans would just begin, begin to drop their bombs. Anything would be better than this freezing cold waiting.

His morning had been filled with training exercises with the ten other members of his gun team, and in the afternoon, he had been detailed to repair the damage to camouflage around the gun emplacements made by the melting snow. He was pleased now to find that the Reading Room was not yet busy, and he could take his tea and ham sandwich to his favourite armchair in the corner of the room and read the book he had brought with him. A welcome moment of calm, of normality. With any luck, it would be a quiet night – no roving German craft flying inland away from the coast, which they hassled day and night, to remind the inhabitants of Albion that they were there, that they were biding time, that their day would come.

He must have dozed off. The white skies in his mind were filled with ominous dark birds, their wings beating and beating, becoming the sound of an aeroplane buzzing, becoming the sound of heated conversation and voices shouting.

"Y'er such a dim-wit, you bloody fool, McAllister," George was shouting, his normally ruddy face reddened further with a burst of flaming anger.

"I'm sorry, George, I didn't mean to knock you," McAllister wined in a tone that only infuriated Woodbridge further.

"Yer never do, yer great oaf. I've had it up to 'ere. Yer never know where to put yer arms or yer legs – or yer 'ead come to that matter."

Albert quickly put his unread book on the coffee table and rose to intervene. This had been brewing all day. Gunner George Woodbridge, an experienced reservist, like he was himself, had little patience with the inexperienced and often inept recruits to the battery.

"McAllister, find Woodbridge a cloth to wipe his jacket down, and then wipe the floor up, don't let the ladies clear up your mess," and placing a firm hand calmly on Woodbridge's wrist, whispered, "we've got to stick it out with the new ones, they'll improve. Go have a smoke. You'll feel better after."

Jean was in the kitchenette, watching all from behind the hatch. She hastily picked up a dishcloth and rinsed it under the running water from the cold tap so that McAllister at least had a chance of completing the cleaning-up successfully. The poor gunner received short shrift from

Woodbridge when he attempted to pat the tea spillage on the gunner's arm.

"I'll do that yer … yer bloody nincompoop!" George swore as he grabbed the wet cloth from McAllister. "Yer could've burned me, yer idiot," he grumbled. "You've been tryin' to kill me all day!" he concluded dramatically.

"But he didn't," Albert said gently, the warmth of his west country accent soothing the riled George. "Here, have one of mine," he continued taking his box of Woodbines from his breast pocket and holding the packet open to his friend. Woodbridge took one without thanks and stomped from the Reading Room to calm down alone outside.

McAllister had turned his attention to the puddle of tea on the floor and was ineffectively mopping it up. Jean wondered if she should offer to help but thought better of it. When McAllister had finished, he stood up and looked around helplessly, unsure of what to do with a dirty dishcloth, deciding after a few seconds to put it on the hatch with a "sorry, Mrs Barnet" and a weak attempt at a smile.

"Do you like Snakes and Ladders, McAllister?" Albert asked. "It looks as if Matthews and Lazenby are about to start a game." He led the young soldier to the long table.

"I do try, Dollis. I'm just not that good, I know," McAllister looked to the older soldier for reassurance.

"We all have our bad days, lad," Albert responded. A fish out of the water, this young one was in the army. But he would learn and maybe become a good soldier. Who knew?

"Look, McAllister, if you promise to steer clear of Woodbridge when he's drinking tea, I promise to run you through the exercises again, slowly, tomorrow – and no one will get killed."

Not such a quiet evening then, Albert thought as he settled himself back into the armchair and picked up his abandoned book. Good job none of the officers was in, and he could sort the spat himself, so no harm was done. He flicked through the book until he came to where he had left off reading. He had not finished the first page before he felt her standing beside him. He saw the grey-green uniform against her legs, beyond the edge of the paper. She was holding a fresh cup of tea and a plate with a second sandwich.

"Thank you, Mrs Barnet," he said, accepting the refreshment and began to search his pockets for coins.

"No. No need to pay for this. I've used the funds," she lied. She would pay the pennies herself.

"Thank you," he repeated. "I hope you're not worried by that little incident, Mrs Barnet?"

She shook her head, but she had been. She found the unpredictability of Woodbridge difficult, joking and teasing one minute and spouting with anger the next. She felt as if she had just received a lesson in how to manage a personality so very different from her own. The quiet, calm, pale Albert Dollis impressed her; she was drawn, despite herself, to know him.

"It's a shame your reading was disturbed," she started, hoping he wouldn't be irritated by her disturbing the activity herself. "What are you reading?"

He held out for her inspection his burgundy-bound book with rich gold decoration.

"*The Life of William Morris*," Jean read aloud in complete astonishment. Her surprise was so acute that Albert laughed.

"Not what you were expecting?"

"Not at all! Oh, I'm sorry, I don't know what I did expect you to be reading."

"I have wide reading tastes," he continued. "Before all

125

of this," he swept the room with his arm as he spoke, "I worked with my father in his book shop – actually, he has two shops, one in Bath and the other in Bristol. I managed the Bristol branch."

Jean looked closely at the book design and turned through the pages as he spoke, her eyes lingering on the frontispiece photograph of the great designer and revisiting his beautiful designs as if walking through a garden of memories in a family photograph album.

"And what do you think of Mr Morris?" she asked.

"A man of great vision; a man who wanted better for the world than what it had. And you, Mrs Barnet, what do you think of Mr Morris?"

Again that evening, she was taken by surprise. Now to be asked what she thought – for it to be taken for granted that she had an opinion on a topic other than domestic life.

"I think he was the greatest designer this country has ever seen, and if ever my designs could be a fraction of his, I would be a happy woman," she had replied.

Jean knelt on the carpeted floor of the study, the burgundy book with swirling gold patterns on her lap. The bottom shelf of the bookcase in front of her was empty, bar a few books which could no longer remain standing now that their neighbours had been removed, and so they had toppled sideways, revealing balls of dust in the corners of the shelf. To Jean's left, was a wooden crate already half full of books – law books, history books, manuals – Alan's; and to her right, was a small pile of novels – hers.

Eleanor stood on the other side of the crate working on the higher shelves, quick and efficient in taking each book from its home, flicking through the pages, and deciding if its destination was to be the crate for disposal, the 'inheritance' stack on her father's desk or the pile on the floor for her mother to keep. She picked up a blue bound tome.

"No, I don't think any of us will want *Corpus Juris Volume 40*," she said, and she consigned the tome to the crate.

And a little later.

"Now this is interesting, *Ivanhoe* – look, Mum, it was Dad's school prize for history in 1908. That would be great for one for the boys to keep," and she deposited Walter Scott's classic on the desk.

"What are you looking at, Mum?"

Jean was still sitting quietly, turning the pages of her book on her lap, seemingly uninterested in her daughter's narrated decisions.

"*The Life of William Morris,*" she replied softly.

An art book, no wonder her mother's mind was elsewhere. She knelt beside her mother to look at it.

"Are you going to keep it, Mum?"

"Yes. It was a present." As she spoke, she turned to the inside front cover where Eleanor read, "To Jean, Happy Christmas 1941, with fond regard, Albert Dollis."

"Who was Albert Dollis?"

So, Eleanor didn't remember. Jean felt the tension she had been holding in her shoulders since selecting the book subside.

"He was one of the soldiers at the canteen. You don't remember?" she checked again.

"Well, I do remember some of the soldiers. Bob, I remember Bob. I remember when he helped me down from a tree I'd climbed when I got stuck. I loved his accent – it was so different – where was he from?"

"Liverpool."

"Ah yes, Liverpool. And I remember Alf Long. He had a little girl, Jane, who I played with."

"Yes, that's right, he lost his wife at the beginning of the war, and he was bringing Jane up by himself, except that he was in the battery, so his mother was looking after her. Alf became great friends with the Fieldings and came back with Jane a few times to visit after the war. That's when you would have played with her."

"What happened to them?"

"I believe he married again, and I suppose the families lost touch."

Jean looked at Albert's handwriting – 'with fond regard' he had written.

"I have a photograph of the soldiers in my box. I saw it earlier. Would you like to look at it?"

Why was she doing this? Jean thought to herself as she sifted through the W.V.S. box in her bedroom. Why was she sharing a memory that didn't need to be shared? Eleanor had only asked about the book, not the photograph. But Jean wanted to look at the photograph.

It was a square snap that had been folded in half years ago to be fitted into an envelope. The picture was of seven soldiers in their tent. It must have been winter, for they all wore their army overcoats and in the foreground was a heater. The tent was their quarters. The men were sitting on iron cots with wooden planks for a mattress and military-issue blankets folded neatly at the ends. In the centre of the picture, one of the gunners was having his hair trimmed by a fellow trooper. Beside him, four soldiers were looking at a newspaper. The seventh gunner was sitting at the back of the tent, watching the haircut and laughing.

"Which is Albert?" Eleanor asked, scanning the men's faces for a childhood memory.

"This one," her mother replied. "He's looking at something. I think it could be a letter. It's difficult to tell because George Woodbridge's newspaper is in the way."

"Who are the others?"

"The man having his haircut is Alf Long."

"Is it?" Eleanor looked more closely. "So it is! I would never have known if you hadn't said. This man's handsome, Mum," she said, pointing to the man watching the haircut. "He looks like Clark Gable, doesn't he?"

"Yes, it's the sleek moustache," Jean giggled. "I have no idea any longer who he is."

"How could you forget Clark Gable?" Eleanor teased and turned the photograph over. There were no names written on the back.

"What a shame you didn't write down who they are."

"I probably didn't think I would forget them at the time," Jean defended herself. "And there were a lot of soldiers here during the war. Albert's battery was the second to be stationed here. There were two more that followed. That would have made at least four hundred soldiers who just stayed in the village camp – and I met plenty of others from the other half of the batteries stationed near the airport when I helped with the mobile canteen and not to mention the troops passing through the city who came into the office for assistance."

Eleanor examined the photograph where the fold through the middle had damaged the paper and caused minute cracks to burst from this false spine into the picture.

"This is history, Mum," she said. "There's no evidence that the soldiers were here now apart from the cricket pavilion. The camp's gone. The field where the guns were has all grown back. You need to look after what you have carefully, so people can remember in the future."

"I don't think people want to remember," Jean replied.

"That's not true."

Seeing that her mother would not be drawn further, she continued thoughtfully,

"It's an interesting picture. It's not a snap. It's more like a scene from a play. It's as if someone has composed the photograph. I wonder who took it and why? It's almost like the men are aware they are recording history."

That would have been Albert. Of them all, he would have been the one most likely to think that such an intimate scene would be worth recording. He would have been the one to arrange all the men in position, and they would have taken direction from him because they all liked and respected him. It was Albert who had sent her the snap after the battery had left and were stationed on the Essex coast – that was before they were sent to France. Her eyes lingered on the face she hadn't seen for so many years – so many years; the pale, fine features, the short sandy hair parted on the left of his head and swept across his crown to the right. His was not a particularly handsome face, but an intelligent face – a thoughtful face.

She wanted to be alone with him. She no longer wanted to share his image with her daughter.

"I think I'll go and write the names on the back before I forget – if you can finish the books, darling – and then I'll make us both a bit of supper."

14.

ALICE

BETRAYAL

June 1940

Although Alice and her staff at the Cambridge W.V.S. office, like sister offices all over the county, had been working hard for the war effort, in truth, not that much had happened. The Bragg children had been sent away, as Sir William Spens had recommended, first to Alice's sister Enid in Newport and then to friends in Herefordshire, but as no war on British soil or airspace had erupted, they had returned home after a few weeks, having very much enjoyed their extended vacation. The same was true for the London evacuees, who, finding that the capital was not under attack, trickled home. Alice was pleased that Maggie's baby had been delivered safely – a very large boy – and equally pleased when her, not exactly unwelcome, but all the same uninvited, lodger departed, as clearly London was perfectly safe, and Maggie explained that she'd rather be together with Alf and the baby in their own home.

A phoney war. A phoney war that was becoming daily a real war as Hitler's troops pressed into France. Lawrence, who had been inspecting sound-ranging equipment on the French western front for the British military, escaped from Paris by aeroplane with only days to spare before that great nation fell to the occupying German force. Alice's heart was in her mouth when he confessed. Lawrence would be a great Nazi prize. The possibility of his capture was too terrifying to contemplate.

It wasn't long before the guns of France could be heard even in Cambridge, as the German invaders pushed the

British Expeditionary Force and the French army to the western shores of France. And then the guns fell silent. The heavy artillery was abandoned, as their operators, along with thousands of other troops, barely escaped with their lives across the channel, rescued by sheer British will. Only 21 miles of sea – a handful of minutes of bomber flying time – now separated Great Britain from her enemy.

Late on Sunday evening, shortly after the evacuation of the Dunkirk beaches, a car drew up outside the Bragg's house in West Road. Lawrence and Alice had not yet retired for the night and were enjoying a lively discussion with Harold Robinson, Lawrence's great friend from the '14-18 war, head of Physics at Queen Mary College London, and billeted with them now that the QMC had been relocated to Cambridge.

Lawrence answered the door returning quickly to the drawing room to fetch Alice, who hurried in equal measure to her unexpected visitor, whom Lawrence had shown into the morning room.

A man in uniform stood waiting for her.

"Mrs Bragg, good evening."

He addressed her as if it were the most natural thing in the world that a policeman should visit this late on a Sunday.

It was Police Sergeant James Rutherford.

"Orders," he announced as he handed Alice a short document that she returned to him once read.

"I see," she commented. "Is there any explanation?"

"Not yet, I'm afraid, Mrs Bragg."

"So, am I correct in understanding that twelve volunteers and I must be ready tomorrow at first light with no explanation?"

"That is correct, Mrs Bragg. But an intelligent lady like

yourself will undoubtedly put two and two together as tomorrow progresses."

"How long shall the women and I be needed?"

"Most of you only for the day, but at least six of you will be needed for twenty-four hours, maybe more. I advise those six to pack an overnight bag as you will not be in Cambridge."

"I see," Alice repeated calmly, yet her mind racing.

"Pick the most discreet," he continued, and with that, he made to leave. He turned from the door, "I can show myself out. And, good luck!"

Alice remained alone in the middle of her morning room, running through the list of volunteers in her head. The most discreet. Jean Barnet, then, not her friend Fiona, who let anything slip from her mouth despite being a Trojan worker. Heather Miller and Valerie Richards – those two could be trusted not to let words slip. Enid, her sister, was staying with their parents in Cambridge – Enid could be relied upon too. Alice went to the study, where she telephoned her way through eleven names and numbers.

At six o'clock the next morning, Alice and her eleven volunteers, Jean and Enid included, reported to St Andrew's church hall, where a harried official and a policeman met them. The church warden's wife had unlocked the hall and was busily loitering, eager to discover what was about to happen and probably equally eager to repeat her information to the neighbourhood. Alice took matters in hand immediately.

"Thank you so much for rising this early to let us in. It is very good of you. Perhaps you could show a couple of my volunteers where the kitchen is to make tea, and we would be very grateful if you could arrange for a milk delivery from your milkman. How many pints? Oh, shall we start with the amount he has spare this morning and take it from there?"

The churchwarden's wife found herself busied away with an important task about which she had not an ounce of understanding.

At half-past six, the first police van arrived outside the church hall. The policeman in the passenger seat descended and went around to the back of the vehicle. He opened the doors and helped a middle-aged lady in sensible shoes with a nervous, anxious face descend. She was carrying a carpet bag and held it close to her chest as if worried it would be snatched from her. She looked uneasily around herself with the same shell-shocked expression as a survivor emerging from a bombing. Next to descend was a grey-faced young mother holding a baby in her arms and a toddler by the hand. All three were crying.

"Now, now, love, just go inside. The ladies will sort you out," the policeman said sternly, but not unkindly, and he steered the group firmly towards the entrance where Enid led them into the hall and did her best to calm and settle the distraught family.

The young family was followed by assorted women and children of all ages. Not one man was among the human cargo deposited by the constant stream of police vans that morning. Some of the women carried small luggage cases, and some carried nothing. All were anxious. Many were crying. None were British.

Inside the hall, Alice quickly set up zones using the benches usually reserved for Sunday School. One large area was created for mothers with small children, so that crawling babies or escaping toddlers could be safe. Another zone was set up with tables and chairs, and another with chairs in groups. It was the best they could do to make use of the space and to provide a tiny bit of comfort. At least it was possible to serve cups of tea. Jean and Valerie kept up a constant service throughout the morning.

"I have nothing. They came for us too quickly. It was so early – we weren't even properly awake. I couldn't think what to take. Can you buy me baby milk? I don't have any," one of the young mothers asked Jean at the hatch in flawless English with the slightest continental accent that Jean found impossible to identify.

"I don't know," Jean replied. "I'll find out."

Leaving Valerie to continue serving cups of tea valiantly, Jean approached Alice.

"Alice, what are we to do? These poor creatures have come with nothing, not even baby milk."

"I know," Alice replied grimly.

Suddenly there was a scuffle by the door.

"*Nem! Ne nyúlj hozzám.* No, I will not let you treat me like this. What have I done?" A well-dressed middle-aged lady shouted at her policeman escort, who remained tight-lipped.

"It is not a crime not to be British. I have committed no crime."

Enid, closest to the door, intervened calmly, trying her best to soothe the angry, desperate woman, conscious that over a hundred, even more angry, desperate eyes were upon her.

"Where will they take us?" the woman begged Enid.

"I don't know," Enid replied. "We will find out soon, come and sit down, have a cup of tea." She attempted to steer the lady from the door to an unoccupied seat by one of the tables.

"Please help," the lady begged. "Please help get a message to Miklós. Tell him I'm safe. Tell him I'm here."

"I'm so sorry I can't," Enid had a lump in her throat, and

135

the lady sat down, the fight taken from her and rested against the table with her head in her hands.

"This is pitiful," Enid whispered angrily to Alice. "What have these poor folk done?"

What had they done indeed? Other than all be the wives and children of European refugees or immigrants, who were being rounded up and interned that day, the men taken to one hall, the women and children to another. None had been given the time to pack properly or bring necessities. And the cause? The Fall of France, the encroaching danger, the possibility of treachery from within the country's borders, the fear that information had already leaked to the Germans. They might be innocent. Then again, they might not.

"Alice, if these women are going to be here much longer, we're going to need more supplies. Some of the women don't even have nappies for their babies," Jean said softly.

If only the authorities had given her a bit more of an idea about what was going to happen, it would have been easier, Alice thought regretfully, before organising Jean and another W.V.S. volunteer, Mildred Hughes, to be taken by one of the empty police vans to the central office to bring back whatever blankets, nappies, toys and packs of cards could be found in their store. Once it became more apparent how many internees needed to be fed, Alice arranged for rolls and soup to be delivered to the hall by the W.V.S. mobile canteen, followed by a hot meal in the early evening ordered from a nearby hotel.

There was little else they could do other than try to keep the women and children calm and comfortable; play with the babies and children, play cards with the older women, and offer innumerable cups of tea.

The police action had been swift – the last van arriving before lunch. A lady in her early forties entered the hall. She had had more time to dress that morning than the others. Her arrest had been later in the day, as her hair was immaculate, and she had already applied her make-up. She wore a pretty, mauve print summer dress, lace gloves, hat, and handbag. She must have been on the point of going out, perhaps to meet a friend for lunch or a shopping trip in the city, when the police had arrived.

Alice was supervising a small team of her volunteers who were taking details from the women at one of the long tables. By mid-morning, it had been established with the police that it was permissible to get messages to the internees' neighbours – many had pets which, without anyone to feed them, would starve. There were the water, gas, and electricity supplies, too, which would need to be turned off in homes that were likely to stand empty for many months to come. Communication had to be minimal, unemotional, and essential. But at least it brought internee and volunteer alike a little comfort.

The well-dressed newcomer stood in a daze at the door, surveying the hall full of women and children, some crying, some sitting with their eyes closed, imagining themselves elsewhere, mothers trying to look after babies and small children without proper resources, elderly women feeling small and frail without their husbands or sitting resolutely trusting to the good sense of their adopted country. Despite the activity, an eery calm of resignation hung in the hall like an oppressive fog. She saw Alice and moved towards her.

"Alice," the woman said quietly, her eyes wide, reaching out seeking sympathy and friendship.

"Tanya! – Oh my goodness!" Alice was caught off-guard.

Tanya, it was Tanya Popova – her friend, wife of one of the Cavendish scientists who worked alongside Lawrence.

"Alice, we haven't done anything wrong, you know that, don't you?"

137

Alice fought to prevent tears from coming to her eyes or a tremble to her voice. She had a job to do. A verdict of innocence or guilt was not hers to make.

"Come and sit down, Tanya, let me get you a cup of tea," Alice felt foolish, slipping into her society hostess role in a church hall full of internees, but what else could she do? What else could she say?

Tanya hesitated, scanning Alice's face and features for a different reaction. Seeing none was to be had, she pulled her spine up straighter, held her chin up higher, and sat down where Alice indicated, turning her face away from her friend.

Late in the evening, Alice received further instructions: 6 of her W.V.S. volunteers were to stay with the police guard in the hall with the internees overnight. The remainder could leave and return home. Four of those W.V.S. allowed home were to return at first light in the morning to assist the police escort the prisoners to their destination.

Knowing she had a long day ahead of her the next day, accompanying the group to a mystery destination so far away it required an overnight stay, Alice went home to bed with a heavy heart and an aching head. Lawrence was quick to read the tiredness and angst in her face.

"You've had a hard day, my darling?"

She nodded.

"Can you tell me about it?" he asked.

She shook her head silently.

He had never known his gregarious wife to be lost for words, and he wrapped her in his arms.

"I understand."

Thank goodness he did. She couldn't get through any of this if he didn't.

She rose early the next morning and returned to the hall to find a weary, unhappy group of prisoners who had slept badly, either perched on chairs or curled on the floor, covered with loaned W.V.S. blankets, disturbed by babies and children who could not sleep in the strange, fearful surroundings. Only a few had a change of clothes, and there was nowhere sufficient to wash, even if they had brought towels. Tanya's eyes were smoky and grey as the rubbed mascara blended with the bags below her sockets, evidence of little rest and much anxiety. Like the other women, her skirt and blouse were creased from a night's wear.

Soon the police vans returned, and without more than a cup of tea, the whole sorry party was taken in loads to the station, where they were all herded onto a train. No one knew where they were heading other than to London, but that was merely an interchange. Alice and her W.V.S. helpers tried their hardest to keep up the women's spirits, but there was nothing they could answer to the anxious questioning: "Where are we going?" "Where are they taking us?"

At King's Cross, the party was shepherded the short way along Euston Road to Euston Station, and breakfast rolls were distributed on the platform while they waited to board another train, this one heading north, to Liverpool, where Alice and her volunteers left the Cambridge internees with the Liverpool W.V.S. and the Liverpool police.

It was a strange goodbye to these women and children. Alice could hardly wish them luck – they could be enemies for all she knew, although likely as not, they weren't. Yet she felt the weight of her betrayal to her friend on her all the long way home to Cambridge. Later, Alice learned that the party's destination was not Liverpool but a bleak internment camp on the Isle of Man. Such is war. Such is the price to keep the population safe.

15.

JEAN

CHRISTMAS SHOPPING

It was still dark when Jean woke. The kitchen kettle's whistle cut into her dreams, severing their delicate thread. She reached for the small square alarm clock on her bedside table and squinted at it in the darkness. The lime neon dots showed it was early, 6 a.m. She put the clock down and slipped her hand under the pillow to reassure herself that the envelope was still there. Of course, it was. She lay with her head resting on the pillow, resting on her hand, resting on the letters and his photograph, listening to Eleanor in the kitchen below.

Albert had been good at writing letters. He was always writing letters back home to his family or helping fellow troops less literate than himself compose their necessarily anodyne scrawls to wives, sweethearts, or mothers. She had wondered if he had a sweetheart or a wife as she had served him tea and sandwiches from the hatch. He was old enough to have a wife and several children. If he did, he never mentioned them to her or anyone else. She concluded that he was a bachelor – a book bachelor. The thought had made her smile.

"I'm in a spot of bother, Dollis," Jean had heard McAllister say in a low voice to Albert as he carried his plate and cup away from the hatch in the Spring before the war came to Britain. The young gunner's eyes were like pools of limpid water that threatened to spill beyond their rim at any moment.

"What's the problem?" Albert asked kindly, taking a seat at the long table where McAllister had been sitting in front of note paper with a half-written and half-crossed-out letter.

"It's my mother. She wrote and told me she's got shingles. She's in a pretty bad way."

"I'm sorry to hear that."

"My Pa passed away a while back, and she's only got me."

"I'm sorry," Albert repeated, wondering where McAllister was leading the conversation and what the problem really was.

"The landlord has put the rent up, and she can't afford to stay in the house, she's going to have to move, and I've no leave due to go to help her. She's not well, and there isn't anyone else. My parents were both only children too – funny how it runs in families. I've tried to write to the landlord to see if he will reconsider, but I don't know what to say. I never was very good with letters …" and he hung his head, ashamed at his confession.

"Of course, I'll help," Albert smiled. "Do you mind?" he added, reaching for the note paper, and in no time at all, he had written a simple letter, urging the landlord to be compassionate, for McAllister to copy out.

Jean felt sorry for McAllister. He was not alone in being far from home with domestic troubles on his mind. There was a lull in serving, so she left Mrs Appleby in the kitchenette, washing up a stack of dirty cups and saucers and went over to McAllister and Albert at the long table.

"Excuse me," she said nervously.

The two soldiers looked up from the letter. McAllister was surprised but Albert, Jean thought, seemed pleased.

"I'm sorry, I wasn't eavesdropping, but maybe the W.V.S. can help your mother."

"Oh, I don't think so, Mrs Barnet. Mother lives a long

way from here."

Jean saw that Albert pulled in his lips to keep them tight so as not to remark on McAllister's ignorance.

"We have branches all over the country, you know, and we exist to help anyone who needs help," she explained kindly.

"Really? I thought you ladies only helped us soldiers or folk caught in air raids."

"Yes," Jean replied. "That was at the beginning in '38, but so much has happened since then, hasn't it? Lady Reading, our Founder, says that W.V.S. must never say 'no'." She blushed, falling over her words. She was glad Woodbridge wasn't in the Reading Room that evening, or he would have teased her. "Lucky chap ter 'ave a gal that never sez 'no'." She could just see him grinning and laughing at his innuendo.

"And we are so glad of that!" Albert rescued her.

"Thank you," she acknowledged. "Where does your mother live, McAllister?"

"Worcester."

"Well, it's simple then. If you like, I will write to the Worcester office and explain that your mother needs help as she is alone and sick with shingles. They will surely be able to bring her comfort. Perhaps even resolve the problem with the lodgings. Would you like me to write? If you give me the details, I will write tomorrow from the Cambridge office."

"Thank you, Mrs Barnet, that would be very kind. Mother's a lucky woman, and I'm a lucky chap to have you and Dollis to help us."

Jean had been pleased to help and pleased too with the calm look of regard in Albert's steady blue eyes as she returned to the kitchenette to resume serving.

The door opened, and Eleanor switched on Jean's bedroom light.

"Good morning, Mum," she said gently. "I know it's early, but I thought you'd like a cup of tea in bed before I go."

"Thank you, darling."

Eleanor put the cup and saucer on the bedside table between the alarm clock and *The Life William Morris* that Jean had placed there the night before. Noticing the book, she picked it up and sat down on the bed next to her mother.

"Did you sleep well?" she asked.

"Yes, thank you, darling, did you?"

Eleanor nodded and then added tapping the cover of *William Morris* with her neatly manicured fingernails.

"I know it's hard, Mum," she said, "but you've got to try and finish the sorting. It's not long until Christmas, and you know we've planned the move for the 16th of January – that's only just over a month away – there's a lot to do still."

Eleanor was always the efficient one, the tidy one. The daughter who liked to have everything planned and organised so that nothing could take her by surprise. But it wasn't fair of Eleanor to suggest that she wasn't making an effort. She was. It was just at her own pace.

"I spoke to Barbara yesterday about asking Sally's Girl Guide pack to collect the boxes. They are having a jumble sale next Saturday. Someone will call during the week to collect them."

"Thank you, darling," Jean said, genuinely relieved that the filled boxes, that horrible kettle included, would soon be leaving the house.

"I'd better go. The train won't wait."

"Thank you, Eleanor. Thank you for all your help."

143

"See you at Christmas, Mummy," she said, kissing Jean goodbye.

Jean sat propped up against the pillows, drinking her tea, and pondered for a while on what she should do. She got out of bed, standing up slowly, her back still ached from the acrobatics on the chair to reach the W.V.S. box down from her wardrobe on Saturday afternoon. Now that Eleanor had left on the early train for London, Jean could safely return his letters to the box, still resting on the dressing table where she had left it. She opened the lid and placed the envelope on top of the newspaper article with the photo of Alice Bragg, the Mayor.

Looking through the box with Eleanor on Saturday afternoon hadn't been so bad. She'd quite enjoyed it, more than she'd expected – showing her daughter her posters, remembering the escapade with the piglet in the market. The war hadn't been all bad. Not all the memories were sad ones. Maybe she would take some time to look through the box a bit more later, over a cup of tea.

In the meantime, there were things to do. Eleanor was correct that the house move was close, but Christmas was closer. That's what she would do this morning. She would do Christmas. She had been so caught up in thinking about moving, in denying that she was moving, in being forced by her daughters to go back to thinking about moving, that she had neglected to get ready for Christmas. And it had the benefit that sorting out Christmas meant not sorting out her house, her papers, or her life.

Cambridge city centre was busy with only a couple of weeks left before the festival. Jean took the bus from Grantchester. She had never learnt to drive – she had always been too nervous, and the bus was much easier, especially as everyone said that car parking was becoming more and more of a problem in the university city. Most of the students had already left for the Christmas vacation, but a few, probably post-graduates, were in evidence around the university buildings.

It was a cold but crisp December morning. Jean was wearing her shopping suit. A green tweed ensemble that she had made a good ten years ago, her winter coat – the first significant piece of clothing that she had bought once rationing had finished after the war – hat, gloves, and scarf. Her feet were chilly in stockings and shoes, and she had to move her weight from side to side, stamping the ground discreetly to keep warm as she waited at the bus stop and sat on the bus for the few miles of the journey. Perhaps she ought to buy herself some new boots, she thought to herself as she looked around at the young women in the city with long boots and short skirts – although she would never wear a skirt with a hemline so daringly above the knee as the youngsters wore today.

The Christmas lights in the shop windows and the streets were cheerful. There was a pleasant hum of commerce as shoppers browsed and bought. Jean first went to her favourite stationery shop not far from the station, where she ran her eyes over the Christmas cards on the stand. She picked up an attractive view of King's College Chapel from the Backs. The familiar scene was covered in fresh white snowfall. It was a pretty card, but what would be the point of sending a view of Cambridge to people who lived in Cambridge? She only had a few people to send to who lived elsewhere: Eileen and John in Chester, Tom and Pippa still in Catford, Fee and family in Canada, the Fieldings in Bournemouth, definitely not a whole pack's worth. She replaced the view of King's on the shelf. The only other card she liked had a rabbit, a candle and a manger which, although well-designed, was quite frankly ridiculous. Then the idea struck her, why not draw some cards herself this year? Yes, why not? She could certainly do better than a holy rabbit.

She used to paint Christmas cards when she was a little girl. Edwardian Christmas trees with Edwardian gifts. Edwardian St Nicholases descending Edwardian chimneys, looks of surprise on their faces when they got stuck. One Christmas, before the first war, she had painted a scene where she, her brothers Nicholas and Tom and her sister Eileen had all smiled out from a sleigh trailing a banner wishing the world a 'Happy Christmas!'

When the twins were little girls, she had made Christmas cards with them – 1930s snowmen and 1930s robins. She couldn't remember painting Christmas cards with Eleanor. She must have been too busy with her war work. That was a shame. Eleanor had missed out on a lot. But, thinking about it a little more, she had made cards during the war. In 1944 as victory was in sight, she had painted two dozen images of Grantchester church and sent each with a letter to those soldiers that had been stationed in the village with whom she still corresponded. Some of them, including Albert, had written back in January, touched by her thoughtfulness.

She left the shop without a purchase and continued along Downing Street until she came face to face with Emmanuel College, where she turned left onto St Andrew's Street. She knew this street so very, very well.

The Robert Sayle Department store, her next stop, thronged with Christmas shoppers. Jean bought three attractive brooches for each of her daughters: a heart-shaped gold leaf ornamented with diamond paste for Barbara, a silver Scottish thistle with flecks of amethyst for Maeve, and a gold flower, whose petals were entirely turquoise beads for Eleanor. At the back of the display case, nestled in the corner, there was a sweet black and sparkling red ladybird. Sally would love it, Jean thought, and she added the pretty, sparking insect to her purchases. In the menswear department, she bought a tie for both of her sons-in-law. The new patterns amazed and delighted her, so much so that it was harder for her to choose the ties than the brooches. Eventually, she picked a maroon and silver diamond-patterned tie for Christopher and a turquoise and brown striped one for Bill. But what about Kurt, Eleanor's German boyfriend? She still hadn't decided what to do about Kurt. If she bought one, she could give it – or not give it, but if she didn't buy a present, then she wouldn't have that choice. So she picked out a plain tie in a very dark purple and took them all to the counter to pay.

Before leaving the store, she decided, on a whim, to go to the haberdashery department and look at dress fabrics. It was a treat she gave herself sometimes when she was in the department store. She was in Aladdin's cave. She admired the fabrics, the patterns, the textures – but hardly ever bought any since she took such good care of her clothes that they rarely wore out. She had not needed the wartime message 'make do and mend' preached to her. She had been born with that philosophy.

Long bolts of fabrics were laid out on display stands by fabric type. She took several moments to walk around the stands, lightly brushing her hands over crepes and jerseys, picking up the corners and gently twisting chiffons and silks between her thumb and fingers to gauge and enjoy the quality. She was particularly drawn to a stand of fine wool weaves; they were gem coloured and displayed together, looked like a windowpane of stained glass.

"Oh my, they're lovely," she whispered.

A neat shop assistant hovering close to the fabrics commented,

"Aren't they beautiful, Madame? The best wool challis. Would you like to look?" And before waiting for an answer, the shop assistant picked up the nearest bolt and with an expert flick of the wrist and a turn of the elbow, several yards of fabric fell in gentle folds almost to the floor.

"It's a very versatile fabric, and it hand washes well …" the shop assistant continued.

"Yes, it's very nice," Jean agreed.

The shop assistant picked another bolt, a cobalt blue, like the Virgin Mary in a pre-Raphaelite painting and then another, a gorgeous amethyst. The fabrics hung, already imaginary skirts or dresses, from their position on the stand to a hairsbreadth from the floor.

"Our customers tell us that these fabrics are excellent for this season's winter dress shape and just the thing for 1964," the shop assistant continued, moving to the nearby table where packets of dress patterns stood on display like books. She picked one up and brought it over to Jean. The drawing of three slim young ladies modelled the styles. One wore a simple shift dress with darts, a belt and capped sleeves, her hem modestly, a smidgen below the knee. Another wore the same dress but with a beautifully cut box jacket with a wide collar and a large button at the neck as its only means of fixation, allowing the jacket to swing at a fashionable angle and reveal a small amount of the dress below. The third picture showed the same ensemble in a different colourway.

"You don't think I'm a little too old for this?" Jean asked the shop assistant.

"Of course not, Madame. It's a classic design but with a very pleasant modern edge – don't you think?"

Suddenly Jean felt very old and shabby in her green tweed suit and post-war coat, both of which must look so dated to this young woman. She had never followed high fashion styles, but neither had she felt old-fashioned – until now.

She looked at the pattern closely. She was a little out of practice with dressmaking these days, but even though the jacket was striking, the pattern wasn't too tricky. The shift dress was easy – a few hours of work only.

The shop assistant, realising that a sale was very close, held out the fabrics to tempt Jean further.

"Perhaps you would like to see them in the mirror, Madame?"

From then on, it only felt like minutes until Jean had made her decision, the fabric cut, the lining, thread and large ornamental button chosen, and the cheque written. A new amethyst dress and jacket for Christmas and for 1964. How exciting! What would the girls say? Jean felt more light-hearted than she had done in months.

It could have been a different woman who left Robert Sayle's an hour after she had entered it. With her purchases in her cloth shopping bag and a new buoyancy in her step, she continued along St Andrew's Street and passed what was once the W.V.S. central office and was now a bank. So much had changed since she used to work there. Cambridge was changing more than ever now that the post-war austerity had eased. Time passes – people move on – as Maeve had said.

She continued along St Andrew's Street until Sidney Street, where she popped into Woolworths and bought pick-and-mix Christmas sweets for her grandsons before doubling back on herself through the market to finish her loop to the Bateman Street bus stop. Shoppers in the market were combining day-to-day housekeeping with Christmas. She skirted the edge of the square keeping away from the crowds. As she did, a stall she had not seen previously caught her notice. Flat on the table in front of the stallholder were small wooden toys painted in bright colours. Pinned to boards, dangling from slivers of shiny red satin ribbon, small wooden Christmas decorations were for sale – little reindeer, snowflakes, nutcracker soldiers. They were enchanting. She had never seen anything like these charming toy decorations before.

She approached the stall and picked up a wooden truck from the table. Perhaps Trevor would like it, she thought.

"They're German, madame. From Freiburg," the stallholder explained.

Jean's hand with the truck dropped suddenly to the table as if it were a pound of lead weight and not the ounce of wood it surely was.

The stallholder didn't seem to notice.

"Handmade. Everything is handmade. Perfect for Christmas presents."

Jean felt stupid. What did it matter if the toys and trinkets were from Germany, made by Germans? She scolded herself. What had she been thinking just a few moments earlier? Life moves on.

"They're very pretty. I'd like to look at the hanging decorations, please," and she bought six, one for each of the grandchildren and a special one, a robin with a red painted breast, for the new baby.

16.
TERRIBLE FOR
THE CHILDREN

Jean let herself into her house shortly before midday. All the way home, as she travelled on the bus from Cambridge to the village and as she walked from the village bus stop back to her house, she had thought about Albert and his letters. The ones in the Cambridgeshire paper manufacturer's box, in the dog-eared envelope, on top of the newspaper report of Lady Bragg, Mayor. She promised herself she wouldn't read them all. She wasn't ready yet. But there was something in them she needed to check.

She freshened up and made a pot of tea, covered it with the sheep tea cosy and waited for it to brew. Then she took Albert's letters and placed them on the table. Next, she removed the German Christmas decorations for all her grandchildren from her shopping bag and laid them carefully beside the letters. She opened the envelope and took out half a dozen or so pieces of creamy paper with faint blue lines covered with copperplate blue ink handwriting.

The letters were so light. The paper was so thin. It felt like there was not much in her hands, but she knew that there was. She passed over two of his letters – the two that he had sent from the East Coast of England in '43 and '44 – seeking his later ones, the ones from the Liberation.

Gnr. A. Dollis
D Troop
387/121 HAA. RA
B.L.A
Friday 26th Jan. 1945

151

Dear Mrs Barnet,

Thank you for your Christmas card and all your good wishes. I can see that you painted it yourself. Grantchester church in the snow looks so peaceful and reminded us all of the very good times we had in the village. A quiet corner of England and a place of friendship if ever there was one. When I passed the card along to the boys in my tent, each and every one said, "That's the only place we've been really happy during the whole of the time we've been in the Army!" And that's not just because Grantchester is idyllic. It's also because you and all your W.V.S. ladies were so very, very welcoming and did all you could do to look after us.

I remember how you weren't impressed with the camp conditions at Grantchester, but believe me, Mrs Barnet, that posting was a piece of heaven compared to what we all endure now. We live in conditions that would horrify you, but we are used to it. It's cold, of course. Last week a barn owl froze to death in the Sergeants' Quarters. All the Sergeants are still with us, though!

So far, I'm glad to say, the Troop has had no casualties from enemy action. There have been a few cases where the blokes would get worried. It's a constant anxiety, as you no doubt would understand, and of course, although they are grown men, most of them are but children. We did have a big event. We shot down a Jerry craft. We now have the propellor in camp to prove it. Woodbridge swears blind that it was all down to him and honestly, he would take the propellor to bed with him, if he could, to prevent the other chaps from claiming credit for it.

Christmas in Holland was nowhere near so good as Christmas in Grantchester. Still, we did very well with the food – each man had a nice helping of chicken, an apple, orange, pear, a packet of sweets and seven cigars that were captured along with a lot more booty from the Germans.

The people out here have suffered badly, especially the children. They have nothing, and, Mrs Barnet, they are so thin, so very thin. The week before Christmas, the blokes and I started a subscription in the camp, which raised 3,252 francs and 200 odd bars of chocolate. We

152

bought toys with the money, little handmade wooden ones. Then we organised a party for the local children with the help of the Mayor. It was nice to see the children and the blokes, too, enjoy themselves.

None of us know what 1945 will bring, but I sincerely hope it is victory and safety.

Woodbridge and McAllister send their best wishes.

With fond regard
Albert Dollis

GNR A. Dollis
387/121 HAA, RA
BLA
24th May 1945

Dear Mrs Barnet,

Thank you very much for your letter. It was so good to learn how successful your elder daughters are at their studies and how little Eleanor is growing up fast.

The troops and I are faring well. Woodbridge and McAllister send their very best wishes. At the present moment, we are stationed at a place named Hildesheim near Hanover. It is a medium-sized town, though now, more than half of it is nothing but rubble, and it surprises one how the people here find places to live in. Really Hildesheim didn't see much of the war. All this fearful damage was done in one raid. The Americans, on reaching a few miles from the outskirts of the town sent in for its surrender, but the Germans refused. So for eleven minutes, close on one thousand British and American bombers pounded the place and killed or injured seven thousand, we were told. Then, of course, as the troops moved up, escorted by tanks, out came the white flag. Had it come twenty-four hours earlier seven thousand people would not have suffered. But such is war.

The food problem for the Germans appears to be getting rather severe now and is expected to only get worse. The population has *suffered, although many, to my mind, asked for it. But it does sicken one to see the little children waiting outside the dining halls to see what the soldiers might throw into the waste bin. They are so thin, Mrs Barnet, so terribly, terribly thin, with huge saucer eyes reflecting fear and tragedy. When I was based in Grantchester during the Blitz of London, I sometimes saw the little evacuated children from the East End. They didn't have very much and weren't in the same kind of health as the town or the country children, but even they, scared and far from their home as they were, do not compare with these poor German mites.*

It feels as if the last six years of war are soon going to draw to a close. Lazenby and Stewart have already received their demob papers – lucky fellows. I try to prevent the thoughts of when I might receive mine and what I will do when I return from entering my mind. If I did dwell on these questions too much, I wouldn't be much use to anyone, for I confess, the thought of returning to normal life fills me as much with fear as it does with hope.

I will sign off now, Mrs Barnet.

Fond regard
Albert Dollis

She returned the letters to their brown home, afraid to read any further, and poured herself a now, rather strong, cup of tea. Then one by one, she picked up each Christmas decoration and laid it down in a straight line on the table in age order of who would receive it, starting with the swan for Sally and ending with the robin for the new baby.

If Albert hadn't written about the suffering in Europe, Jean wouldn't have believed it. How could anyone have suffered as much as the poor people in the East End or Coventry had? She had heard of a little boy who had been caught in a different set of streets from his own when the air raid siren sounded and was forced to shelter with strangers. When the all-clear sounded, he had gone above ground to his street to find it all gone and, with it, his entire family and extended family. He had nothing. No one.

The war had been terrible for the children. Kurt, she knew, was about the same age as Eleanor. He would only have been a very little boy during the war. He had lost his parents, which is why he now lived in England. Eleanor had told her that a second cousin of his father's, now fully anglicised, had sought the child out in '46 and brought him to London. Wembley, she thought. Eleanor was a war child too. Did she and Kurt talk about their war childhood? Or had they put it all behind them as she had tried to put the First World War, as it was now called, behind her as she moved into adulthood? Was it ever possible to put anything behind you?

The telephone in the study had sounded late in the evening. Alan, who was reading legal papers at his desk despite it being a weekend, answered it.

"Jean," he called out. "It's Mrs Bragg for you."

He got up from his chair stiffly when she came and thrust the receiver ungraciously into her hands before removing himself pointedly to the hallway, where he waited with irritation while she took the call.

"Hello, Alice," Jean said limply, aware that Alan was standing in the hall and listening to her conversation through the half-open door, only feigning an attempt at offering her privacy.

"Jean, I'm sorry to telephone you so late in the evening, but Sergeant Rutherford has instructed me to form a team of volunteers for an important job tomorrow. I have no details other than please can you be at the Cambridge office by 6 o'clock in the morning. I know it's early. I don't suppose you might be able to stay on overnight?"

"I'm not sure," Jean replied slowly. "It's difficult with children."

"Yes, of course, I understand. Never mind. But please

155

come prepared for a long day, and you must be discreet. You must say that I have had to call you in to go through the clothes at the depot as we have had an urgent request to send clothing to London by tomorrow night and that it will take all day. Whatever our task is tomorrow, you must not tell a soul. I am sure you understand."

"Yes, Alice, of course," Jean stated quietly.

There was a hint of anxiety in Alice's voice that Jean hadn't heard before, and it alarmed her. Everyone was living on their nerves. The Germans were now in France, Belgium, and Holland. The enemy was closer to Cambridge than Cambridge was to Manchester, Leeds, or Liverpool. The German invasion of the British Isles was hours, minutes, perhaps even seconds away. Until now, Alice had always sounded efficient and cheerful, never anxious and serious.

"What did she want?" Alan asked when he heard Jean had put down the telephone.

"Nothing much," his wife replied. "She needs me to help out all day tomorrow at the clothes depot."

"Well, that's ridiculous," he said. "She can't expect you to work all day, and surely it's not necessary to telephone as late as this on a Sunday evening. It's very inconvenient. I hope you said 'no'."

"No, I didn't. I said that it was fine, and I could help."

"Don't you be as ridiculous as she is! You simply can't volunteer for the whole day. It's not necessary."

"I'm sorry, Alan," Jean said firmly. "I have to go and help tomorrow."

Something in her quiet determination stopped him from asserting his authority any further. Instead, he didn't speak to her for the rest of the evening, and they went to bed in silence.

Alan hardly greeted her when she returned home the following evening, weary and depressed. The girls were already in bed, and her mother looked tired. Jean felt sorry that she had left her mother to look after the children all day and, despite her exhaustion, guided Anne to the drawing room to take some well-earned rest.

"Thank you, my dear," Anne said gratefully. "How was it at the depot? There must have been a lot of clothes to go through."

Alan snorted from his chair and deliberately held his newspaper up high so as not to see Jean, even though she was in the same room and was standing scarcely more than a couple of yards from where he was sitting.

"Yes," she replied. There was nothing more she could say and so much more that she wanted – needed – to say.

She slept fitfully, dreaming about the poor women, worrying for the children snatched from their fathers. She was as clueless as them about where they would go and what would happen to them.

Alan had been icy when she went for her shift at the Reading Room canteen the following evening, but it was too late to arrange for anyone to switch with her so that she could stay at home and give him wifely time. She felt miserable, worried for the foreign women, worried for their children, worried for her children, worried for herself and Alan. He had never been like this to her before.

The Reading Room was empty except for a couple of gunners playing chess on the long table. She hoped it would be busy to keep her mind off it all. The quiet unnerved her, like a calm before the expected storm, so she decided to make herself busy and clean out the cupboard in the kitchenette where all the cups and saucers were kept, even though it was spotless thanks to Mrs Appleby's high standards. Cleaning the cupboard turned out to be a mistake.

Before she had finished the job, dozens of the battalion had come into the canteen, and they all wanted refreshments. Mrs Harding had left a message to say that she would be at least a quarter of an hour late this evening, and Mrs Fielding hadn't yet arrived with the food from the vicarage. Only one plate of shortbread left over from the day before would not fill the appetite of all the boys in the queue at the kitchenette hatch.

"I'm sorry," Jean apologised, yet again, to the next soldier in the queue as she had to wipe up the cup and saucer before she could pour a cup of tea. "The sandwiches will be here any minute. Perhaps you'd like a piece of shortbread?"

The queue was long now, and a couple of soldiers were beginning to grumble, even though they all liked gentle Mrs Barnet a lot.

All of a fluster, she was refilling the kettle when one of the gunners entered the kitchenette, taking her by surprise, jacket off and sleeves rolled up. It was Albert Dollis.

"Don't worry, Mrs Barnet. I can see you need a hand."

He picked up a tea towel and quickly dried up the cups and saucers on the draining board to the sound of playful banter from the troops at the front at the serving hatch.

"You'd better watch your lip, Lazenby, if you want one of Mrs Barnet's excellent cups of tea, and you might find that I give a piece of shortbread smaller than the rest and charge you the same," he quipped.

"Come on, Mrs Barnet, we make a good team, you pour the tea, and I'll serve the shortbread."

Working together, Jean and Albert served the gunners, keeping them happy until Mrs Harding and Mrs Fielding arrived, carrying three very large plates of sandwiches.

"Albert, what are you doing in the kitchen? Is everything

158

all right?" Mrs Fielding bustled immediately, shocked to see one of the troops working in the place of a village W.V.S. volunteer.

"Yes, Mrs Fielding. It got a bit busy, so I stepped in to help Mrs Barnet. I hope you don't mind?"

"Mrs Barnet?" Mrs Fielding turned from Albert to Jean, "Are you all right? You don't look well."

It was true, Jean was pale, and her aching head was written in her eyes.

"I'm just tired, that's all."

"Maybe you should go home?" Mrs Fielding suggested kindly.

"No, I'm fine. Perhaps if I just sit down ..."

Albert led her to the comfortable chair in the corner by the books. The gunner who was sitting there vacated it immediately for nice Mrs Barnet. Mrs Harding followed with a cup of tea. It was quiet in the corner, most of the gunners choosing to eat and drink or play games on the long table or perch around the coffee tables elsewhere in the room.

"Mrs Barnet, I don't think you are all right," Albert said simply, his blue eyes searching her peaky face for a reason.

"Can you keep a secret?" she whispered.

"Yes."

"Yesterday, I did something dreadful. I did something that I will never be able to forget."

It was no use. Despite the promise of discretion, she had to share the burden of knowledge with somebody. Her mother wouldn't understand, and Alan – well, Alan was out of reach.

Albert watched her intently, waiting for her to find the

words, not forcing any confidence or expecting anything from her.

"The police rounded up all the foreigners in Cambridge in the early hours of yesterday morning. We had to look after the women and children all day. It was dreadful. Dreadful. They had no idea what was happening to them or where their menfolk were. They had nothing at all to speak of with them. The mothers didn't even have nappies or milk for their babies. They were taken away this morning to some camp or other, who knows where for who knows how long. Children, Albert, children, and babies too – in prison." She felt burning tears of sorrow and anger spill out onto her cheeks.

"Are you shocked?" she asked.

"No. It's war. Any one of those women could be a 5th columnist."

She nodded sadly.

"Jean," he said, "may I call you Jean?"

Again she nodded.

"You're right not to talk about this. You mustn't confide in anyone else. Jean, it's going to get worse now. The war is here now. All these months have just been buying us time."

It was only a matter of days before the Luftwaffe attacks intensified over the country, their target the airfields, the ports. Bombs fell. Citizens died.

Night after night, day after day, the air raid siren sounded. Night after night, day after day, 387/121 D troop fired their enormous guns into the sky at the evil death engines. The roar of the heavy artillery was thunderous – both exhilarating and terrifying. Shrapnel fell like rain and littered the village and the countryside around.

How many hours had she spent during those long months of nights cowering in their cellar with her family and the two war workers, Daisy and Jenny, who were now lodged in their spare room? Or was it Daisy and Penny? She had forgotten. She could only recall the frightened faces of the two young women, unknown to each other before they had arrived a few weeks ago at their billets, huddled together on a bench next to old packing cases which had never been removed, sharing a blanket as if they were sisters.

Jean held little Eleanor, just four years old, in her arms, the child's face nestled into her bosom, golden curls tucked safely under her mother's chin. From time to time, Eleanor would whimper and look up to her mother for reassurance.

"It's all right, darling," Jean would soothe, stroking the child's head. Amid the sound of the huge guns, Jean would softly sing Eleanor's favourite lullaby with her lips and with her heart, and she would hope and pray that they would all stay safe. That the battalion would stay safe. That Albert would stay safe.

When Eleanor slept, Jean would cuddle into her own mother, Anne, a child herself needing her mother.

Alan sat with pale-faced Barbara and unusually still Maeve on the bed opposite, an arm around each daughter. The twins clasped hands with each other resting four hands on his lap. Protecting his daughters, Alan was stiff and straight. He hardly moved, hardly breathed. He looked ahead into the gloom of the cellar seeing more than just the dark.

In September, their Cambridge guns took a turn at silence, but the terrible sound of the London guns reached far into East Anglia. One awful September night, Jean, Alan and Anne came out of their house and stood in the midnight garden. The arc of the sky was black, decorated with pinpricks of ancient starlight – but the southern horizon blazed blood red.

"London, Alan, is it London?" Jean cried in alarm.

"The bastards," was all Alan could reply.

"God save those poor souls," Anne wept, a hunched old lady in a nightdress and slippers on the grass.

London's Burning, London's Burning, Call the Engine, Call the Engine – the child's nursery rhyme – turned around and around in Jean's mind as she watched the horizon, spellbound and sick to her core. Those poor people. Those poor children.

War had been terrible for the children.

Everywhere.

17.

ALICE

October 1940

"Mrs Bragg, I've finished typing up your report," Shirley Cooper, one of the part-time typists, said as she placed a handful of thin paper with dense typing on Alice's desk at the St Andrew's Street W.V.S. office.

Every month each W.V.S. office was required to produce a narrative report using a specific template of headings to send to the Headquarters in London. These reports gave Lady Reading and her national leadership team an understanding of how the W.V.S. was operating across the land and offered an exchange of ideas and best practices. Alice often wondered if Lady Reading and Mary Smieton did indeed read all the reports or merely flicked through them.

<u>W.V.S.</u>
<u>REPORT FOR OCTOBER 1940</u>

<u>GENERAL</u>

'The deluge of work this month has been very great,' Alice reread her opening statement.

Deluge, earthquake, tidal waves – there weren't words to describe the misery and problems of hundreds of families fleeing from the pounding of London night after night for the past two months. They arrived in organised evacuation or of their own accord, with nowhere to stay, nowhere to live, flooding into the city, hoping it would offer refuge. Unaccompanied children of all ages, even babies and toddlers, needed to be cared for. Unhappy children, with or

163

without their unhappy parents, were now Cambridge's responsibility. Quantities of war workers arrived daily, pouring into the Borough as industry and agriculture stepped up their response to potential invasion. Each man, woman and child needed a new home, needed food. Many needed medical care. Most needed distraction and entertainment.

Hester Adrian, aided by Mrs Constance Farthing as deputy, was the woman in charge of untangling this mass of misery and finding happy, workable solutions to each person's homing need. The Local Authority ought to have shouldered the responsibility, but they didn't. They left the work to Hester and her team, giving the ladies space in the Guildhall buildings and claiming credit for the team's success. No one could seek glory in war, so Alice bit her tongue and looked for small opportunities to give credit where credit was due. She picked up her pen and added to the first sentence, and then read it through:

'*The deluge of work this month has been great, particularly in Evacuation, where Mrs Adrian has worked tirelessly.*' Alice wondered if the correction to the sentence would require the report to be retyped but then rejected the thought. There was neither enough paper nor typist time.

EVACUATION

We were informed at extremely short notice that we were needed to look after a party of 150 women and children evacuated from London for 48 hours in the Leys School while billeting was arranged. 300 evacuees arrived, needing our assistance. A team of 40 W.V.S. volunteers worked in shifts – providing meals and helping the families to find lost luggage, acquire nappies and toothbrushes etc. On the first night, many of the London mothers were very much disturbed to hear the sirens as they had believed Cambridge to be free from air attack; they took quite some calming down.

Our helpers were a very mixed band. It was a charming and heart-

warming sight to see a chemistry Professor's wife prepare a baby feed, a Member of Parliament's wife run out to procure nappies, and a refuse collector's wife organise the children into team games of charades.

Although situations like this were stressful, there was satisfaction in that they all coped, that the evacuees were well looked after, and that everyone was safe. She always liked to include a little story, a little drama, in her reports. She thought of Lady Reading and Mary Smieton reading the narrative and imagining the scene. Perhaps it would bring a little light relief in what would be pages and pages of a United Kingdom's united woes.

AUXILARY NURSING

It is a shame that despite the urgent need for Auxiliary Nurses, we have not been able to provide training for all the 274 persons to date who have put their names forward for training. This is not from a lack of efficiency on our part but because no money has been allotted by the Ministry of Health to this vital part of our work. However, a reorganisation of our space at 64 St Andrew's Street allows us to have a room where nurses can meet to practise their skills with friends and attend lectures.

Alice took her pen and underlined 'not from lack of efficiency' and 'because no money has been allotted' – she might as well stress to Headquarters the cause of the blockage. It was always possible that Lady Reading and Mary Smieton between them might find the right ear at the right government department if they knew what was needed.

OFFICE

As none of our office staff is permanent, we have appointed deputies so that each area of our business has a full-time equivalent woman and no one becomes indispensable. This has left the Centre Organiser free to concentrate on policy and not on details of delivery. It also means she has the time capacity to attend Borough meetings and to visit the different areas of W.V.S. activity.

Alice was proud of her office reorganisation, a necessary one. It would have been unhelpful to say to the now several thousand evacuees, as well as to the war workers, and to the Cambridge families that opened their doors to them, "We're so sorry, we can't help you until this afternoon as Mrs Such-and-such is only able to volunteer in the afternoons," or, "Mrs So-and-so in charge of clothing only comes in on Tuesdays." Furthermore, it would have been all too easy for Alice herself to have been pulled into the nitty-gritty of sorting out where the poor, frightened London children should be lodged, or offering to help a refugee mother, who had lost everything in the bombing of her home, find shoes for her children, a pram for her baby. It meant that now she had time to ensure all the W.V.S. departments in her care ran smoothly – auxiliary nursing, canteens, nurseries, transport, salvage. The list seemed never-ending.

She read the rest of the report, the lists of canteens and rest centres and the solutions to problems, silently blessing the army of volunteers hidden behind every action of help delivered and every idea of assistance planned. At the end of the report, she signed with a flourish *a. Bragg, Centre Organiser,* forming the 'a' of Alice in lower-case and making it the size of an upper-case letter, as she always did, and put the report in her out-tray for Nancy Cuthbert, her Friday and Monday volunteer secretary, to dispatch to London.

18.

Jean

Good News

The afternoon passed slowly. Jean was tired and restless after her shopping trip. Experimenting with some designs for her Christmas cards – robins, snowflakes, nutcrackers – filled some of her moments but not her attention. At 6.30 p.m., she judged that the time was finally right to pick up the telephone and dial Eleanor's London flat.

"Hello, Eleanor Barnet speaking," Eleanor answered efficiently, carrying her office tones into her home.

"Hello darling, it's me."

"Mum?" Eleanor was surprised, "I only saw you this morning. Is everything all right? I didn't expect you to call until later in the week."

"Everything's fine. I was so sleepy this morning when you came in to say goodbye that I forgot to ask you whether you would like to invite Kurt to come and spend Christmas with us. It's the last time we will all be together in the big house. He might like it."

Jean could hear Eleanor's intake of breath at her words. She understood her daughter's astonishment in the fraction of a second of silence.

"That would be great!" Eleanor replied, her usually clear voice strangely cracked. "Are you sure?"

"Yes, of course, darling, it would be a shame for him to be alone."

"Thank you, Mum. Thank you!" If she could have kissed her mother through the telephone line, she would have.

"And Eleanor, I'm sorry – I'm sorry I haven't asked you to invite him before now. It's just that it's been so hard …"

"It's all right, Mum," she said gently, "I know things have been hard for you this year with Dad …"

"Yes. But …"

She couldn't say it – even to Eleanor –she couldn't say it. She couldn't say that what had prevented her from acknowledging Kurt, who was a victim, not a perpetrator, was that it was so hard to forgive. It was just so hard to forgive when people she had loved had been taken from her in two wars – when a version of herself had been taken from her. And it was almost impossible to forget however hard she had tried.

"I love you, Eleanor,"

"I love you too, Mum."

"Now, will he like the traditional Christmas dinner? Roast Turkey? Christmas pudding?"

19.

ALICE

MORE GOOD NEWS

December 1940

It was nearly Christmas. Britain was under attack, but there would still be Christmas. Alice was sitting at the desk in the study, writing a few last cards which she would hand-deliver when she went to the city centre to the office in an hour or so's time, when the telephone rang.

"Hello, Alice Bragg speaking."

"Good morning Mrs Bragg. It's Brenda. Mr Bragg has asked me to telephone you to see if you could come to the laboratory this morning."

Brenda Smith was Lawrence's highly experienced and extremely likeable secretary at the Cavendish Labs. She was cherished by both the Braggs as she was so magnificently efficient and good-humoured at keeping Lawrence's professional world running like clockwork at a time in history when every day was a predictably unpredictable challenge. To receive an unexpected request from her was, therefore, somewhat alarming.

"Is everything all right, Brenda?" Alice asked immediately. Lawrence knew she was busy today. Something urgent must have come up that couldn't wait. But then, why had he asked Brenda to call her rather than speak to her himself on the telephone?

"Yes, Mrs Bragg, it's just a normal day here at the labs, although we are all winding down for the holiday."

When she arrived at the Cavendish Laboratories, squeezed into tiny Free School Lane, Lawrence had a curious expression on his face. From the way he pinched his lips together and furrowed his eyebrows, anyone who didn't know him would have said he was in a furious temper, but his eyes were sparkling with repressed merriment. He looked like an obedient schoolboy who had been told a jolly good joke by a classmate and was now trying his hardest not to laugh in the sight of the headmaster.

Lawrence ushered his wife into his office and shut the door remaining for a few seconds to check that Brenda had returned to her desk. Then he hesitated a moment longer, taking deep breaths to compose himself, preparing to reveal his secret.

"Lawrence, whatever is the matter?" She was captivated by his pantomime. Evidently, she had not been summoned for a matter of life or death. She wondered if it was a scientific piece of news – a breakthrough in his research – which she would likely as not have to pretend to understand but would nevertheless loyally venerate. But why would that need to be a secret from dear Brenda?

Meanwhile, Lawrence looked as if he were about to burst. He came towards her with his arms outstretched and whispered,

"My darling, I have just learnt this morning that I am to receive a knighthood!"

Alice's mouth formed a perfect and kissable O of surprise, which Lawrence immediately took advantage of before whisking her off her feet and leading her in a polka celebration around the room.

They laughed and danced and twirled as if they were young lovers.

Brenda opened the door to see what all the noise was about, and her astonished face made the Braggs laugh even more.

"We're sorry, Brenda," Alice said, wiping tears from her eyes and catching her breath following her impromptu celebratory polka, "it's just that we've had ..."

"... a very important, but as yet confidential piece of family news," Lawrence interrupted. "Please could you make us a cup of tea, Brenda? Thank you."

He waited until his secretary had shut the door, and he could hear her footsteps fading in the corridor as she made her way to the kitchenette.

"It's not public knowledge, darling, until the full list is published in *The Gazette* on the 30th. Do you think you can keep the secret?"

"About as well as you can!" she replied with a kiss as a promise. "I'm so proud of you, Sir Lawrence Bragg. You deserve this honour – you really do."

"And I am proud of you, Lady Alice Bragg, so very, very proud."

20.

ALICE

CALLED TO CANADA

January 1941

Those happy minutes of celebration with Lawrence at the Cavendish Laboratories before Christmas of 1940 stayed with Alice through the long months ahead. So much of our lives, we forget, but there are moments filled with feeling and significance that remain with us forever.

She wished she could have gone with him to Buckingham Palace. She was desperately disappointed not to be by his side, her natural place, as he received his knighthood from the King, but she was laid low with a horrible bout of flu.

"I'm miserable, Lawrence," she groaned from the bed, trying to sit up a little on her pillow as he dressed that morning.

"I know, my darling," he soothed. He stood in front of the mirror, tying his tie. He looked over at her anxiously. Always inclined to be thin, she was positively peaky, and the fever reddened her usually lustrous skin.

"I'm so sorry. I so wanted to be there – you will tell me all about it."

"Every detail." His eyes were twinkling in anticipation of the honour ahead. He was still so handsome. She was so proud of him. She fell back on her pillows, the effort of sitting up too much for her.

It was a long day of fitful sleep and broken dreams – Lawrence waiting in a line to be presented to the King turned to lines and lines of evacuees waiting for their billets at Hester Adrian's desk in Cambridge. The King's kind, distinguished face transformed into the aristocratic features of Lady Reading, exhorting her, "never to say no." She must still be running a temperature, but she wasn't sure. There was no nurse to look after her, and her thermometer was out of reach in the medicine cupboard in the bathroom. Nellie, her cook, ascended with hot drinks and jugs of water. But to ask her for any more assistance was quite beyond her remit, the cook's dark brow semaphored as she stalked into the sick room and stalked out.

Days rather than hours seemed to pass before Lawrence returned in the late afternoon. He immediately saw that she was still poorly and made her a cup of tea. She refused a sandwich but nibbled a biscuit. He sat on her bed and stroked her feverish brow,

"My poor darling, you do feel bad, don't you?"

"Wretched," she said weakly. "But I'm dying to know, how was the King?"

"He was very well and sends his regards, wishing you a speedy recovery, Lady Bragg."

"I bet he did!" she snorted, provoking a cough that would not stop until Lawrence had sought her out a fresh glass of water.

As she sipped, he told her about all the different types of people who had received their awards alongside him at the palace; soldiers, sailors, candle-stick makers. A newsreel team had filmed the crowd outside the palace, and many families had cameras taking snaps as mementoes of the special occasion.

"And the bombing, is it very bad?" she asked.

"The damage to the palace seems to be quite cleared up now," he said, referring to the strikes of the previous

173

autumn. "It's strange. There are places which are untouched and other places where nothing stands."

He had walked through St James' Park, where, close to the splendid lake, it still appeared to be a park, with passers-by lingering to look at the birds or take a moment to sit on one of the benches, whilst in other regions, the grass had been dug up and vegetables planted. He passed the Admiralty into Trafalgar Square, which had remained curiously unscathed, and seemed just as it had been even a few years ago, whereas Charing Cross station, only a few yards away, had been badly damaged. As too was a stretch of Victoria Embankment where he had his lunch date arranged with his old friend Sir Edward Appleton, fellow physicist and now Head of the Government Department of Scientific and Industrial Research. The people of London scurried around, getting on with their daily business, listening all the time for the air raid sirens and ever conscious of where they were to the nearest shelter.

"How is Edward?" Alice asked.

"He seemed very tired but full of plans."

"Did you send my regards?"

"Of course, I did, my sweet."

"That's good." She lay back and rested her head on the pillow, her eyes shut. Lawrence had had a wonderful day. That was a relief. When she felt stronger, she would question him further. She thought he would get up and leave the room, but she could feel his weight remaining beside her on the bed.

"Alice," he said softly.

"Yes," she murmured.

"I know you're not feeling very well, but I've got to tell you about what Edward said."

Startled, she opened her eyes and tried to raise herself up on the pillows. He reached forward to help her and then took her hands in his. What on earth could Sir Edward Appleton have said to make Lawrence behave so seriously? Her fluish temperature made her thoughts slow and her movements sluggish.

"Appleton has asked me to go to Canada to represent the Government – to be our Chief Scientific representative."

She felt confused. Canada? That was a long way away – it would take more than a weekend.

"Will you be home by Easter?" she asked bravely.

"No, sweetheart. I will probably be away for most of the year."

"Most of the year?" Panic rose in her voice and her eyes.

"Yes. I'm sorry."

She slumped back on her pillows and fought back the tears, struggling to comprehend what he had said fully. Canada? For nearly a year?

"But it's dangerous, Lawrence," she protested, remembering reports of German submarines and bombers which struck at will to disrupt trans-Atlantic shipping.

"Perhaps," he replied, not too disappointedly, as he secretly liked an adventure.

"At least there isn't any war in Canada, so you won't face bombs when you are there," she conceded.

She took a deep breath – he had to go, it was important. She would never do anything to hold him back in his career.

She squeezed the hand she hadn't let go of throughout.

"We'll be fine. We'll miss you, but we'll be fine. I hope you said yes?"

Lawrence had said yes. He knew his duty and was lucky

that duty aligned with his academic interests and sense of adventure. There was no delay to his departure, and before the end of February, he had left.

He telephoned from Liverpool on the eve of his embarkation. All was fine. He was excited and happy and missed them already. Fourteen nerve-wracking days later, he sent a telegram. He had arrived in Ottawa and was safe. It was followed in a matter of days by a letter which, as he was on government business, had travelled by air rather than by sea.

… We sailed on the 'SS Baltrover.' She is a steamer which in peacetime, traded in the Baltic. She was far too small for us all, with only half a dozen cabins for passengers, and we numbered more than sixty. Some of the cabins were constructed in the hold – but these are airless holes, and I was relieved not to have been allocated one.

What a motley assembly we were! Airmen who had flown bombers over were now returning home, civil servants with their families bound to positions in the US, and businessmen. The most interesting among us was a party of seventeen fashion models and their chaperone, a female civil servant. They were heading to South America, sent out by the Board of Trade to get orders for British factories to make and export clothes to pay for this wretched war. All their clothes were being sent behind on a separate ship – no use in losing all the supplies and the personnel in one bombing raid.

Now I can see you are worried that I am speaking about bombers, but you needn't, because as you are reading this letter, you will know that I have safely arrived in Canada. Although we were attacked several times, we were not struck, and our escorting destroyers did a marvellous job in protecting us. Seeing all the mannequins in their pastel-coloured trousers lining the decks and waving as the destroyers passed on their routine checks on us was quite a pretty sight. The party of models were a real entertainment throughout, although it has to be said their presence did put a strain on the bathrooms. I had only one of two cabins with bathrooms and you will be pleased to learn that I was quite the gentleman loaning my bathroom out very frequently, as I do understand how essential a bath is to women-folk.

Alice finished reading the letter aloud to Stephen, Margaret and Patience, emphasising his final words, *'with all my love to my precious family,'* trying to be his voice and not a radio newsreader.

"Daddy's so good at telling us stories. He makes everything sound so much fun," Margaret observed when Alice had come to the end of the letter.

"Mummy tells good stories," Patience added, sliding down from her place at the table and climbing onto her mother's lap now that the meal was over and the letter read.

Stephen was silent, thinking about his father. At eighteen, he was beginning to understand just how important his father was, just what a difference he had made and was continuing to make, not only to British science but to the scientific community of the whole world.

"Do you think Father will write his autobiography?" Stephen asked.

"I don't think he'll ever find time for that," Alice laughed. "But it would be a very full and interesting book if he did."

"What's an auto-bia, an auto-bia -gravy?" Patience asked.

"An autobiography, darling, it's a story you write about your own life," Alice explained.

"I'd like to write that book about Daddy," Patience cried brightly.

"That wouldn't be an autobiography," Stephen corrected his little sister. "That would be a biography."

"Mummy, I can write a bia-gravy about Daddy, can't I?"

"Of course, you can, sweetheart, maybe when you are

big."

"And I'd write one about you, too," the five-year-old added.

"That's very kind, but there's not much to write about me."

"I beg to differ, mother dearest," Stephen said. Although he was still a student, he understood that his mother, like his father, was outstanding. He got up to leave the table and return to his books. He had another exam looming.

Alice didn't consider herself outstanding, but she realised that she had become a hard worker. How different from those university days, when her tutors had predicted that she wouldn't amount to anything, as she was continually distracted from her studies by parties and young men.

She folded up Lawrence's letter and returned it to its envelope before putting it in a special compartment of her writing bureau – a shelf where she kept the letters he had written to her when they were engaged and on his, thankfully, few absences from her since their wedding day. Later, she would copy sections into her next letter to David at Rugby. She put Patience to bed, reading her a story, saying her prayers, and singing her a goodnight lullaby. She checked that Margaret was ready for bed, had said her prayers and was reading to herself. Then she readied herself for her evening meeting at the council. She felt a pang of regret as she walked away from the house. Children needed their parents to be at home, and Lawrence, like so many fathers, had been taken away by the war. She felt guilty that instead of being at home looking after her children, she was working with the W.V.S. all hours through the day and, now that she was on the Cambridge Civil Defence Committee, late into the evening too. But it was war. It was inevitable. She'd make it up to them somehow, but how, she wasn't sure.

21.
ALICE
BOMBED

The streets were blackout dark, but the way was familiar, and her night vision was good, so she was able to make out the recognisable shapes of buildings and street corners. She did not fear being a lone woman out in the night. What she did fear was an air raid, and even then, it was more the debris from British anti-aircraft guns than the likelihood of being an enemy target herself. So far, the city had been hardly touched by the bombs. As she hurried along the dark pavements to her meeting, she pondered why this was. There was a rumour that Hitler planned to live in King's College when his forces had successfully occupied England, but this was no doubt a rumour – and would never happen! She clenched the fist of her right hand into a ball at the thought of such an abomination.

Alice was one of the first to arrive at the meeting at the Guildhall. This was now the second meeting of the committee that she had attended, and she was beginning to learn her colleagues' names. It was easy for them to learn hers as she was the only female committee member – all the rest being male town councillors or male representatives of the University.

"Good evening, Lady Bragg," Mr Kemp, the town clerk and secretary to the committee, welcomed her as she entered the room. She was one of the first to arrive.

Mr Thornton, an affable man of about fifty-five, was already sitting and welcomed her too, adding:

"I trust you have fully recovered from your 'flu, Lady Bragg."

"Thank you, yes. I'm much better, Mr Thornton," she replied, taking the seat next to him, the same place as at the last meeting.

More men arrived and helped themselves to a cup of tea from the urn on the trolley that an administrator had left ready for them. A few glanced in Alice's direction as if to say, "you are a woman," or, "you are a W.V.S. – you should be pouring us our tea." But Alice resisted. Here, on this council, she was their equal, she was not their servant, and she was not their hostess. So she sat tight in her seat and conversed with councillor Mr Thornton on her left.

Amongst the committee members was Sir Montagu Sherard Dawes Butler, a former Governor of India, Master of Pembroke College and Mayor-elect of Cambridge. He was small and somewhat overweight, but he was formidable. The committee, both town and gown, deferred to his forceful opinions. He was also very deaf. His place at the table was to the right of Alice, and he was not particularly impressed with this arrangement, although he understood, as they all did, that she was an asset to the council. Not only was Alice exceptionally well-placed, knowing Cambridge citizens – women and men – in all quarters of the town through her work at the W.V.S., but she was also well acquainted with the University thanks to the status of her husband's position. Sir Montagu didn't talk to her but acknowledged her presence with a gruff nod.

The meeting was important but tedious. As Sir Montagu was profoundly deaf, he constantly punctuated the debate with his bad-tempered, "what did you say?" "speak up, man," "what on earth are you mumbling about something important for?"

Alice, thinking that she could be helpful, started to jot down on her notepad points that she felt might be important, details that she thought he might have missed, and surreptitiously pushed the pad towards him at opportune moments. She was well-practised, having heaps of deaf aunts and uncles. He didn't acknowledge her action but occasionally glanced at what she wrote. He departed without thanking her or even bidding her goodnight.

"A useful meeting, I think," Mr Kemp commented as she prepared to leave the building. It was already 9.30 p.m., and she had been working for most of the day. More than anything, she wanted to be back in her own home, but she stopped for a few moments to speak to Mr Kemp.

"You don't need to make notes for Sir Montagu," he said dryly. "He knows what everyone is going to say before they say it," and with that, he left, having made Alice feel rather small. But she didn't dwell on it. Her humour saw the funny side, and she stepped out into the dark street more buoyed up than disheartened.

Mr Thornton had not yet left and was standing in the doorway to the street, doing up his coat and putting on his gloves.

"It's busy tonight, Lady Bragg," he said, motioning to the skies outside. "Will you be all right returning home?" he added kindly.

It was no more dangerous for her than for him, but she appreciated his thoughts and said so.

She hurried back home, alarmed at the whizzes, crackles, and bangs in the air around her. The anti-aircraft guns protecting the airport had been firing. She looked nervously at the sky and prayed that the city would be safe.

It was not. The air raid sirens howled. Alice ran the last yards to her home. The children and nanny Hilda, as well as cook Nellie, were already up and pulling on dressing-gowns, slippers and jumpers, their faces white and fearful. Patience, in Hilda's arms, was more asleep than awake. Margaret was bleary-eyed and scared. She rushed to her mother's side.

"Quick, everyone to the cellar," Alice commanded, leading the family down the stairs, joined by Stephen, who had effected a personal raid of the kitchen for midnight supplies before joining his sisters. Alice tucked the little girls into their shelter beds around the Kings College crates of glass. Hilda and Nellie lay down on the beds that had been provided for them. Then she sat down next to Stephen, who put his arm around her in a protective, manly fashion now that his father was away. She hugged him, grateful for his unspoken thoughtfulness. Somewhere above them, over their house and city, shells fired into the sky to thwart the craft with their cargos of explosion and fire. She listened and prayed until the thick darkness of the cellar and the fatigue of her day overwhelmed her, and she slept.

She woke to the sound of a deep, echoing thump. Her neck was stiff from the awkward position in which she had spent the night. She moved her head slowly to stretch out the pain as, in her first waking, she wondered where she was and what had happened. The banging continued. It was coming from up the stairs. The children, Nellie and Hilda, were all still asleep, although Patience was beginning to stir. Slowly, she climbed the cellar's stairs, fearful of what she might find when she reached the top.

The house was still standing, with no damage here, at least. The thumping was coming from the front door. Automatically, to be well-presented, she straightened the creases out of her skirt with two deft downward strokes and ran her fingers through her hair before opening the door.

On the doorstep stood an ashen-faced warden, his hand still raised to bang on her door. She wondered vaguely why he hadn't rung the doorbell. The tiredness in the creases around his eyes prevented her from asking.

"Can I help?" she asked.

"I've come from the city, Lady Bragg. It's bad. You're

needed right away."

"I'll come directly," and she would, but first, this poor man needed some comfort.

"Are you all right? Would you like a cup of tea? You look like you need some."

"I'm fine, thank you, Lady Bragg. Your ladies already have your mobile canteen out in the centre. I'll pass that way. It will be quicker."

She nodded and watched him briefly as he collected his bicycle and cycled off to wherever he was needed next.

Quickly, she changed into her W.V.S. uniform and coat, brushed her hair with a comb rather than her fingers and descended to the cellar to give her little girls a morning kiss and leave them in the care of their capable nanny.

The streets between her house and the city centre were eerily quiet. She could smell acrid ash in the air. Thin wafts of smoke were rising behind the buildings still standing in front of her. Flames had been dampened thanks to the hard work of the firemen, but fingers of smoke lingered. She cycled quickly to the W.V.S. office on St Andrew's Street, her anxiety about what she would find mounting with each rotation of the pedals, at each junction that she approached. The office was empty, which was why she had been summoned in person and not by telephone, unless, of course, the lines were out, which was a possibility.

Alice wasn't sure where she was needed, so she followed the smoke and the ambulance sirens. In the district running from the large and imposing Catholic church of Our Lady and the English Martyrs on Hyde Park Corner and along the Hills Road as far as the war memorial, buildings had blazed. The enormous church itself had taken a direct hit. The roof was badly damaged, and the windows shattered. Avoiding the debris on the road and skirting around firemen dampening the smouldering remains of the night's fires, Alice made her way to the station rest centre.

Grey-faced volunteers in their grey-green W.V.S. uniforms distributed cups of tea and comfort to individuals and families in various states of shock, fear, and worry. As Cambridge had been scarcely touched by the bombs before, and as Alice, as Centre Manager, did not take a role on any of the rotas to assist neighbouring towns in the event of a large raid, she had never seen at first hand the impact of Goring's Luftwaffe.

A large family group had made a camp from the rest centre chairs in the middle of the room. The father, the head of the family, sat with his head in his hands, elbows on his knees, eyes closed, not in sleep but in an attempt to shut out the night just past from his thoughts and feelings. A frail old lady, possibly his mother, sat beside him, shaking from cold, fright or illness – it was hard to tell. She was already wrapped in a centre blanket, and Alice watched as one of her volunteers approached with a thicker blanket and carefully, tenderly, wrapped it around the old woman, who hardly noticed. A younger woman, alongside, who tended to one sleeping child on her lap and two wakeful ones playing on the floor by her feet, wanly smiled her thanks for the blanket for her mother, or her mother-in-law.

One of the area wardens spotted Alice and came over straight away.

"It's been a bad night, Lady Bragg – incendiary bombs mainly."

"Many casualties?"

"Eight so far, but we've heard reports there are still folk missing." He paused. "Lady Bragg, there were two women in W.V.S. uniform among the dead. I'm sorry."

The news landed like a punch, winding Alice.

"Who?" she asked fearfully.

"I don't know. The ambulance has taken the bodies to the morgue already."

Who could have died? With wits dulled by shock, she tried to remember which women she knew from the Mill Road area who could have been on fire warden or air raid shelter duty during the night. She was tempted to make her way directly to the morgue to find out for herself, but there were procedures to follow. Lists of the casualties, some with names, if they could be identified by documents that they might be carrying, would be sent to the Air Raid Information Centre at the Old Post Office. Here, survivors of the raid, who could not locate loved ones, would be anxiously listing the details of those missing to volunteers, who would have the unenviable task of matching names on the lists of where there was still hope, to the names on the lists of where there was none.

Alice and her volunteers had gone through so many drills on what to do in an air raid, on how to solve practical problems faced by raid victims needing medical help, somewhere to stay, new clothes, furniture, and papers. None of the training had prepared her for this – death on duty.

Who could the women be? She wanted to know, but at the same time, she couldn't bear knowing. The poor women. The poor families.

Outside the rest centre, in front of her, stood the cadavers of people's homes, no more now than charred carcasses and patches of smoking rubble. Here and there, the façades of buildings survived, putting on a brave face to the world, protecting the desolation behind from view. Further along the road, in the direction of the station, where the biggest impact of the attack had been felt, Alice could see the grey-green of the W.V.S. mobile canteen. Her volunteers must have been working hard in it for several hours by now, since the 'all clear,' to refresh the wardens and the firemen. Buildings could be rebuilt, as could lives to some extent, but the gap filled by the death of a loved one could never be filled.

She made her way solemnly from the desolation of Hills Road to the information centre in the heart of the town, where, in low spirits, she did what she could to assist while waiting for the casualties to be identified. The word that two W.V.S. were casualties in the attack had got around. Pale faces questioned Alice, but as yet, she had no answers. Towards the middle of the morning, a junior official arrived from the Guildhall with the dreadful list and delivered it to Alice to examine. She quickly scanned the names until she came to Mrs G. Robertson – Cambridge Place (W.V.S. Shelter Marshall), Mrs D. Ghent – Glisson Road (W.V.S.). She took a sharp intake of breath as she recognised the name of her efficient, bespectacled colleague, and her hand shook as she returned the list to the official.

"Are you all right, Lady Bragg?" the official asked with concern.

"Two of these are my ladies," she replied with a choked voice.

"I'm sorry."

Alice scarcely heard the reply. She had mentally moved on and was rehearsing her words of sympathy to the bereaved families, preparing the offers of help and support she would give, considering the impact these two terrible deaths would have on the rest of her Cambridge volunteers and grieving the loss, the very significant loss, of two irreplaceable women.

22.

JEAN

VOLUNTEERING, NOW AND THEN

Eleanor and Barbara had been efficient in the organisation of their mother. The jumble sale to raise funds for Sally's Girl Guide pack had come at just the right time to benefit from Jean's reluctant clear out of her large family home.

The guide captain (Mrs Turnbull) had telephoned on Tuesday afternoon and arranged to come before lunch the next day to collect the boxes. Jean had not left the house that morning, and when the doorbell rang, she had to stoop down before opening the front door to pick up the letters on the mat, delivered by the postman probably before breakfast. She put them on the hall table without looking at them.

A sensible-looking woman dressed in brown greeted Jean.

"Thank you so much for these donations," Mrs Turnbull said in a clipped, clear, teacher sort of way.

"Would you like me to help you put the boxes in your car?" Jean asked. She almost expected the guide captain to prevent her with an, "Oh, you mustn't lift boxes. You have a bad back," as one of the girls might have done, but instead, Mrs Turnbull made no objection.

"It must have taken you quite a while to go through all of this," Mrs Turnbull observed.

"Yes," Jean replied.

"Barbara said you are going to move into the city after Christmas."

"That's right."

Mrs Turnbull tried again to draw conversation,

"Sally is a real asset to our pack."

This was a better direction, as Jean visibly brightened at the mention of her granddaughter.

"Thank you. Sally is a lovely girl. We're all very proud of her."

"She's at the Perse, isn't she?"

"Yes, she's very happy there. She particularly likes French."

Mrs Turnbull liked Sally and her mother, Barbara, very much. She was surprised at how shy the grandmother seemed to be in comparison. But then, on reflection, perhaps it wasn't shyness, as the older woman didn't hang her head, stoop her shoulders, or even turn her eyes away. Maybe Sally's grandmother was just a quiet person. Quiet people can be strong and sturdy support, Mrs Turnbull knew.

Before thanking and leaving, the Girl Guide leader suddenly asked on a whim,

"Mrs Barnet, I don't suppose you might have time to help us at the sale on Saturday? The girls are very good and helpful, but sometimes they forget to concentrate. You know how girls are, and we do need at least one adult at all times on each stall."

"I'm ... I'm not sure ..." Jean replied automatically and then stopped herself. What wasn't she sure about? She was free to do what she wanted. No one at home needed her to look after them. There was no one whose thoughts and feelings she needed to consider before acting.

It had been a long time since she had volunteered for anything. When the war was over, she had been exhausted –

utterly exhausted. For six years, she had volunteered six days out of seven, frequently putting the needs of soldiers and the community before the needs of her own family. Alan had put his foot down. The war was over. They did not need to do anything more than concentrate on returning to normal life. The girls needed their mother back. Anne needed her daughter back. He needed his wife back.

"It's no matter if it's not convenient, I just thought ..."

"Yes," Jean resolved, interrupting Mrs Turnbull. "Yes, I'd like to help you – very much."

The tea party meetings at the vicarage given by Mrs Fielding had become a regular occurrence since that first afternoon back in July 1939 to help establish a W.V.S. canteen for the Heavy Anti-Aircraft battery stationed at Grantchester. On the first Friday morning of every month, the ladies assembled in Mrs Fielding's drawing room to discuss improvements and to decide the upcoming rotas for manning the canteen and supplying the refreshments. Mrs Fielding used the meeting to sign off the month's accounts. They planned Christmas parties and the odd cabaret evening throughout the year to entertain their troops. They organised jumble sales, jam sales and sponsored silences for the village children, all to raise funds for the items they needed to bring comfort to their boys in their battalion. They put their heads together and came up with ideas of how to help in every way that they could.

If the autumn of 1940 had been hell, then the winter of 1941 had been the abyss. Night after night, the Luftwaffe targeted London, and harassing bombers roamed across East Anglia. The HAA guns fired indiscriminately. Their success was more their morale-boosting thunder than the number of German planes they shot down.

Albert rarely came to the canteen during those months; when he did, his face was grey and his eyes bloodshot from lack of sleep. The battalion manned the guns all night and grabbed what little shut-eye they could during the day. The camp was pretty basic, and living conditions primitive, Jean knew. Once a week, she accompanied Kate McGregor, who drove the mobile canteen to all the posts around Cambridge that the battalion manned, taking the watching soldiers hot tea and sandwiches and providing a shop for cigarettes, notepaper, and chocolate.

It was January, grey and freezing. The hardest, coldest English winter in many a year. Jean hadn't seen Albert since the party for the troops in the village hall on Christmas Day. The village W.V.S. had arranged a meal of roast pork, vegetables, and potatoes. The men themselves had organised a cabaret and games. Jean had watched the fun from the back of the room when she arrived for her turn on the rota. She had not dared to suggest to Alan that she miss her own family Christmas dinner so that she could spend those precious hours with the troops.

Hitler seemed to have given them all a few days off that January. But then the weather was particularly bad, which perhaps more explained the frozen quiet. Weary to the bone, Albert had spent several hours already that morning in training exercises alongside the forty other men who manned the four heavy artillery guns at the Grantchester emplacement, ten to each gun. This morning he was less irritated than cold. The men's fitness had vastly improved since the battalion had been formed last year, and some were shaping up to be reasonable soldiers. When he had first met his new team fifteen months ago at the training camp at Weybourne on the Norfolk coast, he had felt insulted by their weediness and their dull wits. Didn't the Army know there was a war and that it took muscle power to man the heavy guns and brains to operate them?

McAllister was the first to see the welcome grey canteen van arrive at the emplacement.

"Hot tea!" his cry went up.

"At ease. You can have your tea, lads," their officer permitted.

"Who is it, McAllister? Can you see?" Albert asked.

"Looks like Mrs Barnet and her friend today."

"What day is it then? Surely not Tuesday?"

"Sure is, Dollis. Comes round fast, doesn't it!" McAllister replied, and he smiled and waved at the welcome sight of the two W.V.S. uniforms descending from the van – one of them particularly welcome.

Albert watched Jean as she opened the hatch at the side of the van and began serving. As much as he wanted to see her, be close to her, he hung back so that he would be the last. If he were the last to be served, there might be more time to talk – unless she had to rush off to another post to help other soldiers such as himself. There wasn't much to look forward to in his life. Seeing Jean, no matter how infrequently or briefly, warmed him like the sunshine on a grey day.

"How are you, Albert?" Jean asked when the queue had subsided, leaving a couple of men standing to one side finishing their hot drinks, stamping their cold feet on the frozen ground to keep the circulation moving in their toes and breathing out dragon fumes with each word they spoke. Kate was already wiping down the serving hatch and closing the urn. Jean only had a few moments to talk to him before it would be time for the mobile canteen to move on to the next post, where searchlight operators would be waiting.

"Couldn't be better," Albert answered grimly.

"I don't think that's true," she said, looking around the emplacement.

Although it was in the centre of the village, in the field

191

behind the Rose and Crown pub, the camp was so primitive it could have been in the back of beyond, away from any human activity. There were three large guns on their concrete standings. Sandbags, sodden from the melting snow, surrounded the guns. In the last few weeks, a properly constructed hut had been built for the command post and another for the artillery. These had joined the hut erected as the Officers' Mess when those superior men had arrived. But there was no shelter for the men on duty from whatever weather the skies threw on them. Worse, in Jean's opinion, was the fact that there were no proper living quarters for the men. They had no huts and still lived entirely under canvas.

"Albert, why haven't the army supplied you with better quarters? It's terrible that you all have to live like this."

"Because we're the forgotten foot of the army," he said bitterly, "and we're not the RAF glamour boys. They send us any old troops and any old bit of tent to live in."

She hadn't seen him as glum or as snide before.

"You're cold," she said sympathetically. "I'll make you another cup of tea."

"No, it's all right. Thank you. I am cold. I'm sorry. I shouldn't have said what I did. It's just so frustrating that we've been here for nearly a year, and there were troops here before us, and we still don't have proper huts to sleep in. You don't even want to see where we wash. And the privy! It doesn't even have a door, or any wall, just a limp bit of canvas. When I came into the army full time, when war broke, I used to dream that I was back at home in the book shop with all the books I could ever want to read. Now I dream it's completely quiet – no planes, no guns, and I'm in the hottest, steamiest bath imaginable."

Jean could see how he had changed from when she had first met him last year. He wasn't dirty, but he wasn't particularly clean. His uniform, on the worn side then, was distinctly shabby now. The lines around his eyes and corners of his mouth were more pronounced. And he looked tired. So, so, tired.

There wasn't much she could do herself about helping him find a bath. She couldn't contemplate asking Alan if Albert and others could use their bathroom from time to time, the answer would surely be 'no', but she could bring the matter to Mrs Fielding and the village W.V.S. committee.

Jean spoke up at the next committee meeting the following Friday when the agenda reached 'any other business'.

"When I was at the gun emplacements this week with the mobile canteen, I had the chance to speak to some of the soldiers," she began nervously. "The camp conditions are still appalling. It would help a great deal if some of us could perhaps lend the men our bathrooms to wash in."

"That's a very generous thought, Mrs Barnet," Mrs Roberts replied. "But the battalion stands at over one hundred men. We can't wash them all in our houses."

"I just thought ..." Jean was crestfallen at her plan of help being summarily pushed aside.

"I think it is an excellent idea. It reminds me how Mary washed our good Lord's feet and dried them with expensive perfume and her hair," Mrs Fielding, the vicar's wife, commented.

"Goodness me, I don't think we need to go that far," Jean countered with surprise.

"But all the same, Mrs Barnet, a hot bath would go down very well, I think. We can't wash them all, Mrs Roberts, but we can wash some. I suggest we draw up a list of who in the village can offer washing facilities at what times, and we take it to the Sergeant."

"I've been itching to offer young Bob Holmes a bath and

a good shave, for that matter," said motherly Mrs Harding, who had an extreme affection for the young man who had recently turned nineteen.

"First on my list will be Albert Dollis," Mrs Fielding added. She knew exactly who Jean had most wanted to help.

It wasn't just baths, Christmas parties, and off-duty refreshments that the committee had provided. They had got the village knitting, using wool supplied by the W.V.S., first, to produce 'comforts' – gloves, scarves, hats – for their Cambridgeshire troops, for troops overseas and later, sweaters too for the desperate in Liberated Europe. Women of all ages joined in, even Anne, Jean's mother, who knitted at speed every evening in a daily competition with herself to knit the world to freedom and the boys to a state of woollen comfort. They mended socks, darned uniforms, and stitched on divisional flashes or other marks of rank or identity. They did everything they could to look after the soldiers in their care.

And now, here she was, over twenty years on, helping again. Jean felt ridiculously excited in the run-up to the Girl Guide Christmas fête. She enjoyed the intervening days. A little thrill of anticipation of having a role, a proper helping job, at a community event made her smile outright, alone in her empty house. The jumble sales with Mrs Appleby in Grantchester and Mrs Finlayson in central Cambridge during the war had been great fun. A Girl Guide sale with her granddaughter would be fun too. She filled the days before the sale with festival preparations – painting her Christmas cards, wrapping her Christmas presents and cutting the fabric from the pattern for her new dress and jacket. She ignored the sorting, the W.V.S. box, and any other thoughts pressing on her mind other than the fun times, the girls when they were little, and the escaping piglet at the salvage drive.

What should she wear? She had never had any concerns

about what to wear in the W.V.S. It was always the same, her grey-green dress with its beetroot red trimmings. On Friday evening, she decided on a navy skirt and a white blouse. But when she got dressed on Saturday morning, she felt like a sales assistant or an elderly Girl Guide. That would never do. She changed to a cherry red blouse and added a silvery scarf to match her silvery blonde hair.

Christopher arrived with Sally at 8.30 a.m. to pick her up and take her to the church hall. Grandmother and granddaughter were in position behind the white elephant stall at 9 a.m. when the doors opened. A trickle of Girl Guide families and locals came in steadily throughout the morning. Jean was surprised at what Cambridgeshire people bought nowadays and did her best to hide her embarrassment when any of her cast-off items were purchased.

The jumble sale was more of a Christmas fête than a wartime fundraiser. Girl Guide handicrafts, perfect for family Christmas presents, were on sale alongside donated books, second-hand clothes, and bric-a-brac, including the odd electric kettle. In the corner of the hall, behind some large screens made of old green curtain fabric, Father Christmas sat cramped and hemmed in by several sacks of presents at his feet. He was obviously in a bit of a draught as periodically he pulled his red coat tighter around himself. Jean watched him as he gratefully accepted refills of hot tea from the guides manning the refreshment stand and pulled his beard away from his face, the elastic stretching tightly so that he could eat two chocolate cream eclairs.

Sally was a stalwart. She spent the whole morning helping her grandmother on the stall, even when a couple of her Girl Guide friends, who had given up helping, tempted her to leave her position and to pay the 3d to visit Father Christmas or to part with 2d to try her hand with them in the lucky dip.

"You can go along with your friends if you like, Sally,"

Jean offered.

"No, thank you, Granny. I'd rather stay and help you with the stall." And to prove she meant it, she said to the gentleman currently browsing,

"That's a unique end-of-day glass candle holder. Don't you think it's worth one shilling? It would make a lovely Christmas present."

The gentleman, impressed with the twelve-year-old's charming smile and sales patter, parted with his shilling to the benefit of the Girl Guide pack. Jean, full of pride, watched her capable granddaughter take the money and wrap up the flecked glass candle holder in a newspaper.

When the twins had been twelve years old, like Sally, they too had been Girl Guides. They proudly wore their uniform, just as Sally did, but it wasn't as smart back then as nowadays. Clothes rationing had been introduced, and when Maeve had a growth spurt, all her coupons were needed for her school uniform, which she then had to wear for all occasions – even as a Girl Guide. Whilst Barbara, who hadn't yet stretched, was still a recognisable member of the pack. It was at that time that Maeve asserted her difference. She didn't look like her twin sister anymore, so why keep up the pretence? And she cut through her long plaits with two decisive shears of the scissors without asking her mother's permission, leaving Barbara with waist-length braids and herself with, when it was tidied up, a shoulder-length bob. If she had dared, she would have cut her hair even shorter.

Jean was shocked. Her child no longer looked like a little girl – the hair, the swelling chest, the level-eyed assertion of a maturing identity.

While Barbara preferred to stay at home, spending time with Anne, playing with Eleanor, practising her knitting, or reading stories, Maeve found a purpose outside the family sphere with the Girl Guides. She sewed medical bags, distributed anti-gossip posters, and helped whitewash kerbs to delineate roads from the pavement in the blackout nights. She collected jumble, took messages, and knitted socks.

Twice a week, she stayed late after school with her guide pack and went to the camouflage rooms in an old building that had once been a billiards saloon. The army provided the nets and the scrim to garnish, and the W.V.S. provided the woman-power. There were so few women available to volunteer by the time Maeve was thirteen, conscription to the forces or compulsory war work having depleted the pool, that the garnishing fell to the very young and the very old. Teenage girls, like Maeve, worked alongside eighty-year-old grandmothers, each doing their bit to support the war effort. The multi-generational female teams produced miles and miles of camouflage nets to hide the troops and all their military paraphernalia in their crawl across Europe from the beaches of Normandy to the Nazi heartlands.

It was messy work; the scrim stained her hands and clothes. The nets hung on improvised frames and spread across the floor like a fragile hull of a boat. Being a young one, Maeve would crawl along the netting on the floor, tying the khaki greens and browns of the scrim to the net in whatever pattern she chose. Later the army gave more direction to the patterns, which was decidedly less fun. The scrim was highly flammable. They all lived in fear of the ongoing night attacks. They nearly lost everything in one raid when bombs fell close by, starting fires and damaging neighbouring buildings. But the old saloon stood firm, and the nets survived. The covering of broken glass and soot was swept away, and the work continued. "You won't get us, you devil!" One elderly lady shook her fist at an imaginary Hitler before picking up a broom and clearing the debris.

Maeve would knot and chat for an hour with the Guides and the grannies before her father came to collect her and accompany her home, the pair cycling through the lanes back to Grantchester. He always came for her, even in the bright summer months when she could have made the journey alone. They would cycle in silence, or they would chat, whatever they both felt like, and they usually both felt the same.

"How was your day?" her mother would ask when she returned to the house, slamming her school bag down on the hall table.

"Fine." Maeve would reply, hunting through the kitchen for something to stave off her hunger before supper.

"Did you make many nets?" Jean would ask.

"'spose so," Maeve would respond, her mouth full of apple, carrot, or if she was fortunate, a piece of bread and jam.

"You are so good to help out," her mother would say in the gentle way that left Maeve feeling cross. Maeve would reply with a shrug of her shoulders and leave her mother standing in the kitchen.

"Do you have any homework?" The inevitable question would follow Maeve up the stairs.

"Periodic table of the elements," Maeve would shout through the closed bedroom door, and then she would finish her apple, carrot, or bread with her beloved chemistry books in the peace of the bedroom she shared with Barbara.

Jean regretted that Maeve wouldn't talk about what she did. She was proud that her daughter, such a young woman – only an emerging woman, had flung herself into war work. She would have liked to have talked about it. She would have liked to have shared it.

"Thank you so much for helping today," Mrs Turnbull said as Jean was preparing to leave.

"Thank you for asking me. I enjoyed it," Jean replied truthfully.

"You've been a great help. The white elephant stall has no white elephants left. There's nothing more annoying, you know, than having to store jumble to carry over to the next sale."

Jean smiled and nodded. She'd caught herself thinking about the war again. How strange, she pondered for a moment, that all these memories were tumbling out, like a bottle uncorked, from the deep recesses of her mind where she had banished them. She had a headache from the noise in the hall and was hungry. She wanted to go back home for a late lunch. She had some soup ready in a pan. It would only take a few moments to heat up.

"… help out again?"

"Excuse me?" Jean asked

Mrs Turnbull repeated her question:

"I was just wondering if you would be able to help out the pack again. Sally has told me that you are an excellent artist and you are also a dressmaker. Perhaps you could come along and help the girls with their badges. Not all their mothers are good with pencils or needles, and some of the girls struggle to complete their tasks."

Jean thought for a moment.

"Yes," she said. "Perhaps I will find time in the New Year."

23.

POST

Jean let herself into her house and waved goodbye to Christopher, who had dropped her home. Her back ached from too much standing around behind the stall. She felt tired after her morning volunteering. She never used to feel tired after a morning of helping out. Perhaps that was what being nearly sixty years old meant, or maybe she just needed some vitamins, or a good rest.

On the doormat were two envelopes delivered by the postman while she was out. One was brown, a bill no doubt, probably for the telephone, which would be due about now. Alan had always been the one who paid the bills whilst she saw to the housekeeping, but since he had died, she had been forced to learn how to manage all her money. It was confusing at first, but she was beginning to understand, and although she loved her sons-in-law very much, she didn't want them to run her finances for her. It was one thing for your husband to control the money in the marriage, after all, he earned it, but it was quite another for sons-in-law to undertake the task.

The other envelope was white with a Canadian stamp. How lovely, Jean thought, that would be from Fee then. She hoped Fee had found time to write a letter along with the card. She wasn't the best letter writer, so news from Canada was patchy. There was a pile of post waiting for her on the hall table. She had been adding to it all week, every time the postman arrived. She might as well open it all up this afternoon, and if there were cards amongst it, she could put them up in the drawing room over the mantlepiece to start to make the house feel Christmassy.

There was a lot of post. As she picked up the envelopes,

a few jumped out of her hands onto the floor, down behind the table.

"Drat!" she said, bending down to pick the supposed cards from the floor.

In the kitchen, she lit the gas under the pan of vegetable soup for her lunch. She took a slice of bread from the cream-coloured bread bin. She had stopped eating butter on her bread when it was scarce during the war and had never regained the habit. While she waited for the soup to warm, she started to open her post – a full dozen Christmas cards. She began with the envelope from Canada. Shepherds offering sheep on a winter's night to the Holy Family greeted her, but inside, the only words aside from the printed 'Merry Christmas' were:

Dear Jean and Alan, with much love, Fee, Jonathan and family.

Jean slumped slightly in the chair. Surely she had written to her friend to tell her about Alan's heart attack? Perhaps the letter had got lost? Or maybe she hadn't written? Those months were now such a blur. And as she was so late in getting round to sending any Christmas cards herself this year, Fee had not found out that way either. She was disappointed too. She wanted more than a greeting that could have been sent to anyone. She wanted news. She wanted friendship.

A second card, a Parish church in the snow with a Christmas tree at its entrance surrounded by choristers in their white robes and stiff collars, came from Mrs Fielding and her Reverend husband from where they had retired, somewhere near where their son lived in Bournemouth:

Dear Jean, wishing you and all your family a very Happy Christmas

Along with the seasonal greeting, Isobel had written a few words detailing the Reverend's failing health.

Jean worked her way through the other cards where there was the odd brief note, the odd embarrassed words of reiterated sympathy at her loss. It was so strange that people you could be so close to, so very close to, at a particular time in your life could just drift out of it – Fee, Alice, Albert – when times changed, when normality returned. It was strange too that people you spent your whole life with, 37 years to be exact, could be snatched away from you unexpectedly, without warning, all of them leaving you equally alone.

She ate her lunch and took the cards to the drawing room, where she arranged them on the mantelpiece, ready for Christmas. Then she went upstairs to her room and put her war box, which had been sitting on her dressing table where she had left it, into the bottom of her wardrobe, under her shoes, to await the removal men. She would recork the bottle – if she could.

24.

ALICE

LADY READING'S VISIT

March 1942

Lady Stella Isaacs, Dowager Marchioness of Reading, descended from the London train onto the platform at Cambridge station. Dressed simply in the W.V.S. uniform and coat, which she had commissioned a London couturier to design, she could have been any one of the millions of the service's volunteers, not its chairman. She had no insignia, no armband, no badge or colours to mark her out as important – none of the women did, they were all equal in rank and in value. However, no one could mistake Lady Reading. She simply was not ordinary. Her high Turkish cheekbones and eagle-sharp eyes marked her out as different, of notice. She stood tall and regal with an aristocratic aura, a mantle which she had assumed upon her short marriage to Rufus Isaacs, Lord Reading and which she had never taken off.

Her tall, imposing stature belied the spinal troubles that had plagued her childhood. For months on end, for years in a chain, she had been confined to her bed. For many, this would have been a prison, but Stella had a core of iron that held her magnetic personality. Her bedroom, into which the sounds and smells of the Sea of Marmara close by, and the great city of Constantinople beyond poured, was the centre of the household. It was the place where four younger and four older siblings brought her their games, their news, their ambitions, their woes and Stella, from the bedsheets, wove it all into a great family cloth. She became wise beyond her years, an expert in diplomacy and determined – grittily determined – to have a purpose on the planet once her

203

fragile spine was fully formed and her bones strong enough to support her mind and her character.

She now wove a different cloth, a war-time cloth. Like a monarch on a royal tour, Lady Reading visited the corners of her immense Women's Voluntary Service, checking that each piece was woven tightly, rousing spirits, flying the flag high. Today it was the turn of Cambridge and the baby she had left in charge of Alice, now Lady Bragg.

Despite her busy schedule, she regularly read the monthly reports that Alice Bragg sent to headquarters, like centre managers all over the country. She was pleased to find that the Cambridge branch appeared to run smoothly, although there were the usual difficulties of not having enough volunteers and too much work. Today, she would have the chance to see for herself as she visited the borough, Alice's realm. She would observe and ask pertinent questions, not holding back her criticism if that tool were necessary for the improvement of the operation.

Alice was on the platform, ready to greet Lady Reading. Mrs Finlayson, her deputy, and Mr Charles Kemp, representing the Council, accompanied her. It was a typical, busy weekday morning with passengers arriving and departing, soldiers returning from or beginning their leave, visitors, and businessmen – all at the transit lines of a bustling wartime city.

"Lady Reading, welcome to Cambridge," Alice greeted her chairman warmly.

"I am delighted to be here," Stella Isaacs responded.

After the necessary introductions, the day began with a tour of the station canteen. It was an efficient enterprise. Today it was calm with only a handful of soldiers present, but a troop train could pass at any moment. Then it would be all hands to the deck as hundreds of men would need to be refreshed in no more than fifteen minutes. The volunteers would push trollies and urns along the platform to serve the soldiers in their carriages, as that was quicker than allowing troops to descend and queue at the canteen or try to offer an onboard service. All the men received their tea and departed refreshed, frequently still holding a Cambridge cup in their hands as the train drew away, attempting to keep to the timetable.

"And apart from the missing cups, have you had any particular problems?" Lady Reading enquired.

Mrs Carnegie, who had volunteered at the canteen since the start of the war, replied,

"No more than many big stations, Lady Reading. Although we have had some trouble in the evenings, sometimes the soldiers can get – a little worse for the wear, shall we say, and they have caused some nasty mess."

"Drink?"

"Sadly, yes."

"What did you do?"

"Lady Bragg met with the Brigadier and the Station Manager. The Brigadier said we'd have to close the canteen for an hour between 10 and 11 on weekend nights."

"That's not ideal, is it," Lady Reading observed.

"Not really," Mrs Carnegie continued. "But word got around the soldiers that it was Lady Bragg and the other W.V.S. ladies were so upset by the soldiers' bad behaviour that we'd closed the canteen. I think the soldiers felt like their mothers had told them off. They were embarrassed when they thought about how much we all help them – and it all being voluntary. Since then, the evening behaviour has been much better, and we've been able to keep open as usual."

"Excellent!" Lady Reading was pleased with the gentle

solution. "And what do you serve the troops to eat?"

"Sandwiches, soup and cake mainly," Mrs Carnegie replied.

"Have you thought about baked potatoes?" Lady Reading suggested. "The station canteen at Paddington has recently started selling baked potatoes, served hot, with a little lard or butter – cheaper than sandwiches and less of a supply issue. And pies? You should consider pies."

From the station, Lady Reading was taken to view the camouflage nettings, where she complimented the enthusiastic elderly volunteers, who demonstrated how low they could bend, how high they could reach, and how fast they could tie on the scrim, despite many of them being over eighty years old. She visited the billeting office where she administered sympathy to Mrs Adrian and her team for the ongoing difficulties of finding accommodation for war-workers and evacuees and boosted their morale; it wouldn't be forever, the end was in sight, all the hours the volunteers gave freely to help fellow citizens claim their basic right of a roof over their heads and food in their bellies – everything they did was so much appreciated. At the example war nursery, she was almost the Queen herself, a very special, awe-inspiring visitor, and one little chap gave her his drawing of a cow and a horse as a memento.

Wherever she went, almost at a glance, she could sum up the effectiveness of the activity. Where necessary, she suggested improvements, although these were so slight, they were icing on the cake more than fundamental changes. It was a smooth operation in Cambridge. What was more, all the volunteers spoke highly of their Centre Manager. Clearly, the women participating in each activity felt supported and enabled. Alice had done well. What a good thing it was Sylvia Moulton Fletcher had introduced her back in '38, Lady Reading reflected.

It had been decided in advance that Lady Reading would lunch at the British Restaurant at the Pitt Club. Situated on Jesus Lane, it had been built almost a century ago to resemble a Roman temple. For most of its life, it had been a political dining club for the male undergraduates. Commandeered by the Borough when the first flood of the bombed arrived in the city, it was now harnessed into the national war effort and was a restaurant for mass feeding. The bust above the entrance of William Pitt the Younger, in whose honour the club had been formed, seemed to sneer at the sign 'British Restaurant' placed below his breast and regretted that all and sundry could now enter his home.

Inside the club, the British Restaurant served cheap and nutritious meals, although there was no choice of menu. Lady Reading took her tray to the hot counter as if she were any other member of the public and not the dignitary that she was, handing over her 4d from her purse for a plate of two sausages, potatoes, carrots, mushrooms, and gravy.

"The Borough has chosen particularly good china," Lady Reading commented to Alice as they sat next to each other on a long table between the internal columns of the large room.

"Yes indeed," Alice replied, waiting for the comments of constructive criticism, which surprisingly didn't come.

The large dining hall echoed with the clatter of knives and forks tapping plates, spoons scraping bowls and the hum of scores of conversations.

"You have done an excellent job here in Cambridge, Lady Bragg, and I congratulate you wholeheartedly."

"Thank you, Lady Reading."

"Particularly when I know you lacked your husband's support for much of last year."

Alice frowned imperceptibly. Stella Reading spoke as if

207

Lawrence had abandoned her, which simply hadn't been the case.

"Lawrence has always supported me entirely. It was his duty to leave the country."

"Canada, I heard?"

"Yes, that's right. He represented the British Government. He was our Scientific Liaison Officer with Canada."

"For the whole year?"

"He was away for eight months."

"That must have been very hard for you and your children."

"It was."

It had been a terrible separation. Alice and Lawrence had never been apart for more than a few weeks. They buoyed each other up. They nurtured and loved each other passionately. Half of herself sailed with him across the Atlantic in the winter of 1941.

"But so many people have to bear so much more. At least we all knew he was safe."

"Indeed," Lady Reading agreed, lifting a fork full of potato and gravy to her mouth and savouring the flavour.

"Speaking of safe," she continued, "the Cambridgeshire Regiment, is there any news yet?"

It was the talk of the town. It was the subject on everyone's lips. The Regiment, reinforcement to a tired army, had only just arrived in Singapore when the country fell, taken by surprise by the Japanese.

"To our knowledge, all the boys are Japanese prisoners," Alice said quietly. "The Red Cross will no doubt do their best to get messages through, but these are dark days for the town. You know how it is. Many young men join up together, so most of us know someone out there. We have volunteers who are desperately fearful for their sons or their husbands – one hears such terrible stories of Japanese treatment."

Alice's face darkened as she thought of her friend, the shoemaker Mr Carter, who had two sons in the Cambridgeshire Regiment now interned by the Japanese in Singapore. She had cycled past his house each week for a scrap of news, but so far, there was none.

Lady Reading nodded and filed the information away for future use.

"Goodness gracious," she exclaimed, suddenly standing up, her dinner not yet finished. Alice looked around in dismay for what had startled Lady Reading.

At the entrance to the club, a white-haired gentleman and his student grandson had entered. Lady Reading had abandoned her meal and was making a bee-line for him.

"Lord Woolton, how delightful," she enthused.

Lord Woolton, Minister of Food, was enjoying a rare moment of family time in his enormously busy schedule and was visiting his grandson. He had been surprised and rather pleased at the sight of his dining alma mater, the Pitt Club, contributing to the war effort in the guise of a British Restaurant – an initiative of his own Government Department. He was now further surprised to meet inside it Lady Reading, the head of the organisation which enabled the restaurants to operate, thanks to her army of volunteers.

"Lady Reading," he said momentarily, lost for words.

Lady Reading had the upper hand. She was not lost for words. She rarely was.

"Lord Woolton, may I congratulate you on another of

209

your successes," she said, surveying the grand interior of the room thronging with evacuees and war-workers, eating their sausages, potatoes, and gravy. Then drawing his attention to Alice, who had likewise abandoned her meal to greet the new entrants, she continued, "And may I introduce you to Lady Bragg, wife of Sir Lawrence Bragg, the Nobel Scientist."

"A pleasure to meet you, Lady Bragg. I have not had the honour of meeting your husband, but I have heard much about his talents."

"Thank you." Alice glowed at the praise of her husband.

"Lady Bragg is our centre organiser here in Cambridge," and without leaving the Minister space for comment, Stella Isaacs continued to elaborate on the success of the British Restaurants, the Pitt Club and the noteworthy china in particular.

"What a coincidence to meet Lord Woolton here," Lady Isaacs said to Alice as they left the restaurant to head together to the W.V.S. afternoon meeting. "I must say, he is one member of the Government I find extremely easy to work with. Even so, how funny to meet in one of his restaurants."

Cambridge was like that, Alice thought. You never knew who you were going to meet. "You will have an interesting war in Cambridge," Lady Reading had said to her back in '38. It was certainly that.

The Guildhall was full when they arrived for the afternoon rally, packed with a sea of grey-green uniforms. Alice was relieved at the sight of such a large turnout for their chairman. It had been a mammoth undertaking to ensure that all the W.V.S. members in the town and the villages were aware of Lady Reading's visit and had the opportunity to come and hear her speak themselves. Valerie Moss and Jean Barnet had worked tirelessly copying the invitation letters and arranging for their distribution by hand to save the cost of stamps.

Alice remained at the back of the hall for a few moments before taking her reserved seat in the front row. There must have been over six hundred women present – most of the women were middle-aged or elderly. Few younger women were able to volunteer nowadays, since so many were either in paid war work or had been conscripted. But there was still a handful of young mothers who somehow managed to give a small amount of their time, although goodness knew how. Alice scanned the audience and saw some faces she recognised. Jean Barnet, still looking pale and thin from being ill after Christmas, was sitting towards the back with her friend Fiona Larkin. A little further along the same row, Alice recognised Mrs Fielding, the vicar of Grantchester's wife. Alice felt a wave of pride come over her as she looked at the assembled women – her team. She wondered if a headmistress felt the same when she looked out across the school over which she presided.

The loud buzz of conversation which had filled the hall when Alice arrived – women catching up with old friends, introducing themselves to a fellow W.V.S. sitting close by who they didn't yet know – died down with every step that Lady Reading took towards the stage, as the audience began to realise that their honoured guest had arrived.

At the podium on the stage, Stella Isaacs used all her skills as a public speaker to rally her troops – praising them for their hard work, motivating them to continue to give more. She emphasised the rightness of civic duty and the morality of working together, stressing that the strength of the British nation relied on each member playing their part. She reminded everyone present that the W.V.S. would never refuse a request for help.

As the women left the hall, they were smiling and

laughing. They felt appreciated. They felt re-energised. They knew they could face however many more years of war remained as long as they faced it together. The Mayor escorted Lady Reading back to the station to return to London, and Alice remained in the hall, thanking the women for attending and answering any questions.

"That was right good," Fiona Larkin commented as she passed her Centre Organiser at the exit.

"An excellent speech and so encouraging to see Lady Reading in person," was Mrs Fielding's view of the afternoon.

"Thank you, Alice," Jean said as she passed. She was on the point of leaving the hall, but Alice stopped her.

"It's I that should thank you, Jean. Very few people would have known about this afternoon if you hadn't got the invitation letters."

"A team effort then," Jean said quietly.

"Exactly – a team effort!"

And it was.

25.

JEAN

SEWING

A jigsaw of soft amethyst body parts lay on her dining room table. Purple shapes hidden by fly-weight beige paper labelled A, B, C. Assorted pieces that by the magic of the sewing machine would turn into sleeves, skirt, bodice, jacket. Jean worked pinning and stitching, the soft burr of the machine the only sound in the house. Lines of straight seams, zig-zag overcasting, stitch by stitch, locking the pieces together to create something new, something striking, something beautiful.

When the tide had turned, when it had become clear that the country was not going to be invaded, but when the kingdom had settled into a long wait to regroup and become invading liberators, the army officers decided that it would not do for women to mollycoddle the troops any further. It was time these men learnt to stand on their own two feet. It was time these men learnt to darn their own socks!

Jean was overcome with a fit of giggles when she relayed the message from Mrs Finlayson at the central office to the Grantchester vicarage committee.

"So, if I understand you, Mrs Barnet, we are now asked to teach the soldiers to sew?" Mrs Roberts had asked incredulously.

"Indeed we are," Jean replied with merriment.

"We will need the patience of saints," Mrs Appleby commented.

"Mrs Barnet, I think that like poster design, this is a task which most squarely lands with your abilities, seeing as you

213

are so good at making your little girls their lovely dresses," Mrs Fielding suggested. She was an embroideress by preference, and the thought of teaching reluctant soldiers to sew was beyond her capabilities. Jean couldn't quite see the link between being able to make dresses and darn socks, but she was more than happy to take any opportunity that brought her into contact with the troops.

Since the teaching of sewing skills was at the bequest of the army, attendance at the sessions in the village hall was mandatory. Each soldier was ordered to bring his socks to be repaired and was supplied with a needle and thread. Some of the socks were more hole than sock, thus presenting an interesting challenge to pupil and teacher alike.

Jean sat with a group of six soldiers around her, five of whom were either nervous or reluctant or both.

"This is flippin' dangerous," George Woodbridge moaned for the umpteenth time as he waved his sharp needle in the air. "Ow! Now I'm bleedin', look, Mrs Barnet. I'm really bleedin'."

He held out the tiniest prick of red on his finger to prove his injury.

Lazenby was slowly and intently threading a needle next to him and said, "Be quiet, Woodbridge, I'm concentrating."

"But I'm bleedin'!" George moaned and shoved his hand, with sock, into Lazenby's face so he could see.

"I don't care if you're bleedin', I'm sewing," Lazenby retorted.

"Come, come, George," Jean said soothingly. "It's only a little prick, and you're doing a grand job with your darning.

"Wish he'd fall asleep with his prick, like Sleeping Beauty," Lazenby grumbled.

"Language Lazenby!" Albert scolded, deepening his

214

eyebrows in what he hoped would be an officer-like scowl, but seeing the funny side to the comments.

He had nearly finished darning his socks, working quickly, sitting next to Jean. He hadn't needed to come. He had learnt how to darn years ago as a reservist, but when he had heard that Jean was to be their teacher, he had feigned needlework ignorance. There was something about Jean that made him feel better. When he saw her, he felt happier. Whatever he said to her, she genuinely appeared to be interested. When she was nervous or worried, she had a way of fiddling with the fabric on her uniform sleeve or on her collar, and all he wanted to do was to catch her hand in his and hold it still and soothe away whatever it was that made her feel that way. He loved the way she moved, the way she laughed. Sometimes he caught the scent of her hair – it smelt of the spring. He wanted to grab the scent with his hands and keep it pressed in the pages of his book, as if a flower from a sweetheart's posy. First, without realising, and then fully cognisant, he stood or sat as close to her as he respectfully dared.

He didn't think she knew. But she did. Oh yes, she did.

She took his completed sock from him and inspected his work.

"Well done, Albert," Jean said, looking down at the sock. "You've finished – top of the class!"

"Well, if 'e's got A plus, then I must've got an A," George declared, laying an oddly misshapen sock on the table. "But don't none of you lads tell me Missus. She luvs mendin' me socks. It'd be a shame to take away one of 'er pleasures in life."

George had grinned as he spoke and had accepted the thump Lazenby landed on his arm with good grace.

26.

ALICE

BAKING TINS AND COUPONS

May 1942

There were days when holding onto Lady Reading's words of motivation was all that got Alice and her office staff through the hours between letting themselves in with the key in the morning and locking the door in the early evening, and there were other days when what was required was a distinct sense of humour.

It was all very well Lady Reading insisting that the W.V.S. would never say 'no' to any request and that everyone should work together to help their neighbour, but sometimes the requests were just too big. It meant that Alice's office became a problem-sorting agency for anyone and everyone, for any kind of issue that had a home nowhere else, or where it was perceived W.V.S. help would be better, kinder, more efficient.

"Well, that's a bombshell if ever there was one," was Frances Clode's verdict on the letter she had just read.

"My sentiments exactly," Alice replied.

"I just don't see how we are going to manage Lady Reading's request – we don't have the resource," Frances continued, passing the letter back to Alice.

"But I do think that Lady Reading is correct, training is necessary."

Frances groaned.

"But Alice, how many courses does Lady Reading require?"

Alice reread the letter. "She says each woman must attend five courses – Civil Defence, Immediate Aid, Firefighting, A.R.P. and Anti-gas."

It was a mammoth task, she knew. They had more than three thousand members, and each one was to attend five different courses. She attempted to work out in her head how many courses and how many dates would be needed.

"… and we'll need to book the trainers, we may even need to train the trainers as there's bound not to be enough, and we'll need to write to all the women – all three thousand. Goodness, we won't have enough paper. We'll have to shrink the letters and use the duplicator – which you know is on its last legs – and then we'll have to …" Frances' voice was raising a pitch with each new thought as the administrative work underpinning Lady Reading's bombshell became apparent. "… And we don't even have enough help in the office to do all that and keep on top of our normal business."

"I'll see if Mrs Moss has some spare time. She'd be a great help. I'm sure."

"What about Jean Barnet? She was so good at helping when we had to write to all the women about Lady Reading's visit in March," Frances suggested.

Alice hesitated for a moment. She was worried about Jean. She hadn't been very well before Lady Reading's visit, and although her help with writing to the members had been invaluable, she had been far more withdrawn than usual and seemed excessively tired. Alice had put this down to too much work and slow recovery from a winter infection, but it was now May, and Jean didn't seem to be very much better. That poor woman needs a holiday, was what she thought to herself, but she didn't say it – they all needed holidays, and there was no chance of that. No chance.

"Good idea Frances, I'll ask her." She knew this would

mollify her colleague who was worrying about the administration involved. But what she meant was – I'll ask her and suggest that perhaps she doesn't have time because of her other commitments.

Suddenly Frances' face brightened with a new thought:

"There's always the Girl Guides. They would do a very good job of stuffing envelopes. If Mrs Moss can do the copying, I will write the envelopes. I'll ask Mrs Moss to make a start on copying Lady Reading's letter this afternoon as everyone should read it."

The telephone rang, Alice answered, and a young man appeared at the door asking a question about billet payments, Frances attended, and their morning disappeared in the standard round of problem-solving and information sharing.

In the middle of the afternoon, a cheerful woman in a very faded pink dress entered. The dress was too small, and she was bursting from the buttons, forming a placket over her breasts. The fabric had been ripped in numerous places and repaired, not particularly expertly.

She opened the tarnished clasp of her battered brown leather handbag and pulled out a wadge of identity cards and ration books, grabbed in haste and stuffed into the bag in no particular order. She placed them on the table in front of Mrs Finlayson, who was working the afternoon shift.

"I'd be much obliged if you can help me," the new arrival said.

"Of course," Mrs Finlayson replied with a customer service smile, but all the same eyeing the pile of documents suspiciously.

"Me neighbour, Maureen Barker – do you know her?"

Mrs Finlayson shook her head. No, she didn't.

"Ah well, no matter. Me neighbour Maureen said to me

yesterday that the whole family were going to need new ration books and that I should come here."

"Yes, that's true," Mrs Finlayson explained. "The Government is now introducing clothes rationing in addition to food rationing." She was a little surprised that the woman didn't already know this. "But I'm sorry we can't help you here. You will need to go to the Food Office. I will give you directions."

"Oh no, ducky, there isn't any use me going there!"

"Mrs …?"

"Call me Mrs Davies," the woman replied.

"Mrs Davies, I'm very sorry, but we can't issue you with ration books here. You must go to the Food Office," Mrs Finlayson explained again carefully.

"Oh no, Maureen said you would help me here."

Alice, working on the other side of the room, pricked up her ears at the conversation at Mrs Finlayson's desk.

"You see, Maureen said you'd fill in the forms for me, so I can get them."

"You mean the reference sheets?"

"Something of the like, ducky. You see, I can't make head nor tail of it."

"Well, I can explain the questions to you if that would help," Mrs Finlayson offered, trying not to show impatience, as she was very busy checking the lists of names and addresses for the letters about the training courses.

"Won't make no difference," Mrs Davies said good-naturedly. "Can't read nor write, can I?" It wasn't a situation that bothered her particularly, so she wasn't ashamed to admit it.

Mrs Finlayson looked at the pile of identity cards and old

ration books – there were probably enough for ten people. She took a deep breath and went to the file for the reference sheets.

Sitting down again with her pen and the paperwork in front of her, she began,

"Now, Mrs Davies, perhaps you can give me some details? What is your Christian name."

"Jane, but everyone calls me Janie."

"And how old are you?"

"Oh, I reckon about 30."

"You don't know?"

"Nope, me Mum wasn't ever sure. We used to have cake in July when I was a littl'un, but that's more because that was definitely me Dad's birthday and it made sense to share a cake." Again, it was not something she seemed particularly bothered about.

With difficulty, Mrs Finlayson asked the questions on the sheet and worked through documents Janie had bought with her, trying her best to give correct answers. It did not help that although Janie thought her eldest daughter had probably 'gone sixteen,' she wasn't sure. Nor did it help that two of her sons had different names on their ration books from their identity cards, and neither of those sons had the same surname as their mother. None of this administrative chaos seemed to worry Janie unduly, so Mrs Finlayson tried her best to take her cue from her and not to become too upset by the disorder in the paperwork – but this was very difficult for a woman who appreciated order and careful administration.

As Mrs Finlayson was diligently assisting Janie Davies, a woman in a W.V.S. uniform entered the office – with a dog. Alice looked up from her desk and went forward to greet her unknown colleague. She wasn't overly fond of dogs and was a little alarmed that the woman had brought the hound into the office.

"Good afternoon, can I help?" she greeted, keeping her distance from the dog.

"I do hope so, I'm in from Ely and I'm doing a spot of shopping. Boris isn't up to it, you know. So I'd like to leave him here with you. You won't mind, will you? I'll be about an hour."

"Boris?" Alice asked, confused.

"Yes, he's too old to have come. He's fourteen, I shouldn't have brought him, but there was no one to leave him with. I must fly. See you later." And with that, she handed Alice Boris's lead and scuttled out of the office.

"Pleased to meet you, Boris," Alice said, holding the lead and looking down at the dog. He was a Labrador, and he did indeed look very tired.

"That dog could do with some water," Janie observed, finding more interest in the new arrival than the paperwork.

"Come on, good boy, good dog," Janie beckoned the dog, and Boris obediently and slowly padded over to her and sat at her feet, where she proceeded to give him a lot more attention than the paperwork.

Alice went in search of a bowl in the little kitchenette in the smaller room at the back of the large office. Mrs Moss was there doing battle with a temperamental duplicator which was also in need of a holiday. Alice offered both Mrs Moss and the machine some soothing words before continuing her search for a bowl. When she returned holding a dish filled with water, an officer was standing patiently by the door.

"Just a moment," she smiled and gave Boris his water,

which he lapped up vigorously. Then turning to the officer, she asked, "Can I help?"

"Baking tins," he announced.

"I'm sorry?"

"Baking tins. I'd like some baking tins for the troops."

"Of course. Robert Sayles department store is just along from here, and there is a very good hardware shop on the Mill Road. They might have some in stock."

"Well, actually, I was hoping that you might have some lying around that I could have."

Baking tins, lying around in an office, in the middle of a war – whatever next?

27.

JEAN

CHRISTMAS DAY

The frost had been at work overnight, leaving Jean's garden exquisitely decorated for Christmas day with icy jewels hanging from the twigs of every tree and outlining in silver the spiky corners of each holly leaf. Minute by minute, the pale December sun was chasing away a heavy night fog. It was a perfect winter's Christmas day, not a white Christmas, but certainly a frosty, special Christmas. The last in Jean's big family home. She didn't know whether she felt sad about this or relieved that the day had finally come.

The house was completely still and silent. In a few hours, it would be filled with all of Jean's family. There would be presents and food and laughter – and Kurt. She was nervous about meeting him, but not as nervous as Eleanor was about bringing him.

Eleanor had insisted that Kurt pick her up early on Christmas morning so that they could arrive in Grantchester before her sisters and their families. She was pleased he had his own car and that they wouldn't have to travel by train, it was infinitely warmer, and it meant they could make their goodbyes early and return to London if the day got too much. It was fabulous that she could finally introduce him to all her family, but she was only too aware of how overwhelming a mother, two sisters, two brothers-in-law and five children had the potential to be.

"Don't worry, Eleanor," he said for at least the sixth time as they made their way along the A10 out of London.

"I'm not worried."

"Yes, you are, I can tell."

"Well, maybe a bit."

"Shall we listen to the radio?" he asked, and he switched it on when she nodded.

The Beatles were midway through their number one single, singing "I wanna hold your haaaaand," as Kurt turned the dial.

"How do you know I'm worried?" she asked.

"Because you keep buttoning and unbuttoning your coat."

"That could be because I'm cold."

"But you're not, I've got the heating on, and your coat is warm. You are worried."

She started to tap out the rhythm of the Beatles' Christmas hit on her lap,

"I wanna hold your haaaaand," Kurt sang out of tune, "I wanna hold your hand."

She didn't comment. She was lost in her thoughts.

"You mustn't worry if Mum doesn't say very much. She's very quiet, and she's found losing Dad and the move difficult. And you mustn't mind Maeve. She can be a bit spiky at times."

"Eleanor, I can't wait to meet your family. It will all be fine."

"Hopefully," she replied, undoing the lowest button on her camel coat. She had wanted to add, 'and it doesn't help that you are from Germany because she lost a brother in the First World War.' But how could she say that when it was a direct criticism of his identity, and he could do nothing about it? He knew though. Not about the brother, but about the prejudices towards him for being a child of Germany. Not for the first time, he wondered if he should have changed his name from Kurt to Kevin.

They parked outside the large house. The garden was neat and trimmed as always. After Alan had passed away, Old Tom from the village came once a week to help Jean. Eleanor didn't think her mother had arranged it, probably it had just happened. It was likely that Old Tom had taken it upon himself to help Jean out and her mother, finding the help useful, paid him.

"It's very pretty," Kurt said admiringly.

The sunshine sparkled on the frost on the path leading to the house, as if the Almighty had shaken a vial of glitter to guide their way. On the old front door, Jean had hung a wreath of holly and ivy, and she had put up cheerful coloured Christmas lights, which looked like glowing candy, around the hall window next to the door. Not far from the house, Kurt could see the spire of the village church, St Andrew and St Mary. As if on cue, the bells began ringing, calling the faithful to the Christmas Day service.

"Here goes," Eleanor said, reaching her face up for him to give her a much-needed kiss of encouragement. Then with their bags of presents for the family, Eleanor let herself and Kurt into the house.

"Hello Mum, we're here. Happy Christmas," Eleanor called out.

Jean entered the hall from the drawing room, where a welcoming fire was lit almost instantly – as if she had been waiting in anticipation for their arrival.

"Happy Christmas," she replied, kissing her daughter's cheek. "And you must be Kurt – welcome." She wasn't sure how she ought to greet this young German. A kiss might be too familiar, a handshake too formal for her daughter's boyfriend of well over a year. He extended his hand for her to shake, and her dilemma was solved.

"Thank you so much for inviting me, Mrs Barnet and Happy Christmas."

He wasn't a bit as she imagined. She thought that Germans were blonde and blue-eyed, but that was silly really, she knew that couldn't always be the case. This young man had dark brown hair and soft chocolate eyes. He was wearing a suit and tie. Good, Jean thought, that meant that the present she had chosen for him was suitable. He might even like it.

"Mum, you look amazing," Eleanor said, admiring Jean's amethyst dress and jacket. "Is it new?"

"Yes, I bought some fabric at Sayles just after you were up last, and I made this outfit – do you like it?" She wasn't entirely confident that it was the right thing for her age, although she loved the colour and the fit.

"Yes, I do. It makes you look years younger, and so slim, Mum."

"Oh good," Jean was relieved. She could get through the day now that Eleanor had approved of the outfit, and Kurt was not the monster that he could have been.

"Would you like a cup of tea, Kurt?" Jean offered.

Kurt had lived in England long enough to know the expected answer,

"Yes, please, Mrs Barnet, that would be great."

Her daughters sat in the same places for Christmas dinner as they had always sat since they were old enough to leave their highchairs and sit at the long table. Christopher was in Alan's place with Maeve on his left, Barbara on his right, Eleanor – the little one – on Jean's left. Anne's seat, empty for many years, was now occupied by Sally. Maeve's husband Bill and all the little grandsons sat in the spaces in between, with the youngest in each family sitting closest to his mother. Kurt was safe alongside Eleanor, who guarded him fiercely from too much family interest.

As usual, there seemed to be a hundred different conversations all at the same time as adults tried to catch up with each other, children tried to play even though it was lunchtime, and adults told children off for playing and not eating. Jean listened where she could, answered where requested, and deflected any attempt to be brought in as an additional adjudicator in matters of grandchildren's behaviour. It was not until the pudding – a very large apple and plum crumble with an enormous jug of custard – that there was anything resembling a normal level of sound, as all the family, especially the little boys, enjoyed their puddings.

"This is delicious, Mummy, but I'm afraid I can't manage any more of it," Barbara said of the pudding, sliding it away from her towards the centre of the table; her stomach pressed, and appetite diminished by the growing baby.

"Where are you going, young man?" she was interrupted by eight-year-old Trevor's abrupt coincidental departure from his chair.

"You've finished, so I'm going to play," he replied.

"Oh no, you don't. What do you say to Granny?"

"Thank you for my lovely Christmas dinner, Granny. Please may I leave the table?" he mumbled shamefacedly, as he knew what he ought to have said but was in too much of a hurry to go and play on the swing in the garden.

"Boys, you can all go out for a while," Maeve said, nodding to Bill, who was wise enough to know that this meant that he should accompany his sons and nephews to the swing. "But put your coats on. We'll call you in when it's time for the presents."

It was a family tradition to exchange presents in the afternoon with a cup of tea and a slice of rich Christmas cake covered in marzipan and royal icing. It was a long wait for the children, but it was non-negotiable, and anyway, Father Christmas had filled their stockings at the end of their beds during the night with titbits and treats to keep them going.

Maeve began to clear away the pudding plates whilst Eleanor whisked Sally off to the kitchen to make a start on the mountain of washing up at the kitchen sink. Kurt got up to assist but was prevented by Christopher's conversation,

"So Kurt, what do you do in London?"

"I'm in the motor industry. I work for AC Cars."

"Really?" Christopher brightened enthusiastically. He had been worried his prospective brother-in-law might work in finance or accountancy or something else impossibly difficult to understand. But cars – and sports cars at that – now that was quite a different matter.

"And what's your opinion on the Ace? Does it really perform better than the Cobra 2.6?"

Barbara yawned loudly and leaned her head into her hands.

"Excuse me," she said, looking up at the two men. "I don't mean to be rude."

"Darling, you're tired. Why don't you have a little rest? You could lie down on the sofa in the drawing room. It's warm in there," Jean suggested, mothering her vastly pregnant and over-fatigued daughter.

"Thank you," Barbara said gratefully. "I'm not sleeping too well at the moment. I'll be glad when this one makes his entrance," she continued rubbing her swollen belly.

"So you think it's a boy?" Jean asked quickly.

"More than likely, we were all girls, and we girls are having mostly boys. Sometimes it goes like that," she shrugged, almost with indifference.

"But we don't know," her husband said, helping his wife out of her chair. Secretly he rather hoped for another little girl.

"Do you know the hospitals are developing equipment to take ultrasound scans of babies?" Kurt asked. "In the future, they will be able to tell you if you will have a baby boy or a baby girl."

"That's fascinating," Christopher said. "If the Soviets can get men into space, anything's possible. Now, what do you think about the Ace Cobra? I'm really interested. Does it perform better than the Cobra 2.6?"

Jean stayed sitting at the table, listening to Kurt talk animatedly about the motorcar industry. The words washed over her head, but she liked the light in his eyes as he spoke. He was well-dressed, and he had good manners. There was only the slightest hint of an accent now and again as he had lived far more of his young life in England than in Germany. During the Christmas meal, she had noticed that whenever he could, he had reached for Eleanor's hand beneath the table. She saw how they leaned close to each other, allowed their knees to touch beneath the tablecloth, and their feet on the floor. She saw how Eleanor's cheeks glowed and how her eyes were soft. She looked so pretty today, so wholesomely pretty – her face the reflection of the love in Kurt's chocolate-brown eyes.

Had she looked the same when Albert looked at her, his blue eyes filled with unspoken love and desire? She must have done.

It was Christmas 1941. As with the two war-time Christmases that had gone before, Jean had lunched with her family and joined the festivities at the village hall afterwards. 387 Battery D troop of the 121 Regiment of the Royal

Artillery had arrived under the command of Captain Maltby when the winter of 1940 was on the cusp of turning into spring and had stayed longer than anyone had expected them to be stationed, including perhaps the Captain himself. After nearly two years of serving the men at the Reading Room canteen, providing them with hot baths, helping them with whatever need or comfort that could be offered and afforded, these soldiers were friends.

When Jean entered the hall late in the afternoon, the dinner had all been cleared away, and the tables pushed back to the edges of the room to allow for entertainment. A loud and not particularly harmonious rendition of the Andrews Sisters' hit song 'Boogie Woogie Bugle Boy' was being performed by a group of soldiers. The troops and the women volunteers, who made up the audience, joined in the chorus, imitating trumpets when the chorus came around. The battalion had put together a small band, and among the musicians, Jean recognised Lazenby playing his cornet and the large, thuggish-looking man named Thomas playing a tiny ukulele. The song was surprisingly raucous, and it was a surprise to see women like Mrs Harding and Mrs Roberts joining in. The soldiers had been provided with a ration of rum alongside their dinner. Perhaps the older ladies had joined them in a toast – or two.

Her eyes searched for Albert across the hot, packed room. There he was, on the other side. He looked away from the band, and he saw her. It was as if his sixth sense had told him that she had entered.

She stayed where she was at the entrance to the hall, waiting for him to find an opportunity to join her. There were a few more songs, equally amusing, followed by a lad who fancied himself as a stand-up comedian and, being rather tipsy, delivered awful impressions of well-known personalities and a rather good imitation of Captain Maltby. Any other day of the year, this would have been a risky activity, but today was Christmas. Today the boys were far from their homes and their loved ones. Today they created fun with their substitute family – the battalion.

George Woodbridge stood up at the end.

"That's quite enuff of all that, Perkins. We thank you kindly fer yer skill, but lads, it's time now to get movin'. It's time for a game – musical chairs was always me favourite when I was a litt'le chap, so we'll start with that."

With surprising efficiency, Woodbridge managed to get all the troops to construct two aisles of chairs back to back for the party game. Lazenby, Thomas and the other battalion members reprised 'Boogie Woogie Bugle Boy.' A few soldiers, feeling too old or too silly to play the game, hung around the edges of the room. George grabbed Mrs Appleby good-naturedly by the hand and began to whizz her in a polka up and down one of the aisles of chairs. Mrs Harding followed his lead and took the arms of a surprised Bob Holmes. A roar of laughter rose from the dancefloor to the ceiling when McAllister found himself without a chair when the music suddenly stopped, and then the music, the dancing and the laughter began again.

During the party mayhem, Albert quietly moved around the edge of the room unnoticed, to join Jean by the door.

"Happy Christmas, Jean," he said quietly when he reached her.

"Happy Christmas, Albert," she replied equally softly.

They stood so close to each other that the sides of their arms brushed. She longed to reach out and take his hand, but that would never do.

For a moment, they watched the party game in silence.

"I have something for you. Do you think you could step outside?" he said, without turning his eyes away from the game to look at her next to him.

"Yes," she replied, and unobserved, she slipped out of the hall, waiting for him to follow a few minutes later.

"Let's walk up to the churchyard," he suggested. He knew that they wouldn't be seen there.

They walked quickly to the church. It was cold. Jean hadn't taken off her coat when she arrived at the hall, so she had a layer of warmth, but he was only in his uniform.

"You'll be frozen," she said with concern.

"It's no matter. I'm used to it."

The December afternoon was drawing to a close, and the light was fading fast. The shadows of the gravestones made long fingers that merged with the shadows of the trees and the wall.

He reached into his breast pocket and pulled out a rectangular package. A gift in a brown paper bag, tied up with string. Over the paper, he had drawn circles and waves in blue ink to decorate it, to make the ordinary paper bag seem like special Christmas wrapping paper.

"Thank you," she said, taking the package and removing the string.

Inside was his burgundy-bound book with rich gold decoration. It was his *Life of William Morris*. She opened the cover and, on the frontispiece, he had written in his careful slanting copperplate:

To Jean, Happy Christmas, with fond regard, Albert Dollis

Her heart was racing. She was sure he could hear it pounding.

"Thank you," she whispered.

"Do you like it? I hoped you would?"

"I love it, Albert, I do." How she wanted to add, "And I love you too."

He read her mind and reached out his arms for her, pulling him into his chest and holding her close. She didn't resist. She couldn't. She didn't want to.

She felt him kissing her brow. She raised her face to him in the half-light and sought his lips. He kissed her, his tongue searching hers, and she responded, reaching her hand to his head to pull his face closer to hers. The smell of his skin, of his cheeks, his neck, his throat, his chest underneath the jacket that she found her fingers opening without conscious direction, was intoxicating. His hands explored her body, gently and tenderly at first, and then with fiercer desire, reaching for her breasts and cupping his hands around them.

He pulled her closer still, tracing the shapes of her waist and her hips below her coat, his hand gliding up her precious silk stockings, only worn now for special occasions, like Christmas Day. He took her hand and guided her to feel where he most wanted her to touch. Letting her precious book, his book, fall to the grass, she answered his every stroke, his every kiss.

"I love you, Jean, God, how I love you," he moaned as he kissed and stroked.

"I love you too."

She had finally said it. She had said the words out loud that she had held secretly inside for many months.

Never had she felt like this before – never. Alan did not touch her like Albert was now touching her. He did not make her tremble or her heart pound, her senses burst.

"My darling Jean," Albert whispered in her ear. "Say it again. Say it again that you love me."

But Alan was there now, between them. With her eyes

shut, kissing Albert's moist, insistent lips, she saw the look of disgust on her husband's face as if he knew what she was doing with Albert at that moment in the graveyard. She imagined the expression of contempt on Mrs Fielding's face if she also knew.

There were women who did this sort of thing with the soldiers. Women from the village and the surrounding area, who stood with the gunners in the shadows, letting them lift their skirts and slide their hands up stockings with arrows up the sides – marks of their 'profession' that showed they were available for a price.

"No!" she said, pushing him away.

At first, he did not want to give her up. He held her tightly. He tried to kiss her again, more deeply, more passionately.

"No, Albert," she said, this time more firmly. "I can't."

She stepped back from him and into the shadows. She was shaking. The last light from the ending day shimmered on the tears welling up in her eyes. She buttoned up her coat, rearranged her skirt.

He stood silently for a moment, trying his best to pull his emotions back into his body, to regain his self-control.

"I'm sorry," she said feebly.

He said nothing. He was frozen to his spot, the cold December air now beginning to bite him where his shirt and trousers remained undone.

"I'm sorry, Albert," she repeated, unsure what to do next. She should leave, but she couldn't. He had to say something kind to her. He must.

"Don't you ever say sorry, Jean. It was me, my fault. I'm sorry," he whispered fiercely.

She could hardly bear to look at him.

"I'd better go home." Her voice was scarcely more than a whisper.

He nodded, and standing in the shadows, he waited in strained silence for her to leave.

Jean picked up her book and walked quickly in the dark back to her house, her footsteps echoing in the Christmas silence of the street. She wanted to run. She wanted to flee from the man she loved so desperately and upsettingly to the security of her home where she was wife and mother. But to run would be to draw attention to herself. "Why were you running in the street on Christmas Day afternoon, Mrs Barnet?" she could already hear the gossipy question.

They avoided each other after that. It wasn't difficult. He knew the pattern of her shifts at the Reading Room canteen, and without publicity, he chose not to go there when he was off duty, reading on his army bed instead.

Then suddenly, without warning, the battalion received orders that they were to move to the Essex coast. After an unheard-of tour of two years in one base, it was time to leave. Everyone was sad. The soldiers – to leave the beautiful village with the river running through it, an idyllic home where the care they had received from the villagers had been a panacea for their war. The villagers – to lose men they had come to know well, some very well indeed. If anyone noticed Jean looking pale and Albert looking glum, nobody said anything about it. Everyone felt pale and glum.

Within a fortnight, Dollis, Woodbridge, Holmes, Lazenby, McAllister and all the rest had left the life of Grantchester to be replaced with a hundred different men.

Albert didn't see Jean to say goodbye. Instead, a few days after his departure, Jean received a beige army envelope with green stripes through the post.

Essex
20ᵗʰ Jan. 1942

Dear Jean

Please read this. Please continue reading. Don't stop. I'm going to put this letter in a green envelope so that the officers won't read it.

I'm sorry. I am so, so sorry. It shouldn't have happened. I never wanted to hurt you or embarrass you. I think the world of you. God, Jean, I love you, and I think, I believe, that you love me too.

It's probably for the best that the army has moved us on.

I can't ask anything from you, any more than you've already given, but please, please let me write to you just while this wretched war is raging, and please write to me. No feelings. Just words to let each other know that we are still safe – that Jerry hasn't killed us yet. You put yourself at so much risk for the sake of other people. You really don't know what a beautiful and special person you are.

Goodbye Jean, I won't write in this way again – do not fear. And to show how much I mean what I say, I shall sign off the way I mean to begin,

With fond regard
Albert Dollis

She hid away from her family in her room to read the letter. He had gone. He had left her life. For a short time, he had brought bright, dazzling technicolour passion to her black and white passionless world. To him, she wasn't one of the girls with the arrows on the sides of the stockings – she knew that. He loved her, and he understood her. And she loved him – how she loved him. Now he had gone.

Deep, silent sobs wrenched her body as she cried, her face deep in her pillow to suffocate any sound she might make until her eyes were raw and dry, and she lay in anguished stillness.

He had gone – and it was for the best. She knew that.

She was married to Alan and loved him in dutiful friendship, but she knew she had never fallen in love with him, now that she knew what to fall in love was.

"Mummy," she heard Barbara calling from downstairs, "Mummy, I need your help. Where are you?"

"Just coming, sweetheart. Wait a moment – please."

She got up and wiped her eyes with her handkerchief before lightly brushing her cheeks with her compact face powder to try to even out her tear-stained complexion. She brushed her hair and straightened her blouse. With luck, she looked close to normal, and Barbara would not notice that her mother had been crying.

His letter was on the bed where she had been lying. She ought to destroy it. She should rip it up into tiny pieces and throw them in the fire downstairs. But she couldn't. This letter, and any more that he might send, along with the book, were all she had left of him – all she would ever have of him. She folded the army envelope in half and placed it in the third drawer of her chest of drawers under her summer blouses. No one would find it there. It was safe and hidden and could stay there until she decided what she would do with his words.

Then she went downstairs to Barbara and went through the motions of living.

28.

ALICE

AMERICANS

West Road
Cambridge
5th November, 1942

Dearest Sylvia,

Again, my dear friend, I must apologise for the delay in replying to your last letter, but this time you will see that I really do have an excuse. Cambridge was chosen to host your compatriot Eleanor Roosevelt on her whistle-stop tour of Britain. The First Lady is a friend of Lady Reading, did you know? And she has a very great interest in women's war work. She is surely the USA's greatest asset. You have probably read in the papers that she arrived in October and is spending a month touring the country – Glasgow, Edinburgh, London, Bath and Cambridge. Of course, her visit to Cambridge was meant to be a secret, so naturally, the whole town knew she was coming, and a good thing too, in my opinion, as it would have been a very sorry state of affairs for crowds not to turn out to wish such a remarkable woman well.

Now that I have had a full two days to recover from the experience, let me tell you what happened. I know you will be interested, but maybe you will also be a little relieved that Birmingham and Coventry didn't find their way onto the itinerary when you learn all that we had to do.

The guidance we were given for the day was that Mrs Roosevelt was to see both an exhibition of our work here in Cambridge and also to have the opportunity to meet workers more intimately. Of course, all the section leaders wanted to have the opportunity to show off their areas of expertise and hard work. It was quite an effort to steer everyone's enthusiasm into an exhibition of activities that the dear lady wouldn't see at Glasgow, Edinburgh, London, Bath – or Birmingham and Coventry. We put on quite a show (quite the envy of any other branch,

I am sure), and in truth, we did select the least ordinary of our activities. Did you know that we have quite a W.V.S. industry here making cardboard coat hangers for clothing depots? We are also experts in book-binding for the Forces Mobile Library, stitching suits for snipers and making jackets for seamen entirely from old leather glove cuttings and, my personal favourite, creating beautiful toys and doll-houses for the nurseries made from furniture that can no longer be repaired.

Her day in Cambridge started with the official welcome at Queens' College by the Vice-Chancellor, the Mayor, the Regional Commissioner, and the Regional Administrator. I was honoured to be included in this little reception. Of course, it was as stiff and formal a welcome as could be expected. Such a contrast to what happened when she and I left the dignitaries behind and walked together through the streets to our Borough Office. The pavements were lined with our women and their friends to greet the First Lady. It was most festive as we went the short way, and she seemed to appreciate the turnout, smiling graciously and waving in response. Quite a crowd greeted us outside our office, all brandishing Stars and Stripes flags and cheering.

I expect I have told you before that our office is not large but we shoe-horned our exhibition into the premises and the First Lady was greatly interested in our display.

Mrs Roosevelt had sent a message in advance that she wanted to learn about industrial billeting, so we arranged for two Irish girls working at Pye Radio to meet her, as well as a labourer and a Cambridge householder providing billets. The Irish girls were distinctly nervous at first, but Mrs Roosevelt was quite charming in the way she drew them out of themselves and in no time, she had them talking freely. One of the girls plucked up the courage to ask Mrs Roosevelt for her autograph, which the lovely lady gave away to these kind members of the community who had given up their time to meet her. I have to say we were a little surprised when the labourer, having no clean paper to receive her autograph, presented her with a photograph of his wife, which now, surprisingly, bears the signature of Eleanor Roosevelt. I thought you would find that amusing!

Lawrence sends his love.
Best love
Alice

Birmingham
23rd November, 1942

Darling Alice,

Thank you for your letter. I very much enjoyed your account of Mrs Roosevelt's visit. It does not surprise me one little bit that your Borough was chosen for the special inspection. Not only is Cambridge a delightful city for the American visitor, but you, Alice, have always known how to entertain with flair. What is more, you <u>do</u> have a great reputation in the W.V.S. for running a tight ship in the Cambridge Borough. You wouldn't let me say that to your face. You would 'shush' me and change the subject, but it is the truth, and you deserve the credit.

You mentioned nothing of coffee. It is scarcely possible for a Brit to talk about the yanks these days without mentioning coffee — or chocolate.

I don't even want to begin to tell you how busy we are here, so I won't. Instead, I will send you all my love,

Sylvia

West Road
Cambridge
30th November 1942

Dearest Sylvia

What! A letter from Alice so soon! More of a scrawled note than a letter, my dear friend, I couldn't resist your gauntlet in respect of coffee. Last month we had a train of US troops pass through, and we boiled up three hundred pounds of coffee on one small gas ring and served them all with a steaming cup in our usual fifteen minutes. Apparently, our coffee passed muster as we received many compliments.

Much love
Alice

29.
ALICE
D-DAY

June 1944

Mr Charles Kemp, Secretary to the Cambridge Town Council, read two newspapers as a matter of habit. The newspaper boy delivered the papers to Charles' house before breakfast, and he took the time to peruse the columns whilst drinking his morning tea – another long-held habit. The current newspaper boy was a good lad, as the papers arrived every morning without fail, even if there had been disturbances the night before. He would remember to tip the boy well in his Christmas box in December.

Charles' newspapers of choice were the *Daily Telegraph* so that he could keep abreast of national matters and the *Cambridge Daily News* so that he would be informed of how events in Cambridge were reported and sometimes misreported.

He spread the newspapers out on his dining room table and put on his half-moon reading glasses to examine the headlines on the front page of the *Daily Telegraph*:

Allied Invasion Troops Miles into France

Navy's First Invasion Task Successful

Mr Churchill Reports Initial Progress Satisfactory

With each headline, Charles' heart began to pound faster and faster with excitement. He felt light-headed. He needed to grip the table in front of him. This was it, then! The counter-invasion had begun. The end of the war was finally in sight.

"Muriel," he called out to his wife, who he could hear in the kitchen, "Muriel, come here – quickly!"

"I'm coming," she called back with pointed irritation in her voice. Couldn't he be a little more patient? She deliberately took a bit longer to pour their tea into the cups and saucers she had already laid on the tray.

Charles hardly noticed that she hadn't come into the room. Usually, he would be annoyed if she didn't come when he called her, but today he was so drawn into the exciting news that he simply didn't notice. If the reports were correct, it would seem that the Allied troops had landed in Normandy two days ago on Monday but that the details hadn't reached the London press until yesterday and so had only now made the morning editions.

Muriel entered the dining room with the tea on a tray. She had left his porridge cooking on the stove.

"Muriel," he said excitedly, "look, look at the papers."

"I don't have my reading glasses," she grumbled, "I can't see."

"The Allies have landed in France. The war is going to end."

And to her eternal surprise – he kissed her.

He walked to work a little later with a spring in his step. It was a lovely warm June day, one on which Cambridge looks at its best with English roses blooming in abundance. The lawns that he glimpsed as he walked past the old college gates were green and lush. The Cam sparkled in the sunlight. The war was coming to an end. If he were a romantic man, which he wasn't, the birds would be singing the announcement to the world on this beautiful morning. As he walked through the city streets, it was almost as if he had missed the bird-song announcement, as a sense of excitement was on every street corner, at every doorway, wherever two or more people gathered, the news was on everyone's lips. D-Day. It had finally come. God bless our troops. God bless our boys. Let it be over. Soon.

Charles was in such good humour when he arrived at the Guildhall offices that he overlooked both the assortment of boxes in the lobby from a recent delivery, which the porter had not yet tided away, and the fact that his administrative assistant, Miss Jackson, was more than ten minutes late. Perhaps she had been reading the newspapers? If so, good for her. Not much could sour his temper today – even the appointment in the diary with Lady Bragg.

Charles had an interesting proposition to lay before Lady Bragg – something Sir Montagu and several other senior councillors had discussed at length. It was felt that Lady Alice Bragg would make a good Mayor. He had been charged with ascertaining whether she would accept the position if formally offered. Of course, he did have his reservations. This kind of role would be difficult for a woman. A mayor had to play a political game. He had to make speeches. He had to unify the town. A woman would struggle with all of this. However, Charles Kemp did concede, when it was pointed out to him, that yes, in the past, there had been two very successful female mayors of Cambridge; and yes, Alice Bragg's achievement in ensuring that her W.V.S. office delivered everything that was asked of it was astonishing; and yes, (he was brow-beaten by now as his arguments were evaporating) she was completely apolitical, in other words, an Independent, which surely was a good thing when the country was at war. What was more, she was popular. She was popular with the powers at the University and widely popular in the homes, streets, schools, congregations, and offices of the town.

"Good morning, Lady Bragg," the porter greeted Alice when she arrived at the council's Guildhall offices just before

10 o'clock.

"Good morning, Mr Ellis, such wonderful news!"

"That it is Lady Bragg," the porter grinned. "You'll find him in a good mood about it an' all."

She climbed the stairs to his office, almost now looking forward to her rendezvous with the rather fastidious Mr Kemp. She wasn't sure precisely what council business he wanted to see her about, although they had met from time to time over the previous months on ad-hoc matters arising from the larger council meetings which they had both attended.

"Ah, Lady Bragg," he welcomed her with a large smile that banished his habitual sour frown today.

He was not a man to engage with chit-chat. There was simply too much to do to waste time with unnecessary niceties. Alice knew this, and also knew it was not worth irritating him with social questions, those warm-up comments preceding a conversation, which can be so valuable in finding out how a person is feeling, or what lies behind the thrust of the words to come. It was a pity, but better to play by Charles' rules.

"Lady Bragg," he said with gravitas. "Thank you for coming to see me. Now then, what would you say if you were offered the opportunity of becoming Mayor of Cambridge next year?"

This was not what Alice had expected him to ask. An update on relations between the W.V.S. street 'Housewives' and the area wardens, yes; a request for an opinion on billeting, perhaps; the invitation to become Mayor, no. Her heart told her head what to reply, and without hesitation, she said firmly:

"No, Mr Kemp, I'm sorry, I cannot contemplate this position."

Now it was Charles' turn to be taken by surprise.

"Can I ask why not?"

Alice did not need to consider the proposal. She knew she was giving her all to her family and to the W.V.S. Although the end of the war was in sight, there was still so much to do, so much help required. She was exhausted. Her daughters were still at school and needed her, David's health was an ongoing worry to her, and Stephen, although quite a young man now, was still grateful for a parent's guiding word from time to time.

"My children are too young for me to take on extra responsibility," she replied, "I don't have any more time to give without neglecting them further."

"Could you reorganise your time?"

"I don't think that is possible."

"You could resign from your role in the W.V.S. to take on the position of Mayor."

Again, her heart told her head what to reply, and the answer was most definitely no.

Charles Kemp did not look convinced, so she tried a different approach.

"Mr Kemp, I am too inexperienced. I have only been on the council for such a short time, maybe in five years when I have learned more, and I might have properly earned the honour."

"In five years, you will be old. Neither your looks nor your mind will be the same."

This man was too rude! Alice seethed inwardly.

"Thank you for outlining the suggestion, Mr Kemp, but I need to leave now as I have another appointment to attend," she said icily.

Charles Kemp never noticed the climate in anyone's voice and stood up to show her to the door, as was the polite thing to do. He wasn't disappointed himself that she had refused, but as other powers within the council had decided that Alice Bragg should be mayor, it would be a failure on his part if he could not convince her.

"I suggest you think it over, Lady Bragg. This offer might not come your way again. Talk it over with your husband. I wish you a very pleasant day."

Alice did not have another appointment to attend other than to go immediately to the Cavendish Labs to find Lawrence and lay Mr Kemp's proposal and outrageously insulting comment before her husband.

"Good morning, Lady Bragg," Brenda greeted her. Sir Lawrence had not informed her that Alice would pass by this morning.

"Darling?" Lawrence looked up in bewilderment when Alice entered his office. He was deep in a complicated set of calculations, which he was reviewing for one of his scientists. Had he forgotten something important, he wondered with a slight panic. Was it somebody's birthday? Was he meant to be somewhere today other than the Labs?

She read the worry on his face and laughed.

"Nothing's wrong, darling. But I do have something important to talk to you about," and she proceeded to relate the details of the conversation that had taken place not fifteen minutes earlier.

"Darling, that's terrific," Lawrence exclaimed when she told him of the proposal. He was thrilled for her. His wife, his clever, beautiful, efficient wife, to be the next Mayor of Cambridge! He bounded forward to take her in his arms for a polka, consciously echoing the steps they had danced around the room in celebration of the honour of his knighthood.

She did not respond. Her body was limp, and she was not laughing.

"Alice?" he questioned. "You did say yes, didn't you?"

Alice heard herself say 'no' yet again that morning.

Lawrence held her gently by the shoulder and looked into her eyes with great seriousness.

"Why ever not? It's a great honour."

"I can't. There's too much to do with running the house and looking after the children."

"Tush!" he declared. "That's nothing that can't be overcome. Alice, seriously my love, these opportunities don't always present themselves again. It's important to seize them as they arrive."

"Do you think so?"

"Yes, I do."

"And you honestly think I could manage?"

"I have every confidence in your abilities."

"And you will support me if I accept?"

"One hundred per cent."

She smiled and began to let herself agree.

"Do you know what that rude little man said to me when I told him I thought I would make a better job of being Mayor in five years or so?" she asked. "He said that by then, I would be too old, and neither my looks nor my mind would be the same. Honestly, Laurence, how insulting! I'm only 45!"

"Good show, old lady," Lawrence congratulated.

And Alice started to laugh. She laughed at the ridiculous

idea that at 50, she could be too old, and consented to a spin around the room in her husband's arms on this day of celebration – the beginning of the end of the war and that soon she would be the Mayor of Cambridge.

30.
JEAN
CLEANING UP

January 1964

The girls had agreed between themselves that Maeve would be the one to help their mother on the day of the move, even though it meant her taking a day off work. Barbara and Christopher would be focusing on their new baby, who was late in making his or her appearance into the world. Christopher's mother, Margaret, was helping them look after the older children so as not to involve Jean unnecessarily. Eleanor, who had given up so much of her time to help pack up the old house, was only going to come and help unpack the boxes at the new house on weekends that coincided with fittings for her bridesmaid's dress. Jean was glad of the help. She knew she couldn't manage the move alone.

Everything was packed into crates, cardboard boxes, suitcases, and bags. Jean felt that maybe she too should be packed into something, as she stripped her bed for the last time after a restless night's sleep and folded the sheets and blankets into the allocated crate, leaving the mattress bare, ready to be covered and taken with the bedstead to the removal van.

Geoff and Ted from Barker and Sons, the removal specialists, reversed their large apple-red coloured van into Jean's drive promptly at 9 o'clock. Maeve arrived in her car a little later. For a while, Jean watched as Geoff and Ted manoeuvred her bed and then her wardrobe down the stairs and into the open mouth of their van before deciding to clear the final things from her bathroom – her toothbrush, her flannel, the soap. She would clean the bathroom next so that it would be fresh for Mr and Mrs Thwaites to use when it became their bathroom later that afternoon.

Once, she had cleaned a house for its new tenants. That had been towards the end of the war. There was a large house in the city that the military had vacated the week before that was ideal as a hostel for the Belgian refugees being repatriated to their homeland, except that it was filthy, in such a disgusting condition that no paid helpers would touch it.

By then, Frances Clode was the W.V.S. Cambridge borough manager as Mrs Finlayson had been forced to retire due to ill health.

"I'm *so* sorry," Frances had buttered her up through the telephone line. "The building is in an absolute state. We've been told to expect the Belgians tomorrow, and we don't have anywhere else to billet them, so we've no option but to crack on. We'd be so grateful for your help if you could spare the time."

The twins were virtually adults, and her mother could mind Eleanor. The battalion had left, the village canteen was closed and the mobile canteen redundant, and the Queen's Messenger convoy, no longer needed, was on its way to Burma, so of course, she had the time, even for cleaning.

She asked Mrs Appleby to go with her, and the two ladies arrived together, Jean ringing the doorbell of the vast, once-upon-a-time white-painted house. Alice Bragg opened the door, enveloped in a brown hessian apron, hair wrapped in a dark scarf and carrying gauntlet gloves.

"Alice!" Jean couldn't have been more surprised. She would never have thought Lady Bragg would be part of a cleaning party.

"Thank you so much for coming, and you must be Mrs Appleby. We appreciate you giving your time to help," Alice graciously welcomed them.

"Do you like my party wear?" she continued, poking fun at herself in her cleaning attire.

"No doubt it will be handy," Mrs Appleby commented, her nostrils arched by the stench that had greeted them through the open door. She had been looking around the entrance hall since the door had opened and was alarmed at the cigarette buts, lumps of mud, balls of screwed-up notepaper and apple cores littering the floor, not to mention the undistinguishable marks on the walls.

"This is nothing," Alice said, following Mrs Appleby's eyes. "Wait until you see the kitchen and the bathrooms. Frances has made a start in what they must have used as the dining room, and Mrs Moss is working her way through the bedrooms."

As she spoke, she led Jean and Mrs Appleby through the house to the kitchen. The previous tenants had not been too worried about either washing up or cleaning surfaces, with the result that fat, grease, breadcrumbs, and mouldering remnants of food smothered the stove, the counters and the sink. Towers of dirty dishes and pans created a city in the kitchen. Empty packets and opened tins littered the table and spilt onto the floor, which now was brown linoleum – but was unlikely to remain brown once scrubbed.

"I've never done much cleaning," Alice said light-heartedly. "Frances said I would be most effective in the larder. She thinks that is where I will do the least damage. That's where I shall be, do call me if you need me."

Mrs Appleby and Jean looked at each other in disbelief. They had never seen such a filthy kitchen.

"Best make a start then, Mrs Barnet, hadn't we," Mrs Appleby said with grim determination and took out her gloves, an apron, and a headscarf from her bag.

The women worked side by side for many hours. From time to time, Alice emerged from the larder and took a stroll around the house to check that the women in the other rooms were managing and to distract herself from the menial task at hand. Two more women arrived in the afternoon, giving Alice a longer break from the larder, as she directed them to the study and the drawing room to tidy and clean. When she did return to the larder, she kept up a continual conversation with Jean, who was on her hands and knees scrubbing the floors.

"I wonder how they managed to get in such a mess?" Jean asked.

"Too many parties," Alice joked. She was in a flippant mood brought on by the novelty of cleaning and her apron.

"Not properly brought up," Mrs Appleby commented from the sink.

"Looked after too well by their wives," Jean added.

"Or their maids," Alice contributed. "I am so very grateful to all the maids I've ever had."

"How are you getting on in there, Alice?" Jean enquired, standing up from scrubbing and poking her head around the door.

"Very well, thank you," said Alice, turning to look at Jean. "Oh dear, you don't think so, do you?"

The larder was modest for the size of the house. It had enough room for a person to stand in the middle and reach each shelf to the right, left, and in front. A few of the shelves were bare, but many still had empty bottles and packets strewn across them. The shelves on the left were brown and sticky where honey or syrup had been spilt a long time ago and had never been properly wiped up.

"No, you're doing a great job, Alice. With just a bit more

effort, you'll have it spick and span," Jean encouraged.

"And then I'll help you with the floor! I'll turn it from brown to red with my magic scrubbing brush."

It had been such a long time now since Jean had seen Alice Bragg. She knew that her husband, Sir Lawrence, no longer worked at the University. He had taken up an appointment in London. The Braggs were probably living there. But, on the other hand, he may already be retired, she wasn't sure of his age. In which case, he and Alice could now be living almost anywhere. A shout from downstairs broke her train of thought as Ted had found a crate that had not been marked with its intended destination in the new house.

Meanwhile, Maeve had finished clearing up the kitchen cupboards, all except for those items which would be the last to be packed and the first to be unpacked: mugs, teapot, teaspoons, sugar, and tea caddy.

She turned to her mother as she entered the kitchen and said irritably:

"I don't see why you had to get rid of the kettle I gave you."

"I didn't!"

"Well, why aren't you using it then?" Jean saw that her hob-kettle was beginning to boil on the stove where Maeve had set it in preparation for a pot of tea for Ted and Geoff and, of course, her mother.

"I had it in its box, and I think it must have accidentally gone to Sally's jumble sale. I am sorry, darling."

"Mum!" she said crossly. "That was very silly of you."

"I know. I'm sorry."

"Never mind, I'll get you another. It can be a house-warming present."

Jean was about to say 'no thank you,' in the kindest, least

offensive way when Geoff came into the kitchen searching for the tea that Maeve had offered.

Jean made the tea now that she was there, and Geoff took mugs for himself and Ted. Then she poured one each for herself and Maeve, who had turned her attention to the fridge.

There wasn't anywhere to sit down. The kitchen table and chairs had already been consigned to the removal van, so Jean took her cup of tea in search of a chair in another room. The drawing room also was empty, so too was the study. The linen bin from her bathroom had been abandoned in the hall, brought downstairs by the men, but not yet loaded onto the van. It was sturdy enough to take her weight. So Jean sat down in a room in her house, in which she had never sat down before, on the day that she was leaving the house for good.

There wasn't much left in the hall now. The coat stand by the door was bare, apart from the coats that she and Maeve would wear to leave the house for the last time. A houseplant and a lamp poked their heads out from the rim of a cardboard box waiting on the hall table.

From her place on the linen bin, she could see through the open door to the empty drawing room. She had never seen it empty before. Alan had bought the house and moved their furniture while she had taken her little girls to stay with her parents. She had moved from her parents' home to Alan's house, then later, to this house, and she had never seen any of them empty. It struck her that an empty house was one of such possibility but also regret.

After 26 years, it would only be her house for a few hours longer, and then it would become Mr and Mrs Thwaites' house, their new home for themselves and their two teenage children. As she sat on a seat which was not a seat, in a room that was not for sitting in, she felt overwhelmed by sadness.

Her children had grown up in this house, two of her daughters had been married from this house, and her mother and then her husband had died in this house. She had loved Albert from this house. She bent her head and wept softly, not wanting to draw any attention from Maeve or the removal men. After a few moments, she reached for her hankie, tucked up her sleeve, wiped her tears, and stood up. As she did so, she caught sight of a brown envelope stuck between the leg of the walnut table and the hall wall. She bent down and picked it up. Her name and address had been typed on the envelope. It was a bill. There was nothing she could do about it today, so she stuffed it into the box with the plant and returned with the cup to the kitchen.

Maeve turned round and looked up from the fridge, the last staging post in her farewell to the kitchen. She saw at once that her mother had been crying,

"Are you all right, Mum?" she said with an unusual softness.

"Yes. No. No, I'm sad to leave, Maeve."

"Of course you are. That's only natural." She almost made a move to go over and hug her mother, but couldn't. It wasn't her. Barbara was the maternal one who could parent a parent as well as her own children, and Eleanor was the little girl who still found a place on her mother's lap. Maeve was her father's daughter and was at a loss to find the words or actions needed for the moment.

"You'll feel better when you're settled in. The new house is lovely, you'll manage it much better on your own ..." and she continued to reel off the reasons that Jean had heard so many times before as to why she should move, "... and life moves on, Mum, you know you've got to too."

"Yes, you're right, darling," Jean replied, no longer listening, and picked up the broom, dustpan, and brush so she could sweep the downstairs rooms for the Thwaites.

255

Maeve frowned and scrubbed the glass shelves in the fridge more vigorously than they needed.

31.

ALICE

NEITHER THE SHAPE NOR THE FEET
FOR MARCHING

May & June 1945

"Cambridge W.V.S. office, Frances Clode speaking, how may I help?"

"Ah, good morning, Mrs Clode. Charles Kemp speaking, is Lady Bragg available?"

Alice took the telephone receiver from Frances, silently indicating for her to remain working at the desk as the call would not be a long one. Charles Kemp did not beat around the bush after all.

"Lady Bragg. There is going to be a Civil Defence march past in Cambridge on Sunday in three weeks' time. Would your ladies care to take part?"

How nicely put, Alice thought briefly, but she was sure that her ladies would definitely not 'care to take part'.

"Mr Kemp, none of us have the shape nor the feet for marching," she laughed, poking fun at herself and her ladies rather than refusing outright.

"Come, come, Lady Bragg, the war is as good as over. Your ladies, I am sure, would wish to participate in a ceremony marking their contribution to Civil Defence."

Alice detested marching. If the W.V.S. were to march, she would have to lead from the front as Centre Organiser and Mayor-elect. Years before, back in 1938, when she first worked with Lady Reading in Manchester and London, Lady Reading had assured her that joining the W.V.S. would not involve marching. Briefly, she wondered if she could write to Lady Reading for a reprieve – an order from high – 'no W.V.S. member is required to march' and that she could show this precious document to Mr Kemp, saying sweetly, "I'm sorry, Mr Kemp we are not in a position to help you." But that would be saying no. And the W.V.S. never said 'no'.

"Thank you for the invitation, Mr Kemp," she replied politely. "You can count on us."

"Naturally," was his terse response, "I'll have my secretary put the details on a memo and send it over. Good day to you, Lady Bragg," and he hung up as Alice was still saying goodbye.

Frances Clode, who had heard the whole conversation, looked askance.

"You don't mean that do you?" Frances also had a horror of marching.

"Let's let the ladies decide."

"I can't imagine any of them will volunteer, and then you'll have ever such a job trying to persuade them."

It did not prove to be difficult at all. Alice wrote cards to all the members, helped by Frances and Hester, and as the membership was not what it had been in the early years of the war, this was not such an onerous task. Since there was very little time to practise and prepare, the first twenty replies were accepted, and Alice invited all the ladies to a tea party at her house to discuss the arrangements.

Jean knew she would not accept the invitation to attend when she received Alice's card. The thought of putting herself on display in front of hundreds of people made her stomach turn. She read the message and then put the card down on the hall table.

Fee Larkin, meanwhile, read her card with excitement.

"Here, Jonny," she said to her husband, who was repairing yet another radio, buttons, wires, screws and unimaginable parts spread neatly over newspaper on their kitchen table, "What do you think about me marching?"

"You wouldn't manage it, love – you'd have to do as you were told and march in time."

"Ha! That's nothing. I'm going to do it." And he knew that she would.

"I wonder if Jean will come too," she thought out loud. "I'll ask her when I see her later and try to persuade her. It'll be fun."

Mrs Appleby arrived at Jean's house by 10 o'clock to help Jean with the laundry and the cleaning. She didn't go to the Reading Room anymore before going to Mrs Fielding or Jean's house, as the canteen had been closed when the Battalion had left in April '44. Guns were no longer needed to defend the city from an enemy in retreat, but they were necessary in mainland Europe to secure the defeat. She felt sad about that. Not the fact that the war was coming to an end. No, that was a blessing. She was sad that there were now so few opportunities to help the boys. Helping the soldiers, doing whatever she could for them, or assisting Mrs Barnet so the younger woman could help in her turn was what had seen her through these last terrible years.

For day after day, month after month, she had slept badly, dreaming about Stanley, fitfully praying that he was still alive and later, when the extent of Japanese viciousness was becoming clear to those in Europe, demanding of her God that Stanley be dead if that were better than him being alive in a Jap-created hell. Each day she had risen, scarcely refreshed but determined to carry out her personal battle with the day – the battle of just getting through to another night of nightmares. Cleaning the canteen – carefully, methodically, efficiently, anchored her morning. Plumping

259

the cushions, topping up the vase of flowers that Jean placed every week on the long table so that the flowers and greenery wouldn't wilt and would live as long as they could, picking up the morning's papers and laying them out ready to be read, all of this kept her going.

Finally, the Red Cross informed her that if Stanley were still alive, he would be in Changi prison on the Northern tip of Singapore. The Red Cross would endeavour to send him food parcels with letters from his mother if the Japanese permitted. As the Empire of the Rising Sun had not signed the Geneva convention, they could not guarantee that supplies or letters would reach the prisoners, but there was a chance, just a chance, and there was the slenderest of hopes that he might be able to write in reply.

She wrote her letters. Cheerful messages of unremarkable comments relating mundane events in her day-to-day life, giving no details of the war in Europe but assured him that she was safe and silently told him not to worry about her. Bland questions about the weather in Singapore through which she tried to convey her love, through which she tried to reach out to him and put her arms around her precious child, yet put him in no danger from his prison censors.

For months there was no news from the East. For years she heard nothing. But she continued to write her letters, just in case the Red Cross worked their magic and the letters reached him. Then suddenly, out of the blue, a thin envelope arrived with even thinner paper within. It was a letter written in faint pencil – from Stanley! Before she had even read the first line, Mrs Appleby was crying. Tears of pent-up despair burst forth with joy at a letter from her boy. There was little detail other than he was alive. Praise the Lord! She read the short letter twice before running – yes, running – to Jean's house to share the news with her friend.

This one letter gave her more courage to keep going than

she could have thought possible. She needed her strength. The war in Europe was ending, even she could see that, but there was still no news from the East. Hitler was on the run, but not Hirohito.

Jean knew how much Mrs Appleby suffered quietly and the loneliness the old lady concealed. No matter how busy she was, Jean always found time to sit with her in the kitchen with a cup of tea for a few moments. She would have liked to have offered her friend hospitality in the drawing room, but she didn't. Neither her mother Anne, to whom Mrs Appleby was a daily help, a type of servant, nor Mrs Appleby herself, who knew her place, would have been comfortable there. Jean left things where they were and took tea in the kitchen.

While Jean sorted the laundry into piles of different colours and checked for any little holes in the garments – little holes that could become bigger holes, which could spoil clothing too precious to replace now there was rationing – Mrs Appleby dusted and swept the downstairs. She saw the card from Lady Bragg on the hall table. She had received one too. She was not going to march. She might have spent years assisting the war effort in Europe, but her attention, her entire focus, was on Singapore. There would be no marching for Mrs Appleby until Stanley was home. She couldn't imagine Jean wanting to take part either.

Five days after the cards had been sent out and two days after the replies had been received, Alice welcomed twenty W.V.S. members into her large drawing room. She had to confess she had been very surprised at how many members had come and who was among them.

Frances Clode, deputy Manager, the person who would take the reins from Alice at the end of June when she resigned from the W.V.S. to take up her position as Mayor, had grudgingly pledged her support. There were a few ladies from Trumpington but no one from Cherry Hinton. Jean Barnet was among the guests, accompanied by her friend Fiona Larkin, which probably explained why Jean had come. And then there was Mrs Weston, also from Grantchester, who did not look in the least bit fit to march, but whose face was a beacon of enthusiasm.

Jean had known Alice for nearly six years but had never set foot inside the Bragg family's home. The drawing room was a gracious, comfortable room with large French windows that gave out onto an expansive terrace and lawn. There were enough chairs in the room for the twenty-one women.

Alice was a charming hostess, making each volunteer feel especially welcome.

"Thank you so much, Lady Bragg," Mrs Weston clasped Alice's hand and vigorously pumped it up and down. "It's such an honour,"

"Really?" Alice asked in surprise.

"It's such an honour to take part in your last event with the W.V.S., Lady Bragg, when you have done so much. It is such an honour."

"Thank you," Alice replied, quite astonished. Mrs Weston's words were not what she had been expecting but flashing her eyes quickly around her group of guests to read their responses. There were murmurs of support, gazes of agreement.

"Well, I'm just glad the bloody war is coming to an end," Fee added and then blushed at her expletive in a real Lady's house.

"Aren't we all?" Alice replied, politely ignoring her guest's choice of vocabulary.

Now that the war was finally ending, Alice had been able

to secure the services of a housemaid. She was young and, after leaving school, had worked in a munitions factory producing weaponry that was no longer needed. The new maid didn't always act the most sensibly and didn't particularly like domestic service. But for her, any job was better than no job, and for Alice, some help was better than no help, especially on an afternoon like today when the drawing room was full of guests. Alice watched the new maid from the corner of her eye as the girl poured the tea for her guests, ready to jump up and assist if disaster struck. Before the war, at a tea party like today, cook Nellie would have prepared a large sponge cake and biscuits, maybe shortbread, or maybe spiced Welsh cakes. This afternoon there was nothing more on offer than a cup of tea, to Alice's regret as a hostess, but relief on behalf of her new maid.

Twenty women drinking twenty cups of tea listened attentively as Alice outlined the plans for the march. The Lord Lieutenant, Richard Briscoe, the personal representative of the King in Cambridgeshire and a friend of the Braggs, had arranged for a Sergeant Brown to drill the ladies and prepare them for their march. The practice would take place in a junior school playground in the evenings when no one would be around to watch. Alice hoped this would reassure some of the women, who were now beginning to look somewhat nervous at the mention of 'drill' and 'Sergeant' and 'practice'.

"Ladies, I am sure that all of us want to make a good display alongside the other groups taking part in the march."

There were nods of heads and a few murmurs of 'naturally' and 'of course'.

"We will not be permitted to talk to each other during the march, and …," here she paused, wondering which of her two statements her W.V.S. ladies would baulk at the most no talking or what was to come, "… and high heels and jewellery should not be worn."

Mrs Weston's fingers flew to the brooch on her jacket lapel, and Jean began to finger a glass bead necklace at her collar. One of the ladies from Trumpington was looking at the heel on her shoe, assessing if it were too high to be considered flat and wondering where on earth she would find another pair in time if it were not flat enough.

The great marching day was all too soon upon them. Their drill had been, quite frankly – terrible. Sergeant Brown had been visibly distressed at their inability to keep in time. Alice felt quite disheartened, but Fee kept the whole group buoyed with her determination to enjoy the experience.

It had been agreed by all, including Sergeant Brown, who undoubtedly had a little word in the ear of the Lord Lieutenant, that the W.V.S. ladies would join the march at a particular corner en route to render the experience as short as possible for everyone's nerves. All the ladies had family members alongside them, ready to accept handbags and cardigans so that the ladies could march in full and perfect uniform. Lawrence had come to support Alice with Margaret and Patience. Fiona's husband Jonny had changed his shifts to support his wife, finding it almost as exciting as she did and already boasting, to anyone who would listen, what a terrific marcher she was – as good as any WREN or WAF.

Jean's mother, Anne, had also decided to come, bringing all three girls. Maeve looked gloomy about the affair, but Barbara was grinning, caught up in the excitement and Eleanor was manoeuvring herself towards Patience, pleased at the possibility of making a friend about the same age as herself on this great day. Despite her fears that her mother was too old to be standing around outside for a lengthy time, and despite her worry that she would surely be the only one of the women who would be marching on her left foot rather than her right (or should it be vice versa?), she was pleased that they had come. If only Alan had found the time. He never found the time anymore.

They could all hear the rhythmic steps of the marchers approaching and the crowd's encouragement rising like a wave. Sergeant Brown swiftly organised his women, ready for them to step into their positions at the tail of the procession.

"Quick, march!" he shouted, and they were off, Alice at the head of the group.

Somehow, they managed to keep in time. Somehow, they managed to all turn their eyes at the same moment in the direction of the General, reviewing the marchers, and somehow, they all managed to enjoy themselves.

Marching past, Alice turned her eyes to the General as directed. She almost fell over her feet. It was all she could do to keep placing one foot in front of the other. She recognised the General! She had dined with him a year or so ago but had forgotten his name. He had sat through the meal with crumbs of bread roll decorating his whiskers. How funny that she was marching for him! She had to concentrate hard on the direction of her feet to stop herself from ruining the seriousness of the occasion with a fit of giggles.

32.

JEAN

MOTHERS AND DAUGHTERS

The drawing room in the new house was too small to be called a drawing room – but it would, in time, make a comfortable sitting room. The house had only been built a few years before, and although it had a fireplace with a mantlepiece, this was more an acknowledgement of an architectural tradition than a necessity. A modern electric fire was mounted on the wall in the place where coals or logs could just about have squeezed, if given the opportunity. It wasn't very attractive, nor could Jean sit and watch its flame patterns for hours on end, but she had to concede that the room was warm, and the electric fire made considerably less dust.

Neither was the house large enough for a study, so a bookcase and Anne's bureau were pushed into the back-garden corners of the oblong room. The shelves were bare, as no one had unpacked the books from the boxes. The walls too, were bare, except for picture hooks in the wrong places for the wrong size paintings, left where the previous owners had put them.

Jean's sofa, her comfort, was too large for the room. It had been a mistake to have brought it. She could see that now. None of the furniture seemed quite right in the room – the pieces hanging together like borrowed clothes, not an outfit designed for the wearer.

Barbara was sitting on Alan's old chair with high arms and a straight back, her legs raised on a stool, feeding her new baby. Despite her certainty that it would be a boy, much to Christopher's delight, their fourth child was a baby girl –

Sarah. Barbara's hand cupped the little head, but Jean could see a tiny arm in a white babygrow resting against her mother and little babygrow-covered feet poking out from under the blanket that Anne had knitted for Sally, one of the last items she had made before passing away, cherished and passed along to all of Barbara's babies in turn.

"Isn't it a good thing you live here now?" Barbara looked up from her delight and said to Jean. "It's so easy just to pop in like this with the baby." She wasn't yet used to calling Sarah by name since she had been 'the baby' for so many months. "It's beginning to get quite cosy, isn't it?" she continued.

"Actually, Barbara, I don't think it is."

Surprised, Barbara looked around the room to try and understand what was not comfortable. The curtains weren't ideal. They had hung in Eleanor's bedroom in the old house and were the only ones Jean owned that fitted the sitting room window in the new, and the sofa was, frankly, monstrously out of place.

"Yes, maybe you need new curtains, and some pretty cushions for the sofa would help."

"I don't just need new curtains. All of this furniture is wrong here. I've decided ..." and as she said it, she did decide. "I've decided to buy the small floral suite I saw in Robert Sayles last week and some new curtains."

As she spoke, the doorbell rang, and Jean left the room to answer it. Barbara lifted little Sarah from her breast, arranged her clothes to be decent for the visitor and put her baby on her shoulder to caress her back and relieve any wind. She looked around the room. Her mother was right, and Barbara was pleased – pleased that Jean was taking her steps to own her home.

There was no need to have rearranged herself as it was

267

Eleanor. She had arrived earlier than expected. This was the first time she had visited since the birth of her new baby niece, and she willingly took little Sarah for a cuddle, turning her nose into the baby's downy head, shutting her eyes, and inhaling her newborn smell. Barbara watched with satisfaction. Sarah's brothers were several years older, as were Maeve's boys. Perhaps it wouldn't be too long before Kurt and Eleanor tied the knot, and then Sarah might have a cousin closer in age as a playmate. Her babies brought her so much happiness. She wished that happiness for her little sister.

Jean noticed the way Eleanor held baby Sarah too. She had had babies herself and watched the twins with theirs. She knew how to read Eleanor's expression. Barbara caught her eye and smiled knowingly. Jean deliberately turned her gaze away and looked out of the window at her small back garden. She might have met Kurt, she might even have liked him, but she wasn't yet ready to welcome him into her family or to see him as a father to her grandchildren. Not yet. She wasn't ready yet. She looked back at Eleanor, who was rocking baby Sarah in her arms. For the sake of her daughter, she'd have to be ready soon.

33.

JEAN

AN INVITATION TO TEA

Pushed right against the corner, barricaded in by the boxes of books, Jean's hall houseplant withered out of sight. Eleanor lifted the books out of their storage and placed them on the shelves, paying no attention to the order, hardbacks mingled with paperbacks, and reference books took position alongside novels. She could arrange her mother's library on another occasion. This afternoon, her job was to evict the boxes from the sitting room. She found the dying houseplant and doubted the specimen would recover from the unintended neglect.

"Look, Mum," she called. "Someone put the plant with the books – I think it's died."

Jean crossed over to look.

"No matter," she responded, "I never liked it that much."

"Really?"

"No. It was your father who always liked growing things in pots. I've always preferred fresh-cut flowers in a house. Pass it to me. I'll clear it away."

Eleanor lifted the plant out of the box, but even with great care, loose earth from the pot and crumbling leaves fell onto the carpet. Jean took the dead plant to the kitchen and disposed of it in the bin. Eleanor did her best to collect the fragments left behind. Then she picked up the empty box to remove that too. Inside was a brown envelope.

"Mum, there's a letter in the box," she called to her mother in the kitchen.

Jean returned to the sitting room and furrowed her brow as she took the letter from Eleanor, trying to remember how an envelope could be in a box with a houseplant. It looked like a bill. But it wasn't. She opened it and read:

Royal Institution
Albemarle Street
Mayfair
London
Friday 6ᵗʰ December 1963

Dear Jean,

I was in Cambridge recently and was saddened to learn of the passing of your husband. I understand that it was several months ago, and I can only apologise that I recently discovered the news and did not write before to express my sincere sympathy. I do not know if you are still at your Grantchester address. I am sending this letter there anyway, in the chance that if you have moved, the current occupiers will be kind enough to forward it to you. I do hope that you are well and your daughters are too. No doubt you are a busy Grandmother like me. There are some excellent tea rooms in Piccadilly. If ever you are in town, it would be delightful to meet you for a cup of tea and perhaps a slice of cake.

Yours sincerely
Alice Bragg
Ps, please forgive this typed letter. I fell over a few weeks ago and hurt my wrist. Lawrence's secretary is kindly typing as I dictate.

Jean was shocked. To receive a letter from Alice Bragg after so many years! She handed it wordlessly to Eleanor, who read it through quickly.

"This is from Lady Bragg, the Mayor," Eleanor said enthusiastically. "What a coincidence!"

"Coincidence? In what way?" Jean knew she had been thinking about Alice recently. She had been thinking about the war too, but Eleanor didn't know that.

"Don't you remember? We looked at the photo in the newspaper in your box when we were sorting the books and the papers out before Christmas."

"Ah yes, that's right."

"And you said you weren't in touch with Alice anymore but that you'd been good friends during the war."

"Well, I wouldn't say good friends, but yes, we were friends," Jean corrected.

"You've got her address now," Eleanor commented, "and she's asking you to get in touch."

"No, she isn't."

"Of course she is. What else could she mean by 'delightful to meet you for a cup of tea'?" Eleanor said, pointing to the place on the page where the words were written.

"That's only a polite way of finishing her letter. I'm sure she doesn't mean it."

"Whyever not?"

"Look how formally she writes."

"Yes, well, that is a bit old-fashioned, but honestly, Mum, she's positively inviting you to go and have tea with her."

"It's been too long, Eleanor – nearly twenty years – you can't just pick up a friendship you left behind all that time ago and expect it to be the same."

"Well, don't expect it to be the same then," Eleanor argued, "expect it to be a different friendship, but it can still be a friendship."

"Perhaps," Jean conceded. She took the letter back from Eleanor and put it on a ledge inside Anne's bureau.

34.

ALICE

FREEDOM OF THE BOROUGH

September 1946

It was undoubtedly an honour to be the Mayor of Cambridge, Alice reflected. Especially since she was only the third woman to carry the title since King John had created the office in the thirteenth century – but she had nothing to wear! She would be expected to attend a diary full of engagements, and all she had in her wardrobe was her W.V.S. uniform, a couple of well-worn outfits from before the war, her wedding dress, and a wine-coloured velvet skirt cut down from a dress worn by her grandmother in the last century. Nothing suitable at all for the role she now occupied. And there was no likelihood of the council providing additional coupons so she could get anything else. Luckily, her friends came to the rescue and sent her items they could spare. Dear Peggy Shaffner in Chicago came up trumps, posting an elegant dark grey suit and blouse cut to the most fashionable American lines.

The mayoral formalwear was another problem. The bicorne hat was too large and threatened to topple from her head with the slightest movement. It was constructed from a thick, stiff, felt-like material that would accept not a single hatpin. The black robes covered her like a shroud, and the gold chain pushed down heavily on her breasts, making her 1920s-style flat-chested, the links frequently catching and damaging the clothes she wore beneath.

She did not feel at her best, nor her most elegant, wearing this regalia – even though it was an honour. She felt particularly uncomfortable on the day that she granted the

Freedom of the Borough to the Cambridgeshire regiment.

Standing inside the Guildhall, beside the doors which opened onto the balcony, she could hear the hum of the gathering crowd. She began to feel sick. Over the years, she had become an assured public speaker, but she had never addressed a crowd the size of which she could hear assembling outside in the square. Nor had she ever spoken into a microphone. She checked for her speaking notes, screwed up her courage and stepped onto the balcony.

"Lady Bragg," the technician pounced on her, "let's just check the microphone again."

She moved forward, as requested, for him to verify it was in the correct place for her height to catch her words. General Luttark, who was to give the vote of thanks on behalf of the regiment, drew alongside. As Alice was a tall lady, the microphone's height was also adequate for him. The technician tapped the microphone and an amplified buzz echoed around the square. Scores of faces looked up to the balcony in response but, seeing that the occasion was yet to start, turned their eyes away and resumed their conversations.

"Oh my!" Alice whispered. "There must be at least a thousand people down there."

"Likely more, Lady Bragg." General Luttark had caught her words.

"Oh my!" she repeated weakly.

"Nervous?"

"Rather!"

"Wiggle your toes?"

"I beg your pardon?"

"Wiggle your toes and keep wiggling them. It fends off the nerves. So does laughter," the General added when he

273

saw how the ridiculousness of wiggling her toes had captured her imagination.

The Chancellor of the University, the mace bearer and several other senior officers of the regiment assembled alongside her on the balcony. The sound of the beating drum and marching feet signified the start of the procession, and Alice wiggled her toes for all she was worth.

The returning heroes from Singapore were the first to enter the square. Every onlooker remembered the pitiful condition that these brave men had returned in last autumn. Bodies weakened from near starvation, tropical disease, and forced labour. Minds scarred from abuse and fear. In the intervening year, wholesome food and the nurture of their families had filled out their faces. The honour accorded them today was a recognition and a reward for their suffering, and it was an important step on the long road to recovery, a hoped-for destination that some present would never reach.

In the middle of the square was a block of seating reserved for city and university dignitaries who had not been granted balcony space. Alice saw Lawrence sitting in the front row. He smiled at her and waved. She would have waved in return if she could. Just seeing him there made her feel braver.

Soon the procession was complete. All the soldiers, young and old, had taken up their positions in the square. The crowd was silent with respect for the dignity of the occasion, waiting for her to begin. She stepped closer to the microphone and started to read the speech that she had prepared in her soft, light voice.

"Today, we bestow Honorary Freedom of the Borough on the Cambridgeshire Regiment. This is the highest honour that a city or borough can bestow. It is a freedom that is not bestowed lightly. It is only given in recognition of outstanding public service and in real, deep appreciation of our gratitude. The Cambridgeshire regiment, to which a great many of our sons, brothers, husbands, and fathers belong, has a fine reputation and has served Cambridge well, never more so than during the Second World War 1939 to 1945."

She paused and let the speaking notes drop in her hand to her side. She looked out across the square and was no longer addressing the crowd. Now she spoke to each soldier alone, as if he, by himself, were standing in front of her and, with heartfelt love ringing in her voice, she concluded,

"Cambridge is proud of you. Well done!"

Enthusiastic applause resounded around the square, bouncing off the buildings and reverberating along the streets leading away from it, where the crowd spilt over.

General Luttark, the epitome of a British army officer with his large moustache and straight back, stepped forward for his response. He had no notes, he didn't need them, and he was unlikely to be wiggling his toes, although it was hard to tell under his shining polished army boots.

He embarked on his vote of thanks,

"Thank you, Mr Mayor."

A snigger of laughter hummed around the crowd at the masculine address for a female mayor. The General ignored the response and continued,

"We thank the honourable Councillor Bragg, Mayor, Lady Bragg ..." and it was at this point that he appeared to abandon his script – if ever he had had one.

"Today, you have conferred on us an honour. An honour which is enhanced by the honour of the name you bear, a name which is honoured not only here in Cambridge but in the wider circles of the international scientific community, a name which is forever associated with the advancements in modern warfare which made our victory possible …"

The crowd cheered and waved enthusiastically. Alice looked down at Lawrence sitting with his fellow VIPs below, the two on either side congratulating him for the recognition given to him at this public event. She was so proud of him. She would always and forever be so proud of him. But it did seem a little harsh that despite everything she had done for Cambridge during the long seven years of war work and despite her continued dedication now as Mayor, she was only recognised here in front of a thousand people, caught on newsreel for prosperity, for being his wife.

The Speeches were given, and Alice descended the stairs and took her place on the saluting base for the parading of the regimental colours. At the front of the procession were the soldiers of the Second World War, followed by the grey-haired survivors of The Somme, Ypres and Arras and the white-haired veterans of the Boer. If he had lived, if he had returned from Ypres, her brother Eric would have been marching today. But today was not a day to dwell on loss. Today was a day to celebrate the return of the Regiment and the brave service given. She smiled and saluted and gave honour where honour was due.

35.

JEAN AND ALICE

PICCADILLY

Jean was adamant that she could manage to find her way to Fortnum and Mason's on Piccadilly by herself and that she did not need Eleanor to help her.

"Honestly, Eleanor, I'm not an old lady yet. I can manage," Jean had said crossly. But she did have to admit to herself, as she made the journey underground from Kings Cross along the Piccadilly line, that the Tube was busier and dirtier than she had remembered. Piccadilly itself seemed like a different world. The noise of the buses and the cars hit her with brutal force as she came to the top of the steps at the station's exit.

It was raining so she put up her umbrella. She wasn't sure which way to proceed now that she was here and looked nervously from left to right from underneath her brolly, stepping away from the road and into the shelter of the building behind her, trying to avoid the path of busy Londoners and to steer clear of the puddles.

She was overwhelmed by the city's colour. She didn't remember that London was colourful. But it was. Bright red buses, blue, cream, and orange cars on the grey tarmac road. Women in pink, yellow, and green hats and headscarves under their dark umbrellas. Enormous red, green, and blue advertisements, the size of entire shop fronts, decorated the nineteenth-century buildings with twentieth-century products. Theatres, with stage lightbulbs around their entrances, illuminating posters of the plays performed within and lighting up large black and white photographs of the cast treading the boards.

"Sorry, Luv," a man with a cigarette hanging from the side of his mouth muttered amiably as he narrowly avoided bumping into her while she stood stock still, trying to gather her bearings.

"Excuse me, are you all right?" a radio-smooth voice asked. Jean saw that it was a smart young woman in a skirt and light-coloured Macintosh – surely not warm enough for February? She had short dark hair and a friendly smile.

"Not really," Jean said, embarrassed. "I'm looking for Fortnum and Mason's."

"It's over there," the young woman said kindly and pointed along the road to a grand red-brick building with a pale mint-green frontage and arched windows.

"Thank you," Jean said, and the young lady went on her way.

Crossing the road was her next challenge. She had simply never seen so much traffic. There was no way she could cross where she was – the taxis and the motorcycles would run her down. So she walked further to a zebra crossing and crossed with an elderly lady and gentlemen, hoping there would be road safety in numbers.

Fortnum and Mason's grand ground-floor food hall was a feast to the eye. It was an Aladdin's cave of temptation. She would have liked to have stopped to examine the wondrous packaging, to pick up and admire the patterned tins and boxes and imagine what delicacies they might contain. But it was nearly 11 o'clock, and she had to hurry through the glorious food displays to reach the tearoom where she was to meet Alice Bragg.

No single ladies the right sort of age were sitting in the tearoom when Jean arrived. She took a table by the window and waited, looking hard at every new entrant.

She had been worrying whether she would still recognise

her former friend after all this time. What did twenty years do to a face? She thought that Alice was the sort of woman who would have aged gracefully. Alice had always been fashionably dressed – even in her W.V.S. uniform. She somehow managed to appear chic no matter what she was wearing. So that would be a clue. However, glancing around the tearoom, most of the London ladies appeared well dressed, so maybe relying on Alice's style wouldn't be such a help after all. She fiddled with the cuff of her jacket and motioned to the waiter that no, she wasn't yet ready to order.

But maybe Alice wouldn't recognise her? Although blonde hair fading to silver was not the dramatic transition of black, to salt and pepper, to grey. How different would she look to Alice? Maybe she ought not to have worn her new amethyst dress and jacket? It was quite modern. Perhaps she ought to have chosen something more wartime? She fiddled with her pearl necklace, rolling the beads between her fingers to calm herself down.

A few minutes after 11 o'clock, Alice arrived. It was undoubtedly her. Still elegant in, if Jean had known, a navy Chanel suit. Her once dark hair was now entirely grey but carefully styled. Her slightly buck teeth and soft, warm eyes showed that it was her, and so little changed.

Alice caught sight of Jean immediately. It was not hard. She was looking for a slight woman with pale hair of a similar age to herself. She was looking for a woman who did not stand out in a crowd, who would never dream of drawing attention to herself, but who, despite being quiet, contained a solid strength. Jean had not changed.

"Jean!" Alice said with heartfelt warmth as she approached the table.

Jean stood up and was momentarily unsure whether she should shake Alice's hand, but Alice decided for her by greeting her with a kiss on the cheek and an embrace as if

279

they were very old friends.

"It's so lovely to see you," Alice greeted Jean enthusiastically as she settled herself into the chair.

The waiter hovered close by.

"We'll have a pot of tea, please," Alice requested and, without looking at the menu, said to Jean, "The pastries here are rather good. They have a delicious apricot one and quite the most divine apple and cinnamon one – shall we have an assortment?"

It was a long time since her small breakfast in Cambridge, and Jean was hungry and more than happy to defer to Alice's proposition.

"You do look well, Jean," Alice said, admiring Jean's fashionable dress and jacket. The colour suited her very nicely. Alice had been worried that Jean might have been one of those women who fade away once their husband died, but Jean looked very far from fading away.

"I'm so sorry for your loss," Alice said. She had found that it was better to get the sympathy out in the open rather than skirt around it.

"Thank you," Jean replied.

"Was it a long illness?"

"No. It was very sudden – a heart attack."

"Oh, I am sorry."

"Thank you." There was nothing more that Jean wanted to say, so she asked Alice how Lawrence was.

"He's very well. He is the Director of the Royal Institution."

This piece of news didn't mean anything to Jean. She assumed that since it concerned Sir Lawrence Bragg, it was an important position.

"Do you miss Cambridge?" Jean asked suddenly. It seemed so strange to see Alice in London, so out of place.

"Yes, I do, but I didn't always live there, you know. I was in Manchester for many years."

As the tea and pastries were served, the two ladies exchanged news of their families and their grandchildren until they ran out of light conversation, and both women resorted to eating a second pastry, each in slightly awkward munching silence.

"And what do you do now, Jean? Now that your children are fully independent? I'm sure you help them with your grandchildren, but what else do you do with your time?"

Nothing, Jean admitted to herself in a slight panic of impending judgement. She did nothing. The war had finished, and she had retreated into the routine of nothing. Retreated voluntarily, wanting to forget – or forced? Forced by the demands of her husband, who wanted to reclaim his 1930s wife? Forced by the needs of her daughters, who wanted, deserved, a normal at-home mother? Forced by duty towards her mother, who required tender care in her declining years? She hardly knew which.

"I'm ... I'm helping the Girl Guides, my granddaughter's pack, with their badges," she lied, as she hadn't yet followed up her vague agreement of help with the guide captain, Mrs Turnbull, although she did intend to – now.

"How lovely, that will be a lot of fun, I am sure."

"And you, Alice?"

"I'm busy all the time. There are still a great many dinners to host for Lawrence – we host every Friday evening at our apartment at the Institution. There's another tonight. I'm the Chairman of the National Marriage Guidance

Council. I enjoy that. It's such interesting work and so worthwhile. I'm a Governor at Moorfields Eye Hospital, and I'm involved with the Mental Health Association. I still find time to write articles for a couple of newspapers, goodness knows how. I used to write a lot for the *Guardian,* but the current editor is not so fond of my style."

Jean's eyes widened in disbelief as Alice reeled off the list of all her extra-domestic activities. The two women fell again into silence. Jean felt the gulf between them was just as great as before she had arrived. She knew this would happen. She knew it wouldn't be possible to pick up where they had left off, that they had moved too far apart. Alice lived in a world of action, and she lived in a world of torpor. What must Alice think about this dull woman, pretending to be an old friend, sipping tea in front of her? Jean had always known that acquaintances and colleagues aren't the friends you take with you as you move to the next stage of your life.

As if reading her mind, Alice said, "It is a long time since those W.V.S. days, isn't it? I'm sorry we fell out of touch, Jean. I was so busy after the war that I didn't keep up with everyone as I would have liked. Are you in touch with any of the ladies?"

"I hear from Fiona Larkin. She and her husband went to Canada in '48. Mrs Fielding and her husband, Reverend Fielding, retired to Bournemouth, but he's not so well now. And you?"

"I see Hester Adrian very regularly. Do you remember Hester?"

Jean nodded.

"Hester comes up to town at least once a month and stays with us. She uses our flat as her London pad. I do enjoy seeing her. She still works very hard, supporting family mental health services – she truly is a remarkable woman.

And Frances Clode, do you remember her? She's still very active with the Voluntary Service. I wouldn't be a bit surprised if she takes over from Lady Reading when she finally retires. Vera Finlayson died a couple of years ago, did you know?"

"No, I'm sorry."

Jean picked up a couple of crumbs that had fallen onto the tablecloth to occupy the pause in the conversation that had again returned.

"Do you think about the war?" she asked finally.

"Not really, at least not very much," Alice replied. "There's so much else to think about."

That wasn't true, though, and both women knew it. They were a generation that had survived two wars – a generation that had had to try to build a better world twice. The first attempt had not succeeded, but the second, well, life did seem to be improving for many, and mostly, peace had held. They were a generation that had lost loved ones and opportunities. A generation whose daughters, and not themselves, were gaining from the fruits of their labours. Why look back when one needs to look forward? Why dwell on a time when everyone suffered? Why remember a time that everyone just wanted to forget?

"My daughter, Eleanor, says I should write down what I remember about the war," Jean said. "She says what I remember is interesting, and future generations will want to know."

"Why don't you then?"

"Oh, I couldn't," Jean objected, a look of pain on her face.

"Why not?"

"I really couldn't. I don't remember anything in any

283

particular order. I see something in my daily life that sets off a memory that brings another. There's no coherency in what I remember. Even if I tried to write things down, I get the years mixed up, and some things that seemed important don't seem important anymore."

She didn't watch television very much, but a couple of times before he died, she sat alongside Alan in their drawing room, where the new set had a place of honour, supplanting the big wooden wireless, and watched a few moments of a snooker match. The player would hit a ball with his cue, and that ball would strike another, knocking against a central arrangement of balls sending each in an explosion across the table. She assumed it was a great skill, that the player knew precisely what he was doing with each hit and knew in advance the direction each ball would travel. But it didn't seem like that to her. It seemed haphazard and random, like her memory.

Alice nodded thoughtfully.

"I don't think it matters so much how you record your memories, more than you do, because if you don't, who will remember? And maybe your daughter needs you to remember."

"Perhaps you're right," Jean sighed. Yes. It was true. Eleanor at least wanted her to remember – and Sally too. And it wouldn't be a legal document, just a collection of stories. She was under no obligation to remember everything for the girls. She could keep what she wanted hidden whilst still handing over her history to her daughters and granddaughter. There was a lot she wanted to keep hidden – Albert, her pain, her anger, her inability to forgive the nation that had robbed her of her brother and brought so much suffering to thousands of innocent people, her regret that during the war, she had become so much, but since its end, she had returned to being so little.

"Lawrence is going to write his autobiography. He hasn't had the time yet, but I know he will do it." Alice continued after a moment.

"What about you, Alice? Aren't you going to write yours?"

"Good Heavens, I'm far too busy, but yes – yes, I think I'd like to – when Lawrence's is complete."

"I'm sure it would be excellent, Alice. You have done so much with your life."

"I suppose I have," Alice laughed brightly, "and I have so many stories I'd want to fit into it. If I ever do start writing, it will be hard to know what to leave out. Whether that all means it would be good, I can't tell."

"Why did you do it?"

"Do what?"

"Why did you volunteer in the first place?"

Alice thought for a moment and took another slow sip of her tea.

"You know, a little after I finished being Mayor, I attended a dinner at Trinity, and I sat next to the King. He asked me the same thing, and I remember that I replied that I did it because I could not resist an adventure and because I knew it was the right thing to do."

It was a serious point, and Jean knew she should take it as such, but she nevertheless began to giggle.

"You met the King?"

Of course, Alice would have had dinner with the King.

"Yes, he was a charming man," Alice replied and started to laugh too.

The waiter was drawn by their laughter and, noticing

their cups were empty, enquired if they would like more.

"I'd like some coffee, please," Alice ordered and then, explaining to Jean, "my daughters have persuaded me to drink coffee since we've been living in London. They even gave me a coffee machine for Christmas."

Jean could not have been more astonished if Alice had said she had taken up deep-sea diving as a hobby in retirement. Her own banished electric kettle seemed mundane next to a coffee machine.

"Would madame like a coffee?" the waiter suggested to Jean.

"Um, no, thank you," Jean replied, "I'd prefer to stick to tea – thank you."

The Fortnum and Mason tearoom was becoming busier as shoppers searching for an early lunch arrived, coinciding with those lingering over their mid-morning refreshments. Jean noted to herself regretfully that she and Alice would be on their way soon. She had hoped that they would still be friends and had hidden her anxiety under assertions that there was no way that they could. The roots of friendship, in the soil of shared experience, were still there and would no doubt flourish and blossom if given the opportunity.

"What will you do next?" Alice asked as she drank the last sips of her coffee.

"I thought I would do a little shopping and then pop into the Royal Academy to see the Goya exhibition."

"Yes, I remember you have a real talent for art."

Jean smiled her thanks at the compliment.

"And later, I'm meeting my daughter, Eleanor. I've decided to make an evening of it and stay in town the night with her."

"That sounds like an excellent plan, but what I meant

was, what will you do next in your life? I'm sure you will have far more time now that you only have a small house, even allowing for helping your daughters with their children and helping with the Girl Guides."

It was like being back at the vicarage tea party all those years ago when Mrs Fielding attempted to draw Jean into helping with the canteen. Just as then, there were so many reasons why she would not have the time to bring changes to her life, reasons which evaporated under examination.

"I'm thinking about going back to art classes to brush up a bit, maybe learn some new techniques," and as she spoke, she realised that she wasn't lying to Alice or herself. She realised that she was going to do it.

"That's a terrific plan, Jean. The Goya exhibition is outstanding, and it will inspire you. Do send me some of your pieces, won't you? I'd love to see them. You always were so much better than you ever knew."

Alice readied herself to leave as she spoke.

Jean felt a surge of sadness that their meeting was over, yet her spirits were high. She had, after all, rediscovered a friend, and Alice wanted to remain in touch.

"I can't tell you how much I've enjoyed seeing you again, Alice," she said. "If you are ever in Cambridge, please let me know. I'd very much like to invite you to lunch."

Alice said that she would be delighted – and meant it.

36.
DAFFODILS
IN THE PARK

When Jean stepped out of Fortnum and Mason's, it had stopped raining, and even in the middle of the busy capital city, she could smell spring in the air. Although the great Royal Academy was calling to her with its posters of Goya advertising the exhibition within, Jean turned away from Piccadilly, where buses and cars passed in noise and haste, entering instead into the peace of Green Park. Here it was spring. Maple leaves were unfurling, a white cherry was in bud, and early daffodils lined the path down to the palace. Office workers occupied the benches with their sandwiches, lifting their faces to catch rays of the winter-spring sun as they ate. Some were in pairs, others alone.

So, what should she do next? Her daughters had been urging her to move forward for months, and now Alice had also prompted her. Her life was hers to take charge of in a way that it had never been before. She had a reasonable amount of money from selling the big house and Alan's pension and their savings. She was in a good position. She would enrol on art classes. Maybe she would travel. She felt a thrill of possibility and fear at the thought. Maybe she would go to France – or maybe not. Perhaps she would make friends with England first, then Wales and Scotland afterwards.

She spotted a free space on one of the benches with a lovely view across the daffodil paths to Buckingham Palace. She sat down and watched the passers-by; Londoners and tourists of all ages, some strolling and enjoying the spring day in the historic city, some hurrying through the park as they used it as an attractive path to take them from one part of the city to another.

A slight breeze caught the daffodils, and the first bees of the spring flew in and out of the bright trumpets, collecting nectar. Daffodils were one of her favourite flowers. There didn't seem to be very many in her new little garden, so next autumn, she would plant bulbs for a golden display next spring – spring 1965. She would miss having vases of her daffodils from her garden this year, but it was easy enough to buy bunches at the flower stall on the market.

One of her vases of daffodils had been on the table in the Reading Room on the day she met Albert.

What had he done next? She didn't know. After the letters which he had sent as he had travelled with the Battalion across Europe, taking the big guns to protect the troops and pound resistance to submission, he had only sent a postcard – a picture of Dieppe harbour before the war and a brief line:

Dieppe
18th October 1945

Dear Mrs Barnet,

I am de-mobbed and return home. God bless you.

Fond regard

Albert

He had not given her a home address, and she had never attempted to try and find it.

She sat for a moment, her eyes resting on the daffodils but no longer thinking about them, before getting up from the bench and continuing on her walk. A young man with a sandwich wrapped in paper was quick to take her vacated place.

She enjoyed the Goya exhibition more because she was meandering at will through the halls of a great gallery, stopping wherever she felt drawn to look closely at a painting and passing on quickly where another did not take her fancy. Sometimes a portrait of a lady or a child charmed her, and she wondered who the people had been, what their lives had seen. Mostly, although she admired the artist's technique, the paintings oppressed her. She preferred design, patterns, motifs from nature, and clear, bright colours. She liked William Morris. She sighed loudly as she paused before the portrait of a sombre middle-aged official. A woman standing close by, wearing half-moon spectacles perched on the end of her nose so that she could read the exhibition notes and then raise her gaze above the lenses to the painting on the wall, turned and stared at Jean so hard that Jean felt that she must apologise for any offence caused by sighing in the Royal Academy in front of a masterpiece.

37.
EATING ITALIAN

Eleanor had suggested that they dine out since her bedsit was cosy for two but far too small for three. There was a new Italian restaurant around the corner from her lodgings. What sorts of food did Italians eat? Already anxious about the second meeting with Kurt, Jean expressed her worry by homing in on the menu.

"Mum, the food at Antonio's is delicious. The mains are fish or meat with vegetables, maybe some salad. You'll like it. You don't need to have the pasta if you don't want to."

Jean thought for a moment, "We used to eat pasta during the war – noodles and macaroni. It was useful for all the mass feeding we had to do."

"Well, there you go then, Mum. It won't be too strange after all."

Kurt met them at the restaurant, offering Jean his hand, as he had before, in a warm handshake, before turning to kiss Eleanor. When he took off his raincoat inside the restaurant, Jean saw that he was wearing the purple tie she had given him at Christmas. Eleanor was wearing her cornflower blue belted dress, Jean's favourite, a scarf of the softest yellow at her neck and a pale yellow cardigan. She had fixed the turquoise bead brooch that Jean had given her for Christmas just above her left breast. The gold setting glinted in the restaurant candlelight.

Three people sitting down at a table for four is always slightly awkward. Who sits next to who? Who feels like an interviewee before a panel? Who feels like the panel before the interviewee?

The three held back, hesitating to take their seats, not

one of them feeling able, at that moment, to take the lead. The waiter, perhaps well used to the dilemma, held out the chair furthest away from the door and the draught for Jean to sit down. He removed the napkin from the table and, opening it with a flourish, placed it expertly on her lap. Eleanor moved to the seat directly opposite her mother and drew Kurt to the seat alongside her. So positioned, Jean could see both their faces at once. She knew that they were holding hands beneath the tablecloth. The empty space beside her was tangible. She was the third person. She was the odd one out. The single woman. The widow.

Jean had skipped her lunch, as she had been full from the mid-morning pastries. Now, in the early evening, she was extremely hungry. She chose minestrone soup because she'd heard of that before, followed by chicken breast with sauteed potatoes and salad. Kurt waited to see what Jean had ordered before selecting a bottle of white wine from the wine list. It was light and fresh, Jean thought when tasting it, although she admitted she was no expert.

They talked about the Goya exhibition. Neither Eleanor nor Kurt had seen it, nor did either of them have plans to visit, but they expressed a keen interest in Jean's comments. Kurt asked after Barbara and baby Sarah, sending his congratulations to the parents and good wishes to the newborn. He asked if Jean had any plans for a holiday in the summer.

"Yes, I do have some plans, Kurt," Jean replied.

"Do you, Mum?" Eleanor intervened. Her mother hadn't mentioned anything about a holiday to her. Her parents had rarely been away together, only a couple of times since she and her sisters had grown up, and family holidays, other than to visit her uncle and aunt, had not played a part in her childhood.

"I have some friends I'd like to visit."

Jean thought wistfully of Fiona in Canada, but that was ridiculous. Canada was far too far to go when she'd never even set foot out of England. She had not even been to Wales.

"And there are some beautiful towns and cities I'd like to see," she continued. "Oxford – I've always thought about going there. I know Cambridge so well, but I've never been to Oxford. And you? Do you have any plans for your holidays?"

Eleanor and Kurt flicked a glance at each other, and Kurt cleared his throat before speaking,

"I've been looking at Greece for September," he said.

"How lovely!" Jean said brightly, Alma Tadema beauties in smooth white marble settings immediately springing up before her eyes.

"Actually, Mum, we've been thinking about going to Greece together."

Eleanor was looking intently at her mother, scrutinising her face to see if Jean had understood what she was trying to say. She took her hand, tight in Kurt's, from beneath the table and deliberately placed their clasped palms on the white cloth.

"On our honeymoon, Mum."

Jean, who was in a lovely landscape of sun-kissed maidens bedecked in floating pastel tunics, carrying amphora, blinked hard as Eleanor's words pulled her back to the restaurant.

Eleanor and Kurt sat tensely in front of her. Faces hopeful, eager for her blessing, but resolute that they would be in Greece, married, before the end of September.

She could hardly say that she wasn't expecting the news. But it struck her as a strange way to learn that her daughter

293

was to be married. Would it have been different if Alan were alive? Jean wondered. Would Kurt have come to ask his permission for his daughter's hand as Alan had done of her father so many years ago? What would Alan have said, and did any of this protocol even matter anymore? What mattered, more than anything, was that Eleanor was happy and that she would be happy.

"That's wonderful. I'm so pleased for you both." And she placed her hand on top of theirs with a gentle squeeze before opening her arms wide to embrace them both across the table, despite the dinner plates and the wine glasses below.

38.
Spring Snowfall

Jean felt disorientated returning to Cambridge the following morning. When had she ever come home in the morning – apart from those air raid nights of twenty years ago? She made herself a pot of tea and stood looking out of her kitchen window above her sink into her small garden of no surprises, a perfect rectangle where each fence and each corner could be seen. Birds were pecking at the string of nuts she had placed on the bird table a day or so ago, before her trip to London. A pot of primroses smiled brightly up at her from her tiny terrace.

Her box was on the floor of her wardrobe, where she had shoved it in a hurry to get it out of the way when she had moved in, pairs of shoes balancing on top of it and crowding in around it. She took the box out from its burrow of shoes, opened the lid and removed one letter from the dog-eared envelope. Just one. The one he had sent to her when he left Grantchester. She read it through for the last time before folding it over and tearing it in half, putting the two halves together and tearing once more, repeating the manoeuvre again and again until she had created a handful of snowflakes which she watched flutter as snowfall into the wastepaper bin.

Then, climbing up onto her bedroom chair, she put the box on the top of the wardrobe, where apart from the last few months, it had resided for nearly two decades. It would stay there for someone else to decide what to do with it. Someone else in years to come would either consider the contents to be rubbish and throw it all away or piece the letters, posters, and newspaper clippings together to construct a version of her life and her times. Maybe that would be one of her daughters – or one of her grandchildren,

Sally or Sarah perhaps, or maybe one of Eleanor and Kurt's children, not yet born. She was at peace with the thought.

39.

BOURNEMOUTH BEACH

It had been surprisingly simple to arrange. Mrs Fielding had replied by return of post to Jean's letter. Of course, Jean could come and stay with them. It would be no trouble at all. Her husband wasn't nearly as ill as perhaps she had suggested in her Christmas card. It would do them both a power of good to have an old friend come and stay for a few days to take some spring sea air.

The Fieldings now lived in a small bungalow with a postage stamp garden. Yellow forsythia greeted Jean from the front hedge as she opened the wooden gate and walked up the path. A pot of bright red early tulips guarded the front door like a sentry.

Isobel Fielding still stood straight and still carried excess pounds, but now her hair was completely white, and hearing aids behind each ear revealed the damage age does to the senses. The vicar was recovering from another bout of pneumonia. He was very frail and spent most of his days sitting in the bungalow's sunny living room, with a red tartan blanket covering him, head turned either slightly to the right to look out of the French doors onto the garden or slightly to the left to watch the television. But most of the time, he slept.

Rita, Mrs Fielding's daily help, had stayed on to prepare lunch for the elderly couple and their guest. They would manage themselves with sandwiches and cake at supper time, and breakfast was simple. Jean felt guilty. Her visit was more difficult for them than she had been led to believe.

"I hope you don't mind if we rest after lunch?" Mrs Fielding asked. "We have a rule in this house, 'two until four, feet off the floor'." Jean didn't mind. She was tired herself

297

from the journey that morning from Cambridge via London.

Towards the end of the afternoon, when fully rested, Mrs Fielding took Jean the short way to the seafront, where they walked a little before sitting down at an unoccupied bench, looking at the grey-blue seascape that stretched for miles and miles in front of them. There was a chill to the April afternoon, making it feel more like early March, and as a result, there were no more than a dozen or so other locals in view on the seafront or the beach.

"I'm so glad you have come to see us, Jean dear," Mrs Fielding said. "We live very quietly now. So different from those busy days when my husband was in charge of a large parish."

"And you were busy yourself as the vicar's wife."

Mrs Fielding laughed. "Yes, there was always so much to do – then."

Isobel sat silently for a moment, looking straight out to the grey horizon where a boat, possibly a ferry, made a small scratch on the skyline.

"You know, it's not so far to France."

"Really?"

"Yes, it's less than eighty miles from here to Cherbourg and more than one hundred from here to London."

"That's very close, isn't it?"

Looking out across the waves, it could have been eighty, eight-hundred, eight-thousand, Jean thought.

"It was such a threat at the time, wasn't it?" she said.

"What was, my dear?"

"German invasion. It really could have happened."

"Yes."

A gull swooped low in front of them and landed on the sand, where it poked its yellow beak into a tangle of black-green seaweed before taking off into the grey sky, crying harshly. The two women followed it silently with their eyes.

"Do you think we did make a difference?" Jean asked. She didn't feel like she had made a difference, not when she compared herself to Alice and all that Alice had done and had achieved.

"Who?"

"People like you and me and the W.V.S."

"Undoubtedly!"

Jean looked unconvinced by Mrs Fielding's assertion.

"Of course, we did, my dear. Little things count. Caring for the troops the way we did, caring for each other – it all counted."

She paused, looking around at the coast stretching East to West and the sea between England and France, which, twenty years ago, almost to the day, had been a hive of activity as the Allies prepared to push back into Europe.

"You know, some of our HAA boys were probably here."

"I expect so," Jean murmured vaguely.

"Ah, I forgot. You kept in touch, didn't you?"

"Not especially."

Jean felt her cheeks flush. Even now, so many years later, she felt compelled to deflect attention away from herself, away from Albert. She added quickly,

"But you kept in touch with Alf Long, didn't you? I remember he came to visit with his little girl after the war."

"Yes, that's true. But Alf was never on the south coast,

299

to my knowledge. The Battalions were forever being reorganised. The war was on so many fronts by '44 – pushing into France, up into Italy, back against the Japs. Alf was reposted to the Clyde to keep up the defence of the ports. He was pleased to stay on British soil, especially with little Jane at home with her Granny. But Albert was surely on the south coast, wasn't he?"

"Yes, first he was in Essex, and then he went into France from Weymouth," she answered, her guard down, remembering Albert, remembering Alf, remembering the troops with their heavy guns.

"I knew you had stayed in touch with him, my dear," Mrs Fielding said kindly.

Jean was on the point of denying the truth of it when Mrs Fielding added,

"I always knew you were fond of him."

There seemed no point in hiding it now,

"Yes, I was."

Isobel Fielding had always wondered. She had noticed the easy companionship that Jean and Albert had shared at the canteen. She had observed Jean's unhappiness and what could only have been described as pining in the months after the Battalion had left Grantchester. With her expert and sympathetic eyes, she had noticed the distance in the Barnet's marriage.

"I think you loved him, didn't you?" Isobel ventured to ask softly, a mother encouraging the confidence of an adult child.

Jean clasped her hands tightly in her lap and looked down at her cold fingers, willing tears not to flood her eyes in front of the vicar's wife.

"Yes, I did. But I ..."

"Hush now. No need to say more," Isobel interrupted. "You know, I've seen and heard a lot, being married to a vicar for more than fifty years. And all I can say is that life is complicated. But we must always try to do the right thing. I'm sure you did."

"I did."

"Well then, nothing to regret," Isobel smiled and squeezed her friend's hand. "Shall we go home for a cup of tea?"

Jean lay on her bed in the bungalow guest bedroom. The window was open. If she concentrated, she was sure she could hear the sea whispering to her as she struggled to sleep. Regret. She had been full of it. It had filled her and possessed her. The level had risen year after year until it had brimmed over and leaked out of her like tears from her eyes. And now, strangely, it was seeping away, day by day. Her life seemed, little by little, brighter – a grandchild, a new son-in-law, reacquaintance with old friends. She had plans now, springtime shoots of plans for her life. She had hidden her feelings for Albert from the world and even from herself. Never, since that cold Christmas afternoon in the churchyard, had she admitted that she loved him, not until a few hours ago when she had, in some way, confessed to Mrs Fielding on the seafront, and when she had spoken of it, the world had not collapsed, the globe had continued to turn. She knew what she would do next. She rolled away from the window to face the wall, and slept.

40.

THE DOORWAY
TO THE SHOP

From Bournemouth, it was only natural that she should take a few days to enjoy the West Country since there was no particular need to hurry home, and there were so many interesting places that she had never had the chance to visit – Bath or Bristol, for example. She would go to one of them – just one. And if Dollis and Sons bookshop was still trading, then she just might go in and look for a book, and then she just might make enquiries about Albert, and then …

Bath. In the quiet of the early morning, while her hosts still slept, she had held a pin above the map of England that the retired vicar kept in his study, and let fate choose for her.

She found Dollis and Sons in an elegant street close to the Royal Crescent. It was smart, with a well-constructed window display. The business was doing well. Jean paused on the threshold. Through the glass panel of the door, she could make out the shapes of people within – someone at the counter and someone being served.

As she hesitated, the door opened in front of her, and the bell at the hinge jangled its farewell to the departing customer.

"Excuse me," a woman carrying a shopping bag apologised for almost bumping into Jean, and the man at the counter looked up expectantly at the new customer on his doorstep.

There was no going back, only forward. Like pressing the doorbell on that Islington front porch, a lifetime ago. Jean lifted her head and entered.

ACKNOWLEDGEMENTS

Thank you to my publishers, Carl French and Morgana Evans at The Endless Bookcase, for simply being the best.

Thank you to Peter Waine for encouraging me as my story unfolded and to Paul Harrison and Helen Shabetai for helping me iron out its creases.

Thank you to Matthew McMurray, the former Royal Voluntary Service's archivist, whose sterling and dedicated work has made so much historical material available.

Thank you to Professor Lynne Berry CBE, Dr Mike Glazer, Kate Miller, Dr Elaine Saunders, Louisa Treger, Jon Mackley and Charles Bunker, author of the De Gressier quartet novels and former-proprietor of the Orchard Tea Garden at Grantchester.

Thank you to my book club. I couldn't write if I didn't read.

Thank you to my wonderful family: Edgar, Rufus, Conrad, Eloise, Peter, Stuart and, of course, Eleanor, my mother, to whom this book is dedicated.